To Rachel,
with best wishes
George McGuire

# THE DECISION

# THE DECISION

## George McGuire

www.deedspublishing.com

Copyright © 2010 - George T. McGuire, Jr.

Printed in the United States of America

Published by Deeds Publishing, Marietta, GA

First Edition, August 2010

For information write Deeds Publishing, PO Box 682212, Marietta, GA 30068 or www.deedspublishing.com

ISBN 978-0-9826180-3-5

For my daughter, Debbie

# FOREWORD

*THE DECISION* is a story about people who lived during the mid-years of the American Civil War. Facts are intermingled with fiction to create a realistic panorama of that time. Slavery was being brought to an end. Prejudice, perhaps, was being born.

The dreams and wishes of the people of that era were similar to the motivations that bring about our present day mores. Only our progress in knowledge, and the development of a new environment, have changed. The basic instincts of human nature have remained the same.

Dialogue and dialects are intended to place the reader back in the surroundings that would have existed in 1862 and 1863. To fully convey historical truthfulness, a word was used to describe the Negroes that was commonly heard during those years. Also, the limited number of factual events that are described were used to establish a link to that period, a time that may well have been the darkest hour of our country.

# I.

A man came out of the barber shop. A slender individual who was about thirty years old, he was well groomed and had a handsome appearance. He took two steps in our direction, saw us, turned as if he had forgotten something, and walked the other way. I spoke to Sarah.

"Is that him?"

"No!"

She answered too quickly. It obviously was him. She looked at me.

"Let's go, Alexander."

It was all right to go. I had found him and there was no need to stay. I got a good look and would remember him. I tapped "Old Ben" lightly with the reins and we moved forward in the direction he was walking. He was looking into the glass of the store fronts and could see our reflection as we came close. Just as we passed, he turned toward a display of merchandise in a big window so that his back was to us.

Not many people were out. Washington City, a lively place in the past, had been changed by the war. Nearly everyone seemed uncertain about things. Social activities had slowed considerably. Our one horse open top carriage clattered occasionally as the metal rims of the wheels hit rocks scattered through the roadway. Sarah was content to ride along in silence. I glanced at her once and she had a smug look of satisfaction on her face.

It was Phillip who told me that Jennings was always in the barber shop on Saturday mornings. I had deliberately picked a route that would take us there, even though I knew Sarah would not identify him. However, I thought she might show her hand. I had asked if she would like to go for a ride. Then I had conveniently stopped near the barber shop to give our horse a pause. We had been discussing Jennings just before he appeared on the street.

Fancy and Royal, the twins, were waiting on the portico when we got back. Fancy was not a bad looking woman. Her only problem was being too heavy in some places. From what I could see, there was too much weight below the waist and not enough above. Not a good combination. Too bad, because she was attractive in the face. She and Royal had made the trip from South Carolina together. Royal wanted to try his luck playing poker for a few days, and Fancy wanted to visit Sarah and some other friends.

Royal greeted us from where he was standing.

"Ah, there's a handsome couple. And dressed fit to kill I might add. Been over to see the President, have you?"

Then he laughed. I was laughing, too, as I responded.

"That's right, we've been over to see Honest Abe. I told him there's a big, dumb Irishman in town looking for a game."

"Oh yeah? And I suppose he wants to set something up?"

"Absolutely. He's got so much spare time now he's looking for things to do."

Sarah's home, very large and located in a part of the city occupied by the wealthy, was positioned near the street with several acres of land in the rear. She led the way and we all went inside. After pleasant conversations that were brief, Sarah said that she would go back to the kitchen to prepare a meal. It was something that would normally be done by a servant but she purposely wanted to do it herself, and I think it was her way of showing hospitality for Fancy and Royal. Fancy went with her. Royal and I sat in the large drawing room. He looked serious as he pulled out a cigar. He put it in his mouth and chewed on the end. It was only a gesture because he knew that smoking in the house was not done. His appearance was stern as he asked a question.

"Is the war going to mess things up, Alex?"

"I think so. Pretty soon we won't be able to come and go like in the past. I believe they will set up a border somehow, and people going north or south will be stopped."

"Why hell, we haven't done anything. Even if they stop us, what can they do?"

"I don't know but it will be different and could be trouble. I've given some thought to getting away for a while."

"That wouldn't be hard for you. What would it take, one trunk or two?" And he smiled because he didn't believe me.

"It might not be that easy this time."

"What about Sarah?" Now, he was a little more serious.

"I don't know."

Fancy and Royal lived on a big cotton plantation in South Carolina. Their father, Danny O'Brennan, had come from Ireland just before the potato famine and had done well. Sarah's family lived on a plantation nearby. I asked about Mr. O'Brennan.

"How's your father?"

"Fine. Still working the farm. But if they set the Negroes free there won't be a plantation left in the south."

"Yeah, you're right, all the big cotton fields will probably fade away."

"Well, that's what the war is all about. The damn hypocrites, they still have some slaves in the North. Why couldn't they leave things alone?"

"I've thought about it lately, Royal. I think they're right. You can't have slaves."

"What? Are you crazy? You don't mean that!"

"I mean it. The Negroes should be set free."

"Aw hell, Alex, we treat them well and give them things they wouldn't have otherwise. I think you've been living in Washington too long."

"I don't think so. I believe... what was that?"

It sounded like gunfire. Rifles, maybe. I heard it again as I got up and went to the door.

I stepped out onto the portico. There was another shot. Then a man came around the corner, running hard. A black man.

He saw me and came in my direction. He was desperate. I motioned for him to come in and he ran straight toward me. He made it, gasping for breath, and rushed by me to the inside. I closed the door and stayed on the outside.

Soon they were there, three horsemen. They rounded the corner and came in my direction, looked at the open street, and pulled up. One of them reined in his horse directly in front of Sarah's house. He yelled at me.

"Where's that nigger, Mister?"

I didn't speak. The other two men heard, and came over by the first man. He spoke again, loudly.

"That nigger is a runaway, Mister. Property of McCleskey farm in Virginia, not more than a hundred miles from here."

Nobody spoke. The three horsemen moved their mounts close together and whispered among themselves. One, whose rifle was in his hand resting across his saddle horn, moved the weapon slightly so that it was pointed toward me. I eased my right hand up, pushed my coat back and hooked my thumb over the top of my pants, leaving my fingers exposed to the front, and next to the handle of my pistol.

The three stared at me and whispered again. Then they cursed loudly and turned back in the direction from which they had come, digging spurs into their horses. One yelled over his shoulder.

"We ain't through with you, Mister!"

After they turned the corner, Royal came out.

"That was dumb, Alex!"

"Where is he?"

"Out in the garden, hiding. Don't you know he's got a price on his head?"

"I didn't have time to think about it. It doesn't matter anyway."

"They will be back. You can't pull that kind of trick and get away with it."

"You're not in South Carolina, Royal."

"Don't make a damn. Most of the people here are the same."

"All except one."

"What the hell can Lincoln do?"

"He's got the militia."

"Damn Alex, no wonder you've made a fortune gambling. You just can't pass up the big odds."

I smiled at him.

"Don't concern yourself. I'm not worried. I've seen that type before and I don't think they will be back."

We went inside. Fancy and Sarah were standing close to the door. Both looked worried. Fancy spoke.

"Royal is right, Alex. They will come back."

"Not here, not in Washington," I was trying to relieve the fear I could see in Sarah, "they won't try anything here."

I think it worked. Sarah always seemed to believe me. She smiled a little as she motioned toward the back of the house.

"Well, I guess we better go see about him."

As I expected, he was gone. He was taking no chances. He was free and he wanted to stay that way.

Sarah had a delicious meal. Baked ham, succotash, sweet potato souffle and biscuits. She had learned to cook by watching Armeenia. After Colonel Sullivan, Sarah's husband, was killed in the accident, she decided to stay on in Washington and Armeenia was brought up from South Carolina. She had worked there on the O'Brennan plantation along with thirty-four other blacks. Danny O'Brennan had agreed for her to come after making an arrangement with Sarah. Now, she was free. Sarah told her she was no longer obligated to stay and she left for a while, though not surprisingly she was soon back. There was no place to go in Washington.

In the early afternoon, Royal and I went over to Grover's theater to reserve seating for the evening performance, something that sounded like an operetta. It was Sarah's idea. She said it would be a good way to entertain Fancy and Royal. I did not look forward to it. She had talked me into going to an opera on another occasion and I didn't enjoy it. One of the other theaters had that type program once or twice each year. I think it was only to satisfy a few of the "swells" as Phillip called them.

Something else I didn't enjoy was the carriage. Sarah had to have it, of course, and I had become accustomed to being in it when I was with her, or her friends. While we were riding back from Grover's, Royal commented on it.

"Is this the same carriage the Colonel bought her?"

"Yes. It was made in England."

"She's a beautiful woman. No wonder he gave her everything."

"Maybe he just enjoyed making her happy."

"Possibly, but you are doing the same thing and you might be doing too much."

"I know. The problem is, I could turn my back on anything until Sarah came along. And, what I do for her doesn't actually spoil her, it just gives her pleasure."

In the early part of the evening, Sarah, Fancy, Royal and I left for the theater. It was the time of year when the weather was most pleasant in Washington, and we rode in the open-top carriage. Uncle, a black man who worked for Sarah, was our driver, and it allowed us, sitting in the carriage behind him, to quickly become absorbed in happy conversations. Just after we arrived at the theater, and were shown to our seats, the actors appeared on stage and the music began. About midway through the first half of the program, Sarah reached over and held my hand. It made a dull event a little more satisfying.

During intermission, Royal and I went to the front of the theater to stretch our legs. A man in a U.S. Army uniform walked up to us. He was smiling as he spoke.

"Good evening, gentlemen."

Royal and I greeted him and he continued, raising a question as he looked at me.

"You're Mister Fairfield, aren't you?"

"Yes, I am. And this is Mister O'Brennan."

"Gentlemen, it's my pleasure. I am Major Dale."

We shook hands.

"Mister Fairfield, I'd like to talk to you. Not here, maybe tomorrow some time. Would that be possible?"

"Yes, it's possible, Major. However, if I may say so, sir, I think you should be aware that I'm not a military man, nor am I interested in the military at this time."

He smiled.

"Don't worry about it. Recruiting the troops is not my department. I have something else to discuss."

I was puzzled and hesitated. He spoke again.

"It would please me, sir, if we could meet during the noon hour tomorrow. Would it be convenient for you, say twelve o'clock, at Mary Carroll's Teahouse ... I trust you know her place?"

"Yes, I know it. It's a fine place to eat."

"Good. Then I will plan for you to be my guest there tomorrow. Is it agreed?"

"It's agreed."

We shook hands again and he turned away. Royal was suspicious.

"I think he's got something up his sleeve, Alex. You better be careful."

Later, after leaving the theater, we dropped off Fancy and Royal at the Willard Hotel where they were staying. Then, Sarah and I continued on to her house. After Uncle helped us down from the carriage and pulled away, Sarah looked at me and smiled.

"Now, that wasn't so bad, was it?"

"No. Nothing is bad as long as I am with you."

She laughed.

"Well, thank you. And now, since you are being so nice, I will make you a cup of tea."

We had done that before, had tea, and we always sat in the kitchen. After I was settled in a chair next to a table, I watched Sarah as she was moving around. She suddenly turned in my direction with a mischievous grin on her face.

"What would I do without a handsome man to escort me?"

"Oh, I suppose you would just faint at some convenient time and some other man would step up."

She laughed.

"You really think I would need to do that? I didn't meet you that way."

"No, I don't think you would have to do that." I waited a few seconds and continued. "Speaking of other men, what does Jennings do?"

She was surprised.

"Alex, let's don't start on that again."

"I just want to know a little more about him."

"I told you, there's nothing between us."

"Then why can't you talk about him?"

"All right, if you insist, I will talk about him. First of all, he is only a friend. He is from New York but he is here because he has contracts with the government. The company he owns supplies things to the army and he has to spend a lot of time here. He has become acquainted with most of the people I know and he attends many of the same social functions that I do. That is how I met him."

There was a long pause. She had stopped smiling. I knew I had pushed her about as far as I could but I wanted to know more.

"How did you meet him?"

"At a presidential ball."

She answered without looking at me. I spoke again.

"That must have been a year or so ago."

"It was."

She continued to look in another direction and she obviously was getting perturbed. I knew I was on thin ice but it was something that was buried too deeply in my mind, a real thorn in my side, and I just couldn't handle the thought of her being with other men. I asked another question.

"How did you happen to get interested in him enough to start going out with him?"

"He's a gentleman, polite and nice to be with. It's just as simple as that. He's a casual acquaintance and it's foolish for you to worry about him. Why don't you just leave it alone? You don't know him, you don't have to know him, and there's no need for it to go any further."

"Are you going to see him again?"

"Yes! I'm going to see him again!"

Now she was angry and lashing out at me. I was ready to apologize when she suddenly stood up.

"Goodnight, Alexander."

"I'm sorry Sarah, I shouldn't have ... "

"Goodnight."

Even though her tone was a little softer she still meant it. I got up and walked toward the front of the house. She came along with me. At the door I turned toward her.

"I enjoyed the evening."

She smiled very slightly.

"I'll say one thing for you, Alex, you're a good liar."

I reached for her to kiss her. She drew back a little and turned her face slightly. She did let me hug her and I kissed her on the cheek.

On the outside my thoughts turned sour in a hurry. I was thinking about Jennings and how I might be able to provoke him into some sort of confrontation, maybe even beat the hell out of him.

By the time I got home, put the stallion in the barn and walked into my house, I had cooled off. I would leave Jennings alone. If Sarah wanted to see him again there was nothing I could do. Nothing but be miserable. I thought about her. She had light blond hair which blended beautifully with stunningly attractive hazel eyes, a unique combination that was accentuated by a smooth rose-tinted complexion. It gave her a magnetic appeal that grasped the attention of others at a glance. She had the most seductive lips that could be imagined, and any man who could say that he did not want to kiss her would be gallantly untruthful. And she was perfectly shaped with a small waist that captured the envy of other women, and a full bosom that captivated the attention of men. With no flaws Royal was right when he had said, "She is a beautiful woman".

At five minutes before twelve the next day, Mary Carroll's Teahouse was half full. It was a scene that would change quickly. By twelve-fifteen the people from church would be coming in and others would be backed up near the entrance waiting to be seated.

Major Dale was there and had a table. He stood and motioned to me. We greeted each other and sat down. He spoke.

"They have corned beef and cabbage today. I hope you like it."

"I do. I've had it here before and it's very good."

"It seems to have become a popular item on the menu since Mr. Lincoln was served the same dish at the Willard Hotel on his inauguration day."

We exchanged pleasantries and small talk for a few minutes. Then he seemed to open up the subject that had brought us together.

"You know, Mister Fairfield, the war is going to create many needs. We're looking for a lot of people to do many different jobs."

"I can believe that."

"I have a matter in mind that will involve a few questions. I hope you won't mind a personal discussion."

"If you step on my toes, Major, I'll let you know."

"Fine." He smiled and continued. "Let's see now, I believe you have been here in Washington for several years?"

"That's right. I've been here since the summer of fifty-nine."

"And your original home was . . ."

"Savannah."

"I see. And you're about thirty years old?"

"You're one year short, Major."

"Thirty-one. All right. Now, I believe you own a large house sitting on about twenty acres of land here on the edge of the city. And I understand you have thoroughbred horses. Do you ... in other words, it would seem that you might be settled here for good. Is that a reasonable assumption?"

"I'm not sure. I've had some thoughts lately about leaving Washington City, at least for a short while."

"Because of the war?"

"Not really, although that might be part of it."

"What about your house, and your horses?"

"I can leave everything in good hands. I have reliable people working for me."

"Will you go back to Savannah, or the South?"

"No. I might go west."

He seemed relieved. He continued to ask questions, probing delicately and diplomatically. His main thrust, however, was directed toward my attitude concerning the issues involved in the war.

We finished the meal, he paid the amount due, and we walked out together. After we had moved a few steps away from the crowd gathered at the entrance, he seemed ready to get to the point.

"Mister Fairfield, I heard about the way you handled yourself yesterday with the bounty hunters. Can you tell me why you sheltered the Negro?"

"He didn't have a fair chance. And I didn't like the fear I saw on his face."

"But isn't it unusual for a man from Savannah to protect a black man?"

"No, not at all, at least for me it's not."

He pondered what I said. I think he was uncertain about how to proceed. I helped him.

"You're looking for a man to handle a problem that is connected to the war and you need a man from the South."

He grinned.

"I know now why you are a gifted gambler. Will you help us?"

"I don't think so. I don't have slaves, but my roots are in the South. I'll probably just pass it up."

"We all need to take a stand. Excuse me, sir, if I'm getting too personal, but if you leave Washington wouldn't you be leaving Sarah Sullivan?"

"Not necessarily."

"Are you saying that she might leave with you?"

"No, I didn't mean to imply that. I doubt Sarah will ever leave. She still has her husband's assets here and as you might know she is quite well fixed by the value of what she owns here in the city. I suppose I meant that ...well, Major, you might be getting on my toes now."

"I understand. Let's drop that part of the discussion. Let me wind up this meeting today by saying that you can be quite valuable to us. A man of your obvious courage could serve a vital purpose for the Union in the days ahead. Will you think about it?"

"Yes, I'll think about it."

"Good. And will you please keep this confidential?"

"Major, if there is one thing a gambler can do, he can keep a secret."

He smiled as we parted. I thought about him. He was likeable. There was nothing artificial about him. He was straight-forward and polite. His accent was like that of a mid-western person and I would guess that he had come from that area. He was polished and might have been a West Point graduate, a career army man. About forty years old, he was large in size, and he had an underlying firmness about him. I had the feeling that he could be a formidable adversary if challenged.

Back at home I was restless during the afternoon. I couldn't sit still. I went out in the back and stood by the fence and watched the horses. Nothing seemed to bother them. They would eat the grass, move along a few steps, and eat some more. While watching them I thought, `you might be smarter than we are'.

I decided that I wouldn't go to the Sunday evening service at church. Sarah and I had an understanding that we would meet there each week. She would know that I was deliberately staying away. It wasn't because she had sent me home early the night before. She had warned me that she would do that if I brought up Jennings again. It was deeper than that. Sarah had become such an obsession she had taken hold of me completely. And the thought of other men being with her was getting to be too much to handle. She had me backed into a corner. She had said, "Alex, I'm very fond of you, you mean more to me than anyone, but I'm not ready to settle down yet." And I just couldn't swallow that set of circumstances.

Major Dale sent a rider to my home with a message Monday afternoon. The corporal stood over to the side on the veranda and waited as I opened an envelope and read the short message: "Mister Fairfield I would like to meet with you again this week. If you will name a time and place I will arrange my schedule accordingly."

I folded the paper and put it back in the envelope. Then I gave it to the corporal.

"Tell Major Dale something has come up and this week won't be good for me."

"Yes sir."

He got on his horse and left. I sat in the rocker and watched him ride down the long driveway to the road. I picked up a glass on a nearby table and took a sip of whiskey. I was in no mood to talk to Major Dale.

Tuesday morning at ten-thirty I heard a wagon coming up the driveway. I walked out onto the veranda and recognized a familiar voice.

"Aw, how you do this morning, Mista Alexander?"

It was Shorty. A freed black man who worked for Phillip. I was glad to see him. Each time he came he was always cheerful.

"Good morning, Shorty. You come by to pay me that two dollars you owe me?"

"Law have mercy, Mista Alex, aint you forgot that yet?"

He laughed and I did too.

"No. It's time for you to pay me."

He made a loud sound as he laughed again.

"Mista Alex, don't you know black folks aint got no money?"

"Listen Shorty, I'm not interested in fattening frogs for snakes. You're going to have to pay me."

He laughed again. He knew I was playing my usual part. Then he told me why he was there.

"Mista Phillip say he got a game set up tonight at the Blue Star."

"Who's playing?"

"Two gentlemens from Kentucky. And Mista O'Dell, he gon' play too."

"All right. I'll be there at eight. And Shorty, the next time you come by, I want that two dollars."

He laughed hard again.

"Goodbye Mista Alex."

"Goodbye Shorty."

He tapped the mules with the reins and turned the wagon back toward the road. Shorty was quick-witted and bright. His instincts were unusually good. His use of terms and expressions along with his mispronunciation of words only enhanced his personality. He was likeable, sincere and honest, and I considered him to be an enjoyable friend.

The poker game was a disaster for me. I couldn't concentrate and didn't follow my usual guidelines. I didn't watch the faces of the players and I didn't try to remember their habits and tendencies. At the end of the evening I had lost two hundred dollars. Phillip, who usually played about an hour and pulled out, was mystified. He followed me to the door as I was leaving.

"What's wrong, Alex?"

"I've got something on my mind."

"Sarah?"

"Yes, and another matter that has just come up."

"You've got to get yourself straightened out. Why don't you forget about Sarah?"

"I can't."

I thought it would be a good time to ask a question that I had not previously brought up with him.

"Do you think she might possibly feel ill at ease about being with me?"

"You mean because you're from the other side of town?"

"Yes."

"Hell no! She can walk across the stage at Grover's naked if she wants to. She's powerful, Alex. She has banking and railroad money and who knows what else. Money changes everything. Nobody in town is going to question anything she does, trust me."

"Yes, I already thought the same thing. I just wanted to hear it from somebody else."

"She is quite a lady and if you do hang on to her you will be very fortunate."

I smiled at him and turned away.

In the street, outside the Blue Star, there was very little light and visibility was poor. I had to go about a block and a half to get to Kelly's Stables where I had left the stallion. It was after midnight and the street was empty.

After going about fifty paces, I realized there were at least two men following me. I knew because I heard them, and I saw their movements in the vague reflections of the store front glass windows. They were men, most likely, who would try to rob me. It was known to quite a few people that gamblers were leaving the Blue Star at all hours, some with pockets full of money. And for that reason, almost all men carried a weapon.

I didn't change my pace. I had brought my pistol and I moved it over a little, more to the front, still with the barrel pushed down inside my waistband. I looked ahead to see if others were there to try to close off the street. Nothing was in view except doorways that would conceal men, and there was one alley that I would have to pass.

I stopped for a moment to plan my movements. I took out the pistol and checked to be sure it was loaded. I had brought the large Colt revolver that I had won in a poker game with a cavalry officer. It was loaded. I stuck it back inside my waistband and as I did they suddenly came ... from behind and the front. Men were rushing me from all sides, more of them than I had expected. They closed on me quickly, moving to within a few feet, forming a circle around me. They were holding guns and knives.

Then, almost simultaneously, we all stopped our movements. It was obvious that they were in control. I glanced around and counted seven men standing close to me. One of them turned and yelled up the street.

"Okay, Cap!"

A rider came from the alley. The men stood aside as his horse came within a few feet of where I was standing. The man on the horse spoke.

"Well, well, Mista nigger lover, how you gon' handle things now?"

I couldn't see his face well and didn't recognize his voice. I didn't speak.

"Oh, cat still got yo' tongue? Buster, see you can hep him think what he wants to say."

I felt a knife at my back. First there was just enough pressure to touch me, then he gave it a hard push. It penetrated and caused me flinch and jerk. The man on the horse laughed. He opened up again.

"Now, Mista, tell us where you got that nigger hid."

"I don't have him. He kept on running."

"Oh, yeah? Well you better run after him and bring him back. I aint kiddin you Fairfield, that nigger is worth a thousand dollars to us."

"I don't know where he is, he kept going out through the back."

"Okay, in that case, theys only one thing to do. You gon' have to pay us that thousand dollars."

"I don't have a thousand dollars. I got cleaned out tonight."

"Naw, I don't think so, not you, Mista Fairfield. Check his pockets, Buster."

Buster went through my pockets and found nothing. He missed the pistol. He looked up at the man on the horse.

"He's telling the truth, Cap, he aint got nothin'."

"Damn!"

Cap was angry and he continued to swear at me. Then he had another thought.

"Where you keep yo money, boy?"

"In the bank."

He started cursing again.

"You no good bastard, you gon' have to pay for this. I think we'll go on over to the little lady's house and see we can all be accommodated before we head south. Maybe that will keep you from medlin' in the future."

"Hold it." I had to prevent that somehow. "I can get the money tomorrow."

A long wheezing sound erupted from Cap, followed by a chuckle. He knew he had struck a nerve.

"Okay boy, we gon' give you 'til noon tomorrow. You come back to this very same spot and hand me a thousand dollars. You understan'?"

"Yes."

"Let's go boys!"

They left, as quickly as they had come. I pulled my pistol and aimed in the direction of Cap. But he had gone too far into the darkness and I didn't fire.

I ran to Kelly's and got my horse. Pain was now coming from my back, and I could feel that there was a lot of blood. I knew I would need help to stop the bleeding, and I was also concerned about Sarah. Would Cap try to hold her hostage just to be sure I brought him the money? I decided to go to her house. When I got there I knocked on the door, hard, and within just a few minutes she came to the door.

"Alex! What's wrong?"

"Sarah ... can I come in?"

"Yes, of course. Alex are you hurt?" She had a look of fear, as well as an expression of great concern as she spoke further. "You look like you might be in pain."

After I was inside I began telling her what had happened.

"Some men attacked me on the street ...maybe you better lock the door and then I will explain."

She turned and did as I asked and I took a few steps in the direction of the drawing room. She came along quickly behind me and she saw that there was a wound.

"Alex there's blood coming through your coat in the back. I'm going to send Uncle to get Dr. Jefferson."

"No, don't do that ... not yet. Maybe you can look at it. The men who attacked me know about you and they might come here. Let's see if we can handle it without getting anybody else involved. Do you mind taking a look to see how bad it is?"

"No, I don't mind. Come over by the light and take off your coat and shirt."

She cringed when she saw the wound. She tried not to alarm me, though, as she told me how it looked.

"It's not too bad. Still bleeding so we will have to work on that first. Stay where you are and I will be right back."

Even though I was in pain, it was a good feeling to have her concerned about me. The look on her face, as she realized I was hurt, was a silent confirmation of her true affection. She was back in less than two minutes, bringing water in a wash bowl, soap, cotton and bandages.

"This is cold water, Alex. I'll try to stop the bleeding and clean it at the same time. It's a knife wound, isn't it?"

"Yes."

She asked me to sit crosswise in a straight-back wooden chair. She began washing my back near the wound and gradually eased over and very softly dabbed at the wound.

"That hurt?"

"No, it's okay. Thanks for helping me."

"Well, I wouldn't want to do this on a regular basis, but for you, Mister Fairfield, I can handle it. Do you want to tell me what happened?"

"It was the same men who came here earlier. They must have asked a lot of questions because they knew I would be coming out of the Blue Star."

"Oh, that place! When will you ever stop going there and settle down?"

"As soon as you tell me that you will run away with me."

"I'm not ready to run away, you know that."

"Yes, unfortunately, I do know that."

She continued to work on the wound, and occasionally she would blot it with cotton to absorb the blood. Finally she took a hand full of cotton and held it against the wound.

"Tell me if I push too hard. I'm going to see if pressure will stop the bleeding."

After about a minute she took the cotton away. She said it looked better and another minute or so should do it. As she continued to hold the cotton in place she spoke softly.

"I missed you at church Sunday evening."

"I missed you, too."

"I'm sorry, I was out of sorts Saturday night. When you didn't come to church I realized I had over reacted and I felt bad."

"I think it was my fault. I know I go too far sometimes."

After a few more minutes she had the wound taken care of and wrapped in bandages. I didn't want to leave because I felt she would not be safe and I told her.

"Sarah I don't want to leave here tonight, I'm not sure you would be safe. I can sit in a chair downstairs and you can go on up to bed. Will that be all right?"

"Yes . . . it will be all right ... Alex, there are six bedrooms upstairs, why don't you go up there so you can rest? I can prepare a bed for you and get all the things you will need and you can be much more comfortable."

"I want to stay down here, Sarah, it would be safer. I don't think anything will happen, I just feel better being here."

"Well okay. I'll stay and visit with you for a while"

I smiled and she could see that her nearness was comforting to me. She pulled a chair over next to the one where I was sitting and we were very close. She reached over and held my hand. She looked into my eyes and smiled as she spoke.

"Do you remember the evening when we first met?"

"Yes, I most certainly do."

"Did you bump into me by accident or was it on purpose?"

"It was an accident. It was so crowded I didn't see you."

"I never heard so many apologies. It was only a slight thing but you made it seem like you had run over me with your horse."

"I had to keep you there, keep talking. I wanted to know your name and how to find you."

"And how did you know that I didn't have a husband who might suddenly walk up?"

"A gambler's instinct. It didn't matter anyway, I knew that I had to see you again."

"Why, Mister Fairfield, would you try to take another man's wife?"

She was teasing but I was serious as I answered.

"Yes, I would have tried to take another man's wife if it happened to be you."

"You sure didn't waste any time after that night."

She was smiling and enjoying the conversation. I grinned at her.

"You didn't seem to mind."

"No, I didn't mind. Alan had been gone for a while and I felt it was time to become more active... maybe get back to a normal life again."

"Do you want to tell me about Alan?"

"I can tell you about him. He was kind and considerate, and he gave me everything under the sun. We were only married for six months before he was killed in the accident. I think the small problems we were beginning to have was because of the difference in our ages. It had an effect on both of us near the end."

"How much difference in age was there?"

"Twenty four years. I was twenty-two, he was forty-six. He had been married earlier while in his twenties. She died two years after they were married."

"How did you happen to end up with a man who was that much older?"

"Oh ... I don't know ... he was so good to me and I guess I felt like the whole world was at my feet. I could have anything, go anywhere, and it all seemed so thrilling and glamorous. He was tremendously wealthy and he was very generous in the things he did for me."

"Do you miss him?"

"In some ways I do. I miss his kindness. But, in other ways we were never really compatible." She turned and looked at me. "And now I want to hear about all of your lady friends."

"No you don't, it would be too boring. I'll just sum it up by saying that I never considered getting married, I never found the right lady."

"Well, it sounds like you must be kind of picky. And another thing. You sure are sneaky. Who else would get themselves stabbed in the back so they could get into my house in the middle of the night?"

We both laughed. Then she looked over at the big clock nearby and spoke.

"I have to go now. I hope you can get some rest. If you need anything, just yell for me."

She looked at me and smiled. I was holding her hand and I pulled her over gently so that her face was next to mine. We rubbed cheeks and then we were kissing. I raised my other hand and put it on the side of her face, and we were drawn deeply into a passionate moment with an unyielding desire for each other. We were being driven by the tender kisses of a loving affection that was consuming each of us. She finally pulled away and smiled. She stood and spoke.

"I'll see you in the morning. I'm glad you are here."

Then she walked away in the direction of the steps.

# II.

For the next two or three hours, I dozed in a cushioned chair and then fell into a deeper sleep. It seemed like no time had passed before a slight noise awakened me. As I opened my eyes, I saw Sarah at the window, pulling the drapes together. She turned and saw that I was awake.

"Good morning! I was trying to keep the sun out of your eyes so you could sleep a little longer. How are you?"

"Good ... I think. Let me see if I can get out of this chair, and I can let you know for sure."

She came and put her arm around me as I stood. I had been in the chair for a long time, and was stiff. Sarah wanted to check the wound.

"Turn around, and let me see the bandage in the back."

She said it looked alright. there was no blood showing through the bandage. She asked if it was sore, and I said, "Yes."

"Well, we're going to see Doctor Jefferson the very first thing. He lives nearby, and I have already sent Uncle to tell him that we are coming. Doctor Jefferson told Uncle that it still might not be too late to stitch the wound so we need to get moving as soon as possible."

"Okay, we can do that, but I need to send a message to Major Dale. Can Uncle take it?"

"Yes, I think so. What's it about?"

"Last night. I need help to get rid of the bounty hunters."

By ten-thirty we had been to the home of Doctor Jefferson and had returned to Sarah's house. Doctor Jefferson had stitched the wound and had given me an ointment to use. He said that it looked "nasty," and advised me to be careful for a while so that the stitches would not pull apart. He explained that it should heal in a week or ten days. In the meantime, Uncle had delivered the message to Major Dale and had returned with an envelope for me. Inside there was a one-sentence statement from Major Dale: "Be at the location as requested by the bounty hunters at the time that was specified."

I felt good. I knew Major Dale would be there to support me. Sarah was nearby, and she was curious. "What's going on, Alex?"

"I have to go into town, be near the Blue Star at twelve."

"Alex, are you crazy? You can't ride a horse."

"I thought I could use your carriage. Do you mind?"

"Yes! I do mind! You are not going to make that wound break open so you can forget it!"

"Sarah, I'm committed to being there."

"I don't care. You know what Doctor Jefferson said. Maybe we can send Uncle."

"No, that wouldn't work, I have to go."

She thought about it. After a lengthy pause she told me what she would do.

"I will go. And I will handle the reins."

"Sarah, please, be reasonable. Think about how that would look. And it might be dangerous, anyway."

"Alex, I'm going to do exactly what I said. There isn't any other choice for you so take it or leave it."

About forty-five minutes later, we were in the carriage and under way. During the ride Sarah asked me at least five times if I could feel any blood running down my back. I wasn't sure but each time I told her, "No."

We passed Kelly's Stables and turned the corner about a block from the rendezvous point. I took out my pocket watch and saw that we were right on schedule. Sarah did as I told her and pulled up about a hundred feet from the Blue Star. I saw Buster leaning against the front of a building on my right, "grinning like a possum," as Shorty would say. I glanced about and saw what I believed to be some of the others. The street was relatively quiet although there was some activity, including two men on horses, several people in wagons, and one other large carriage. Cap wasn't in view, but that didn't surprise me. When we came to a halt, Buster walked over.

"Where's the money?"

I looked past him as if searching for someone.

"Where's Cap?"

"Don't worry about Cap, give me the money."

"No. My deal is with Cap. I'm not going to pay off twice."

He twisted and turned and seemed to be uncertain. He motioned to a man about two hundred feet up the street. The man responded by holding up two hands, asking for a further explanation. Buster pointed impatiently in the direction of an alley. The man turned and walked into the alley. In a minute or so the man appeared again. He stood for at least thirty seconds looking alternately up and down the street. Finally, he turned and said something to someone out of view in the alley. A rider came out. It was Cap. He was big and heavy-set, and I remembered him at once because of his size. Also, I recognized the horse. He rode up next to the carriage and stopped. He had a simple-looking grin on his bearded face.

"Well now, Purty Boy, looks like Little Mama had to come along to hold yo' hand. Ain't that sweet?"

I stared at him. I wanted to be sure that I could remember him.

"Okay, Fairfield, the game's over. Give me the money."

Looking beyond him I saw the blue clad cavalry soldiers on horses as they turned the corner. They were in no hurry, they were coming at a walk. After they turned the corner they straightened up into formation, six abreast, two lines deep. Cap, who was facing away from them saw something he didn't like coming from the opposite end of the street. I knew without turning he had seen additional cavalry soldiers. The street was sealed off. Cap knew he was in trouble.

"What the hell ..."

It was a highly satisfying scene that I would remember for a long time. Major Dale came from our rear. With two aides he rode ahead of the troopers and spoke sternly to Cap.

"What's your business here, Mister?"

Cap stammered out an answer.

"Well, suh, I was just stopping here to greet this fine gentleman and his lady ... "

"What's your name?"

"C.F.Smith. At yo' service, suh."

"Mister Smith, I know you are a bounty hunter. You're out of your territory. Gather up your men and be quick. You're headed away from here. And don't ever let me find you in Washington again."

"Yes, suh."

Soon, Cap and his men were walking up the street. Major Dale had instructed Cap to get off of his horse and walk too. There were some laughs and loud jokes from the onlookers on the street. The rag-tag group of eight had been pushing their weight around on the street for the past day or so, and now they were shuffling off in true cowardly fashion.

Major Dale told one of his aides to take charge. Then he turned to us. "Good day, Missis Sullivan, Mister Fairfield."

We greeted him and he continued.

"I don't think we will see these men again. I'm sure you can forget them, Mister Fairfield."

"I appreciate your help, Major."

"Any time." He was preparing to leave, then, looking at me, he offered one final comment. "I hope we can have that meeting soon."

"We can. I'll send word."

He smiled and turned away. Sarah wanted to know what he was talking about.

"He's looking for someone to do some work for him."

"Work?" She laughed. "Doesn't he know what kind of work you do?"

"That's enough, Missis Sullivan. Don't underestimate me."

She laughed again and popped Old Ben gently with the reins to get us underway. As we headed back toward her home, I tried to reason with her.

"Sarah, please, let me have the reins. I'm fine. Think how it will look to your friends if they see you driving a carriage."

"No, I'm not going to let you tear those stitches open. I'm not worried about my friends. I drove the carriage over to the navy yard recently when Uncle was sick, so stop worrying about it."

I decided to drop it. She was very kind and could show great tenderness, but at other times she could be strong-willed. It was best during those moments to leave her alone.

After a short silence she turned in my direction.

"Alex, how do you happen to know Major Dale so well?"

"He came up to me in the theater and introduced himself. We met later and talked. He wants me to do something for the Federals, and my guess is he wants me to become a spy. Since I don't know exactly what he wants, I agreed to meet with him again. Whatever it is, he wants to keep it secret, so don't mention it."

"Would you do something to hurt the South?"

"No, I wouldn't deliberately do anything to hurt the South. But we've talked before, Sarah, and we both feel slavery is wrong."

Later, when we arrived at her home, Sarah told me to stay in the carriage and she would look for Uncle. She realized that I had gone about as far as I could. Soon she was back with Uncle who was leading my horse. Sarah spoke.

"Alex, Uncle will drive you home and put your horse in the pasture. I want you to go to bed and rest. Will you promise?"

"Yes, I promise."

At home I found that I could sleep in a new position, on my stomach. I got in bed at five in the afternoon and slept for hours. It was late, in the middle of the night, when a loud knock at my door awakened me. I took a lamp and walked to the door. I put the lamp on a table in the foyer, held a pistol in my right hand, and opened the door with the other hand. I was amazed when the light from the lamp flashed on the man who was there. Ed Jenkins from Savannah!

"Ed! How did you get here?"

"Hello, Alex. I thought you might be surprised."

"Yes, that's putting it mildly. Come in ... before the Yankees see you."

We both laughed. He came inside, and I closed the door. I pointed toward the parlor. As we were getting settled in chairs he began talking.

"How are you, Alex? I heard about what happened."

"I still have some pain and I'm sore. Otherwise the doctor says I will be okay in about a week."

"That's good. I won't keep you up. I know you need rest. Can you put me up for the night?"

"Absolutely. I've got plenty of room upstairs. But tell me, what brings you to Washington?"

"Something important. We have to talk ... in the morning. I took the liberty of putting my horse inside your fence. I hope that is all right."

"It's fine. Would you like some whiskey before retiring?"

"No, just show me to a bed."

The next morning I heard Mary Kate rattling pans in the kitchen downstairs. She did that on the few occasions when I was late getting up to let me know that breakfast was ready. Mary Kate Adams and her husband, Bradford, worked for me. She came each morning and stayed half a day, cleaning the house and cooking meals. Bradford was an expert horseman, and I paid him full-time wages to care for my horses. Mary Kate was unable to have children so both were able to work. They lived a short distance away in a small house that I owned.

When I got downstairs Ed was already there, in the kitchen having coffee and in conversation with Mary Kate. I had the feeling that he was eager to begin our discussion.

After breakfast I suggested to Ed that we take a walk outside in the back of the house. It was pleasant with the sun shining brightly, and there was an early morning freshness that filled the air. We had already engaged in small talk, and as we reached the fence that formed an enclosure for the horses, Ed turned and looked directly into my eyes.

"We need your help, Alex. This war is going to be more difficult than most people in the South realized and we are going to have to do some extraordinary things to win. That's why I came, we need help here in Washington, help you can provide."

"Ed, I'm not a soldier, I'm a gambler. It's the only thing I have done since I was sixteen years old. How can I possibly help?"

"Because of what you just said. You're set up in perfectly. Nobody will ever suspect you are doing anything connected to the war."

"What can I do?"

"Let me back up a little. We've come to realize that we don't have the things needed to carry on a war for a long period. The hot-heads thought it would be over in six months, but we know now that is not going to happen. We're going to need money and war supplies. As you know, our representatives have been to England and France. I feel there is a good chance they will help us. But we have to show them some success. We have to send our armies north into Yankee territory and win a major battle. And, of course, the ultimate goal will be to take Washington. If we can do that, England and France will provide the money and supplies we need."

He paused to get a reaction from me.

"But isn't that a tall order, taking Washington?"

"Yes, a very tall order, and that's one of the things you can do to help us."

"I don't understand."

"We want to know all about fortifications and how many troops are here ... it's information we might need quickly at the right time. We also want to know about the people in the city. We believe at least half of the people would rise up to help if the city was attacked. But most importantly, we need information that would come from high-level people, what moves are being planned by the Union commanders."

"I don't know people like that, how would I get that type of information?"

He paused and took a long look out across the pasture, then he turned toward me.

"Through Sarah Sullivan. She has contacts with everybody from the President on down."

"No! Absolutely not! I would not even consider it."

"Why not? She's from South Carolina. She must feel a loyalty to the South."

"No, she wouldn't do it. Forget it, Ed."

"How do you know? Have you talked to her about how she feels?"

"Yes, we've talked. We both feel slavery is wrong."

"I think it's wrong too, Alex, but it's too late. The hot-heads have already started a war. I think it could have been settled without a war, and there was some hint that Mr. Lincoln felt the same way. He wanted to work out a plan to set the slaves free without bankrupting their owners ... at least that is what I heard. But that is water over the dam now, and it's too late, we're stuck with a war. All we can do is try to win, and it is going to take all of us, plus some help from overseas. You are going to have to take a stand, and I hope you remember where you were born."

I thought about what he said, "you are going to have to take a stand." They were almost the same words used by Major Dale and it was becoming a very challenging situation.

"You're making this very difficult, Ed. I can't give you an answer at this moment except to say once again that I will not involve Sarah. I need time to think about this."

"We don't have time, Alex. I have one operative set up, a woman, and I would like to take you to meet her. She is already established right here in Washington"

"No, I'm not interested in doing that. In fact, I don't want to know her name or anything about her."

"Well, let's forget about that. But I do need to know what you will do."

"I'm sorry, Ed, I cannot give you an answer at this time. I'll have to let you know later."

He was disappointed. However, he accepted my answer. He said that he would leave and possibly return in a day or so. I made an effort to let our parting be agreeable.

"You better be sure the Yankees don't see you. I think they might hang you right on the spot if they catch you."

He laughed. He began making preparations to leave, and soon was astride his horse. A few moments later, with a determined expression on his face, he guided his horse in the direction of the long driveway that would lead him to the main road.

I was greatly troubled. For the rest of the day and late into the evening, I was unsettled and unable to rid myself of the thoughts that were so troublesome. I slept very little during the night.

The next day Uncle came with a note from Sarah. She wanted to know how I was feeling and wanted me to send a note back by Uncle. Also, she said that she would be unable to see me during the weekend because Alan's sister and her husband from Philadelphia would be visiting. She invited me to come for tea Tuesday afternoon, and said she would send Uncle in the carriage to pick me up at two. I wrote a note on the same piece of paper, telling her that I was fine and that I would look forward to seeing her Tuesday.

The next few days passed slowly, although, on a positive note, I could feel that my wound was healing. At times it would itch, and when that occurred I would get Mary Kate to rub on some of the ointment that had been given to me by Doctor Jefferson. Through the weekend, I didn't hear from Ed Jenkins, and I was glad. I wanted to talk to Sarah and get another opinion on everything. And, in having such thoughts, I realized how much I respected her knowledge and her views.

While sitting on the veranda in the rocker early in the afternoon on Monday, I saw a rider turn off of the main road and come into my driveway. As he approached, I recognized him. It was Phillip. I was happy to see him. He waved from a distance, and I waved back. When he got to the front of the house, he dismounted and greeted me.

"Thought I had better come out and see about you - can't afford to have a long-time friend like you go down."

I grinned as he came up the steps and sat in a chair near me.

"Oh, in that case, I believe you might deserve a glass of whiskey."

I poured it for him. He relaxed at once, and we began talking about, among other things, some of the card games that had taken place in years gone by. He said I looked good and he was pleased that the wound was healing. As we talked longer, my instincts told me that he had something to tell me, something that might be difficult for him. Finally he decided to let it come out.

"Alex, I'm going to tell you something that is very difficult for me. I've been thinking about it all during the time I have been here, trying to decide, and I trust I've made the right decision."

I didn't know what to expect. I knew he did not deal in frivolous matters, at least with the serious look he had on his face. I told him to go ahead and let it out, and he did.

"Saturday evening Polly and I dined at the Willard. Sarah was there with another couple, and she was being escorted by Jennings. They were sitting across the room, and I'm not sure she ever saw us." He paused to let his comments sink in and continued. "They were drinking what I assumed to be wine, and ... Alex, I hate to say this because I know it will hit you like a hammer ... she looked like she was having the time of her life. She was -"

I interrupted.

"How do you mean that, was she focusing a lot of attention on Jennings?"

"Yes. She was laughing, reaching over and giving him a little push on the arm, and holding hands."

His words shocked me and came as a great surprise. I was deeply disappointed, and I was angry. I didn't know which feeling was worse, and it seemed like the roof had crashed in on me. I thought I had reached a point with her that nothing like that would happen. Phillip had paused, and I hadn't spoken either, and then he broke the silence.

"You haven't heard the worst. Do you want me to tell you?"

"Yes."

"We were outside later, waiting for our carriage, and they were ahead of us. As the other couple got in front of them, getting into the carriage, Jennings and Sarah were still standing on the street, and they suddenly reached for each other and the kiss of all kisses took place. When they pulled apart they seemed to be quite pleased with each other, and they were smiling. Then they got into the carriage with the other couple and off they went. I'm very sorry to tell you this, my friend, and I very nearly didn't. I know how much she means to you, and I know that I have brought you a sad message. If you want to shoot me, go ahead."

"No. I won't shoot you. If anything, I would probably shoot myself. I just can't believe it. And I'm not saying that I doubt your story, Phillip, it's just impossible for me to reason it out. She told me that she was going to see him again so that's not so much of a surprise. The thing I can't imagine is what happened on the street. If she was drinking wine, I can understand to some degree the way she was acting inside. The rest just seems unbelievable, and it takes away just about everything I had begun to believe about her. Do you think she was intoxicated?"

"Ah ... not likely, although I suppose the wine could have had some effect."

"Thank you for telling me, Phillip. I know it was a hard decision for you. You're a good friend, and you did the right thing."

Not long after that he left. When he did I sank into a greatly depressed mood.

Tuesday morning I made the decision to go through with the plan to visit Sarah. I had spent most of the time since Phillip had come on Monday trying to decide. Thoughts had come to me in the process that ranged from never going back to going there and confronting her in an angry way. In the end I decided to go and act normal, see how she would respond and conduct myself accordingly.

Uncle came on time, and I climbed up into the carriage with him. I wore one of my long dress coats and a new cravat that I had purchased recently in an expensive shop.

When we arrived, Sarah met me at the door, smiling, and greeted me warmly. She seemed happy to see me.

"Do come in, Mister Fairfield, how nice you look today!"

I smiled in return. She asked about my back, and I told her it was much better. She said the weather was so nice she was planning for us to sit on the veranda in the back. We walked through her house to get there and sat in chairs that had been arranged in place next to a table.

We began talking about commonly discussed things and soon Armeenia brought us tea and cookies. During that time I could detect nothing different in Sarah's manner. I knew that she knew, however, that my instincts were very perceptive, and I felt that she would be careful with words. And I was quite certain that she would prefer not to discuss Jennings, or her most recent engagement with him. We talked some about the war, how it was going and how it might affect everyone.

As the time passed, we discussed some of the men she knew, several of the Generals, and it was then that I could sense a slight change in her. She was not quite as carefree as she talked. She seemed a little more tentative. Because our talk had narrowed down mostly to individuals, it was a little more uncomfortable for her.

Maybe she had noticed a change in me, and knowing that I had spent my adult life as a gambler carefully observing the outward signs given off by others, she most likely felt that she could not hide a secret from me. Finally, after a long pause in our conversation, during which time she looked passively into my eyes, she spoke softly.

"Alex ...have you ever made a bad mistake?"

"Yes, I make them all the time."

"No, I mean the kind that keeps you awake at night."

"Yes, I've made that kind, too."

"Since I saw you last week, I have made a bad mistake."

"How bad?"

"Not the worst, but bad."

"I'm sorry. Is it something you want to talk about?"

"I don't know. I do want to talk about it, but ... I'm not sure."

"Sarah, I think I know what is disturbing you. You don't have to tell me, I probably already know why you might be upset."

"But ... how could you know?"

"In my profession I have watched people for years, and about nine-five per cent of the time I know how to judge their thoughts. I know that you are trying to decide whether to tell me something that would be painful for you."

She looked away for a long time. Finally she turned back to me.

"Can we just go on, as we are?"

"Do you really want to go on?"

"Yes, of course, you know I do."

"Sometimes I feel that I might be out of place."

"I don't think I understand that. What do you mean?"

"It seems that most of the people in your life, especially the men, went to Harvard, or the military academy, or a medical school. And the women are from wealthy families, and they are the socially elite here in Washington. Maybe it's just not right for me."

"Alex, you know that I have never let anything like that affect our relationship. I tease you, but I adore you for what you really are, a good and sincere man. I don't know of any man that I respect as much as I do you."

I smiled, and wanted her to know that I appreciated her comments.

"Thank you, that was very nice to hear."

"So can you answer the question, can we go on as we are?"

"Sarah, you know how I feel, and that will never change. I think it's more of a question about how you feel."

"You know perfectly well how I feel. Just because I have said that I am not ready to settle down doesn't change my feelings. When I married Alan I had not previously had a serious relationship with a man, and as I told you, we were beginning to have some differences toward the end. I didn't know exactly what was wrong and wanted to be careful about my future. I thought getting to know other men would help. Can you understand how I feel?"

"Yes, I can understand. But you have to understand me as well. When you have searched for something for a long time and find it, you want to know it is yours and that you will be able to keep it."

She stared into my eyes for a long time with a sweet and tender expression. Small tears began forming in her eyes. I had never seen her cry before, and I knew that she was deeply touched. I reached over and took her hand and raised it up to touch it to my lips.

I felt I should go. To stay longer would make it worse for her, make her even more emotional. I used an excuse and told her that my back was beginning to be bothersome. She asked Armeenia to tell Uncle to get the carriage ready and wait for me in the front. Then we walked through the house together. At the door she spoke.

"Alex, will you kiss me?"

I did kiss her. And as she kissed me in return, it seemed that she was putting all of her heart into it. We held on tightly for a short while and then we moved apart. I touched her face, said goodbye, and walked out to the carriage. Just before I climbed up into the carriage, Sarah called out to me.

"Alex, when will I see you?"

It caught me by surprise. I answered in the best way I could in order to respond quickly.

"It depends on how well my back heals. I'll send a note."

She smiled. Then she raised her hand and waved. I waved back, turned and climbed up into the carriage, and we were off.

All the while, as I had visited with Sarah, I was being pulled in two directions. First, I knew that she had become a part of me that would remain forever. My feeling for her would never change. Whether I could be with her or not, she was buried so deeply in my heart she was there to stay. But, another thought kept coming back that was connected. Could I keep punishing myself as I had for the last twenty-four hours? When Sarah asked, "Can we go on as we are?", she had meant it. She had no immediate plans to change, and there would be occasions in the future when she would spend time with other men.

And even though I felt she cared for me deeply, the possibility would exist that another man might come into her life and take her away. She had told me that she was uncertain about relationships with men because of her marriage to Alan. And she might be right in trying to be sure that she didn't make the same mistake again. It was likely to leave her relationship with me dangling in the days ahead, and it would be necessary for me to make a difficult decision about her.

As I rode in the carriage with Uncle, thoughts occurred to me that were troubling and worrisome. It was as if something urgent had suddenly come about, almost like a desperate situation. I even thought I might leave Washington for a while. I could go back to St. Louis. It would solve two problems. Sarah, as well as the situation that had come about with Major Dale and Ed Jenkins... I would not have to worry about a decision regarding the war or which side I would support.

I had made a great deal of money during the five years I had lived in St. Louis. It had been a gathering place during the time for men of wealth who wanted to gamble. My name and reputation had become known from one end of the Mississippi River to the other and beyond. Men wanted to be able to say that they had beaten me in a game of cards, and they had paid dearly for trying.

Because of my long experience in gambling and a sensitivity that was an inner trait, a gift of sorts, I learned how to win and win big. I still had money in three banks in St. Louis, a total running well into six figures. I had met Phillip in St. Louis. He was working there as a lawyer. He had come to play cards a few times, and we were soon good friends.

After we both realized that he could not win, he stopped playing in the games with me. In those days he was known as a real "rounder," vibrant and always searching for the best of good times. While not in his office, or working in the courts, he stayed occupied with things he found to be thrilling and enjoyable. He was jovial and had a keen sense of humor, and shared those characteristics with me on many happy occasions. He was quite well received with the ladies; he was handsome, and had a personality that kept them laughing.

It was a lady, however, that brought about the reason for his departure from the city. He became involved with a prominent young woman in an affair that somehow went wrong, and he decided to move on. He had heard that there were better opportunities in Washington anyway. One year later he talked me into making the same move. And now, returning to St. Louis would be like going back home for me. Would I be willing to do it?

# III.

The next morning, after breakfast, I walked back into the pasture. We were continuing to have nice weather, so it was a good time to be outside. The mornings, in some ways, seemed to be the best part of the day. The fence that enclosed the pasture formed an outline of the land that was owned by me. The surrounding acres were wooded and not in use by the owners. Walking deeper toward the back, I realized that I had not been there for many months. Actually, there was no reason for me to go there.

At the back of the fenced enclosure, there was a cluster of tall bushes densely grouped together with an undergrowth that made an impassable barrier for the horses, and the small amount of land beyond was unusable. As I reached the edge of the briar patches that formed an outer edge, I got a glimpse of a movement on the far side.

Whatever it was seemed large, and I considered whether it might be one of the horses that could have somehow been able to get through the bushes. I thought it might need further investigation, but I was in no hurry to go back there, and it was only a minor distraction for me at the moment.

I was too involved with thoughts of Sarah. She was taking away everything else, consuming all of my plans and hopes for the future. Nothing like Sarah had come to me in the past. My life, although exciting, had also been unconditionally reckless.

I had been exposed to dangerous individuals and threatening experiences so often that I was conditioned to it, and my lifestyle had become much like my profession: a risk and a gamble. The one thing that I had steadily held on to was the advice given to me by my mother. She had encouraged me to always stay close to the church.

And oddly enough, I had met Sarah in the church. It was at one of the social gatherings, and I had accidentally backed into her. I knew from that point on I would do anything necessary to pursue her so that I could somehow bring her into my life.

I stood in the same spot in the back of the pasture near the bushes trying to think of Sarah in a way that would be rational and not based solely on my emotional state of mind. Each time I thought about leaving Washington and going back to St. Louis, trying to convince myself it would be best, I always came to the same conclusion. I could not do it. Even if I saw Sarah walk away with another man at some time in the future, I could not leave and give up the opportunity to be near her. So, I came to a conclusion that would allow me to put the matter to rest. I would not leave Washington.

I had been standing in the same place for about ten minutes when a voice called out to me from the other side of the briar filled hedgerow.

"Mister Fairfield, may I speak with you, sir?"

What a surprise! I would not have imagined anything of that nature in my wildest dreams. I answered.

"Yes. But who are you, and how did you get back there?"

"I can explain that, sir, if we can talk."

His deep voice sounded like a black man. Nonetheless, I did not believe him to be black because of his manner of speaking and pronunciation of words. I responded to his request.

"All right. Can you come around to where I am standing?"

"Possibly it would be best, sir, if we could talk on this side of the hedges. If you will walk a short distance to your right, I can point out a way for you to get through."

I did as he suggested. After going some twenty paces, I could see what he meant, a small opening that was not as tightly closed up by the vines and brush. I was able to push my way through to a small open area where I raised up and looked at him. And at the first glimpse I was quite surprised. He was, indeed, a black man, and I recognized him at once. It was the man who had been chased by the bounty hunters and had escaped by running through Sarah's house.

He moved toward me, and I walked forward to meet him. He spoke first.

"I am sure that you must be very surprised to see me."

"Yes, I am. How did you happen to end up here?"

"I asked a lot of questions. I believed that if I could get to your place I would have safe refuge."

"I am glad you made that decision. You are safe here. What is your name?"

"Malcolm."

"The men who were chasing you said that there is a thousand dollar reward posted for you. You must be considered quite valuable to the people in Virginia."

"Well, that is possibly true. Unlike most of the other slaves there, I had the opportunity to have an education in England, and when I was brought to New York and sold into slavery, a large amount of money was paid by the bidders. From New York I was taken to the plantation in Virginia. There, among other things, I was to teach the other slaves."

"That's amazing. How long have you been back here in the pasture?"

"Four days." And he turned to point to a shelter made of limbs and parts of bushes. "As you can see, I have set up housekeeping in a somewhat delicate structure." He smiled as he continued. "I hope you do not mind, sir, I had no other place to go."

"No, I don't mind. And I will help you. If we can get you out of Washington, farther north, maybe you will be safe."

"Thank you, sir, I appreciate it very much."

"How long has it been since you have had food and water?"

"I have come up to your barn at night and found some of the dry corn, and I have taken water out of the horse troughs to drink. And again, sir, I hope you do not mind."

"No, of course not. I will put food there for you tonight, something that will be better. Also, there will be a container of water. Tomorrow I will begin making inquiries, quietly of course, on how we can best get you headed north. Oh, I will also put blankets with the food and water. We will have to be very careful, and it will be best for you to stay back here where you are."

"I agree. And thank you again, Mister Fairfield."

"How did you get to Washington?"

"I found help along the way from people like you."

"That's interesting. I don't know much about these circumstances. I have never had experiences with slaves, and most of what I know is what I have heard from others. How many slaves were there at the farm in Virginia?"

"Thirty-eight, counting both men and women."

"How were you treated?"

"That depends on exactly what you mean. The master does, of course, want to keep all slaves healthy so they can be productive. And to that end they are cared for well. Otherwise, there is no freedom, at least with regard to leaving the premises. All work for six full days and rest on Sunday."

"Have others tried to run away?"

"No, as far as I know, not from the McCleskey farm. One of the first things a slave is told is not to run away. A great deal of emphasis is placed on that, and it is made known from the beginning that bad things happen to slaves who try to escape."

I was amazed by Malcom's manner of speech. For the first time in my life, I realized that a black man is as intelligent as anybody else if given the opportunity to develop his capabilities. I wanted to continue the discussion.

"You were very courageous to attempt it. How did it come about?"

"I knew that I could not continue to be a slave. The master eventually placed enough trust in me to give me a good opportunity to get away. The chance finally came that I was waiting for and I used it."

"What do you think would happen to you if you were caught and sent back?"

He smiled.

"I'm not sure. The owner is not a bad person, although there might be some sort of punishment to set an example."

I smiled in return. At that moment a thought flashed into my mind that had never occurred to me. How many others were waiting and hoping to be helped? I thought back, briefly, to the time when I was young and on my own with no place to turn. I had lived from day to day on the streets of New Orleans while still in my teens, fighting and clawing to stay alive. And though I was not in bondage, I was a prisoner of sorts restrained by a wall of insecurity, and at times, a lack of hope. And so, I could relate in a very small way to the feelings of a person who might actually be held in slavery. I continued the conversation.

"You are very fortunate to have a good education. I'm sure it will help you in the future."

"Yes, under the right circumstances maybe it will help. And if I may say so, sir, you seem to have had the same privilege. Did you attend a college nearby?"

"No, I didn't attend a college. The knowledge I have was gained by being a good listener, among other things. In my profession I was exposed to men who were well-educated. I realized that it would enhance my opportunity to become successful by acquiring knowledge, and allow me to associate with men that I would not have otherwise had the chance to know. I listened very carefully to their use and pronunciation of words and watched their body movements and bearing. And it seems to have worked; at least it has opened some doors that otherwise would have been closed."

"Well, I can certainly say that you present yourself as well as any gentleman I have seen in the limited opportunities that I have had, and I believe that your observations of others is very keen."

I expressed my appreciation for his comment and continued the conversation in another direction.

"What would it take to help the others, the ones who are left on the McCleskey farm?"

His eyes brightened. Then, almost immediately, his expression changed.

"It would be virtually impossible, sir. And that would be true even more now since my escape. May I ask the reason for the question?"

"Just a wild thought, I suppose. For a moment I was thinking back to the early years of my life when I could have used some help."

"There is much danger now from night riders, like the ones who were chasing me. They are dangerous men. I have heard they are deserters and rejects from the Rebel army, as well as many other types, and they will kill with no regard to any circumstances."

"Where are they?"

"Scattered across the state in small bands. They seem to appear in many places."

Following my conversation with Malcolm, I pushed my way back through the hedges and walked toward the house. I felt a strong need to help the slaves. I had never felt that way before. Slaves had been a part of my surroundings that had always been there. They were like the cotton fields, the Mississippi River, and it was as natural as the rising sun. Now, with the first hand knowledge provided by Malcolm, I felt differently. Many other people were probably like me.

We did not recognize that we were a part of a mass injustice, a wrong that we were willing to accept. And the hot heads, as Ed had termed them, were going to war for the wrong reason. Probably the majority of the lower-ranking fighting men had no slaves. They were told that the Yankees were coming to take their homes, their land, and their way of life. So they had easily become inflamed. Their concern was not for black people; the Yankees would need to be defeated for other reasons.

When I reached my house, Mary Kate was waiting for me on the outside.

"Uncle is here. He is waiting in the front to see you."

"Thank you, Mary Kate."

I walked around the house instead of going inside. Obviously there would be a message from Sarah, which was not a great surprise, although it did seem somewhat unusual.

In the front, Uncle was standing beside the carriage. We greeted each other, and then he handed me an envelope. He spoke again.

"Miss Sarah say she would like for you to send her an answer."

"Okay, Uncle, let's see what we have," and I took a note out of the envelope.

Sarah had sent an invitation for me to come on Sunday and dine at one o'clock in her home with three other couples. She named the couples and I knew them by reputation. All were among the most wealthy and influential people in the city. Immediately I realized that she was proving a point. She was rebuffing the statement I had made to her about feeling 'out of place among her friends.' After reading the note I spoke to Uncle.

"Tell Miss Sarah I will be at her house at one on Sunday."

He acknowledged what I said, climbed up into the carriage, and left.

I went inside to find Mary Kate. She was in the kitchen preparing a meal. She seemed to recognize the look I had in my eyes and stared at me, waiting for my question.

"I have been invited to dine Sunday with some people who are..." and as I paused she finished the sentence.

"Very important."

"Yes. I need your help with my clothes, I want to be sure I look like a gentleman."

"Oh, that should be no problem. The new long coats and other things you bought recently should be just fine. Pick out what you want to wear and I will be sure that everything is perfect."

She was right. I had bought new, expensive clothing recently in anticipation of playing cards with two wealthy gentlemen who were coming to Washington from another state, and I could be very confident in the appearance I would put forth.

During the following days and evenings, I was careful to be sure that fresh food and water were placed at the rear of the barn regularly for Malcolm. Saturday morning I felt that I could ride my horse without disturbing the stitches that had closed up the knife wound in my back, and I rode into town to see Phillip.

On Saturdays he was alone in his law offices, cleaning up the "mess," as he called it, that he had created during the week. He had said in the past that it was a good day for me to visit. And, as usual, he seemed glad to see me.

"Well, my good man, you appear to be much better. I assume you rode here on a horse?"

"Yes indeed. I'm trying to be ready for the big-time gamblers."

"When are they getting here?"

"Soon. They will let me know when they arrive."

"Is it going to be high stakes?"

"Yes. They travel all over the country looking for big games. I played with them once before and they remembered me."

"Who won that time?"

"Who is sitting in your office right now?"

"I should have known."

Then we talked about other things. Finally I brought up the subject I wanted to discuss.

"Phillip, how do you feel about slaves, and slavery?"

"Hell, Alex, I don't know. Why?"

"Do you think it's right?"

"I guess it's right for some, not right for others. I have just left it alone."

"So have I. But is that right, should we just close our eyes?"

"Mr. Lincoln is taking care of that."

"I know, but in the meantime shouldn't we try to help some of them become free?"

"Alex, if you are thinking about what I think you are, you are about to get your ass shot off. You go messing with somebody's slaves, his property, and he is going to treat you like a thief. Just because you helped one get away doesn't mean you need to organize a crusade. Take my advice, and leave it alone."

I gave him a big smile and changed the subject. His answer made me realize that it was not going to be easy to help Malcolm, much less consider anything else. Phillip and I talked and laughed for about another hour and then I headed to another part of town. I wanted to see Major Dale.

Major Dale was out of his office. I wanted to stay in touch with him, so I left a brief message. In the note I stated that I had come to no decision yet about assisting him, and that I would need more time.

Late Sunday morning I was on my horse again. I was going to Sarah's to keep the appointment at one o'clock, and I had left home early in order that I would be able to walk my horse for the entire distance. In that way I would not become dusty or ruffled en route. For Sarah's benefit, as well as my own, I wanted to meet her guests looking "perfect" as Mary Kate had termed it.

Uncle met me on the outside when I arrived and took my horse. Sarah greeted me at the door and smiled broadly.

"Oh, Alex, please come in." As we walked closely together, she said very quietly, "you look very handsome today."

We walked into her large parlor. Her other guests were there, six in all. Sarah held my hand, and we walked up to each person, whom she introduced, and I exchanged small talk briefly with each one. I felt that I was on equal ground with all, and the situation was not awkward for me. After all, I had spent hours playing cards with people for years who were as influential, if not more so, and I had no feeling of being out of place.

Sarah had tables set up on the veranda for the meal, and we slowly moved there and were seated. Two tables were set, and we separated into two groups. Sarah and I were seated with a man and his wife who each appeared to be about sixty-five years old. The man, who was the president of a bank, was pleasant and content to discuss subjects that were common, primarily the war. His wife was more inquisitive, and she finally got around to a question that I knew she would raise sooner or later.

"And what sort of business are you in, Mister Fairfield?"

"I raise and sell thoroughbred horses."

"Oh, I see," and she almost sounded disappointed, "I suppose you must be very busy now with the need for horses in the war."

"Actually, the war has not changed our business so far. The army needs mules and commonly bred horses, not the kind of animals I have."

I glanced at Sarah, and she was smiling very slightly. I knew she was pleased with the answers I had given, and possibly relieved as well.

Tootsie, a young black girl about fourteen years old who was living with Armeenia, was walking among us with a large fan, using it to be sure that no insects were drawn to the food. It was very pleasant on the veranda. Colonel Sullivan had put a great deal of thought into constructing the house and grounds. There was a walled courtyard covered with cobblestones that enclosed an area of about one thousand square feet. To the right was a building that accommodated five separate carriages. Above that structure were the rooms for Uncle, Armeenia, and Tootsie.

In addition to giving food and shelter to the three blacks, Sarah was paying them wages. She had filed the necessary papers that set each one of them free. Sarah was an unusual woman. She was as caring and tender-hearted as anyone I had ever known. At the same time she could be very spirited in many ways. And, as Phillip had told me, she was very wealthy and powerful. Even though I was quite certain that the other guests were aware that my true profession was gambling, I knew that I would be politely accepted and treated courteously. It was highly unlikely that anyone in the city of Washington would be willing to do anything to arouse resentment in Sarah.

After the meal was finished, Sarah asked the ladies to accompany her inside to the parlor. The tables were cleared and the men were left on the veranda. Sarah had said, "All right, gentlemen, you can smoke your cigars now."

Some did. I had never acquired the habit and did not participate. Talk resumed about the war. The man who was president of the bank raised a question about Mr. Lincoln.

"I think Old Abe is going to have to find somebody in the Union Army who is willing to fight." One of the others responded.

"I agree." And he turned toward me.

"How about you, Mr. Fairfield, how are you planning to become involved?"

"In the way I am presently involved, collecting mules and horses. I am sure there will come a time when these animals will be desperately needed."

He nodded. I could sense that it was not the answer he had attempted to pull out of me. He accepted it, however, out of respect for Sarah, and obviously did not wish to be the cause of a disruption at one of her social gatherings.

A discussion began among the men about the weapons that were in use by the Union Army. One of the men, a Doctor McMillan, said that he had heard about a new hand gun that had been developed by Colt. He looked in my direction as he asked a general question.

"I know very little about it. Has anyone else heard of it?"

The other two men glanced at me and I decided to answer.

"Yes, I have heard of the weapon. It is a muzzle-loaded cap and ball six-shot revolver, forty-four caliber." Doctor McMillan was curious.

"Do you know how it works?"

"It is a single action pistol. It uses a paper wrapped cartridge that combines the ball and powder. A percussion cap, when struck by the hammer, ignites the powder charge and the ball is fired."

"You seem very informed about this, Mister Fairfield."

"I have a friend who is a cavalry officer, and I learned about it from him."

At about four o'clock Sarah came out and made a few remarks that were offered as friendly comments by a good hostess. Then, as she turned to go back to be with the ladies, and in a way that was not intended to be conspicuous, she leaned over and whispered in my ear.

"Can you stay for a while after the others leave? I want to talk to you."

I turned my face upward toward her and formed a "yes" with my lips. She smiled and went back inside.

Not too long afterwards, the bank president and his wife expressed their appreciation to Sarah and departed. The other two couples followed rather soon, and Sarah and I returned to the veranda where we were alone. She was bubbling as she spoke.

"I was very proud of you today, Mister Fairfield."

"Why thank you, Missis Sullivan."

"I told the ladies that we go to church together, and they were impressed by that."

"I'm glad. I wanted to please you today."

"Well, you certainly did." Then she became a little more serious. "I wanted you to stay because I want to explain something."

"All right, go ahead."

"I told you a few days ago that I had made a bad mistake and I want to explain that. I did something foolish, and it was meaningless to me at the time, done impetuously without any thought. It was nothing really wrong. I didn't kill anybody, but you were the reason

I later thought it was a bad mistake. I knew it was something that would have hurt you if you had known, and I do not want to hurt you. So, I wanted you to know ... and I want you to forgive me."

She looked lovingly into my eyes. She was as beautiful at that moment as I had ever seen her. I spoke immediately.

"Of course I forgive you. Forget it and don't ever think of it again."

We stood and embraced. We held each other closely for a few moments and then we backed away. She was happy, and so was I. The day had suddenly become a special one, and I would remember it for a long time.

It was time for me to go. Sarah and I agreed that we would not make our usual Sunday evening visit to church, and instead I suggested that we meet next on Tuesday and go for an early afternoon drive in the carriage. She liked the idea and our plans were set.

A few minutes later we were standing near the front door when Uncle came with my horse. I held her closely again, and we kissed with a new kind of feeling. Then we pulled apart, and I walked to the outside. It was the end of a day with her like no other, more gratifying than anything I had ever known in the past.

At the break of dawn on Monday, I got out of bed and walked to the window of my upstairs bedroom. It had become a morning ritual, looking out to see if the day would be clear, and if it would be a good day for the horses to graze in the pasture. I had slept well, and felt good. Then, as my eyes followed the fence for a short distance to the left, I saw a rider sitting motionless on his horse. Upon close observation I recognized him to be Ed Jenkins.

I dressed quickly, went downstairs to the back door, and called out to Ed. He turned and saw me. He dismounted, tied the reins of the bridle on his horse to the fence, and walked in my direction. We greeted each other, and I asked how long he had been there.

"Only a short while. I camped in the woods last night."

"Why didn't you wake me and come in?"

"I think the Yankees might know about my presence here in Washington now, and I didn't want to take a chance on being caught in your house."

"Are they closing in on you?"

"Not yet, but I am planning to leave today. I wanted to talk to you before leaving."

After we had coffee I decided to open up the subject that obviously had to be discussed.

"Ed, right now, all I can say is that I have to remain neutral. I cannot bring myself to work against what Mr. Lincoln has vowed to do – free the slaves."

"Alex, you have to realize that it is no longer just a matter of freeing the slaves. It is North against South. We have to win to preserve our existence."

"I still don't know what I can do to help."

"Convince Sarah Sullivan that she must help us. I know she has contacts that could provide invaluable information."

"No, that is the last thing on earth I would ask her to do. Even if I did ask she wouldn't do it. She loves the South, but she detests anything that is deceptive. And, she would not betray anyone, regardless of which side she is on, so you will have to consider that a closed matter."

"Okay, since you are putting it like that, I will. We are only trying to counter what is being done by agents working for the North."

We entered into a lengthy discussion about the war. He said there was great confidence existing among the people of the South. Military leaders like Lee, Longstreet, Jackson, Stuart, and others, men with battle experience as well as great enthusiasm among the common fighting men, had created an army that was eager to fight. And they would, indeed, be difficult to defeat. Ed made one final comment.

"I'll be back. I know your heart is with us, and I know you will help us at some time in the future."

And then he was gone.

During the day I walked to the back of the pasture and talked to Malcolm. I told him that my initial investigation indicated that it would be best to wait for a few days to try to formulate a plan for him to get out of Washington. It would be necessary for him to stay put for a while longer. He was agreeable. During the discussion I let him know that most of the people in Washington and southern Maryland were sympathetic to the South.

Tuesday turned out to be another beautiful day. Sarah seemed very happy to see me when I arrived at her home in the early afternoon, and we were soon in the carriage, ready for the ride we had planned on Sunday. And this time, knowing that the knife wound had healed, she let me handle the reins. I asked where she would like to go.

"Out in the direction of the Navy Yard. That road usually does not have as many holes ... maybe it will be a smoother ride."

I tapped Old Ben with the reins and we were under way. Sarah seemed to be relaxed and joyful. Was it my imagination, or was she more settled in her feelings about our relationship? After we had gone a short distance, she had an interesting thought.

"Maybe we will see Mr. Lincoln. He rides out this way sometimes."

"Do you think he would recognize you?"

"I don't know. I've only visited with him briefly at social events. Missis Lincoln might remember me."

"How do you like them?"

"He is a wonderful man. His wife is very devoted to him and their sons."

I turned and grinned at her.

"I could be very devoted to you."

"I know. And I would love that. Just don't rush me."

The carriage we were in was the one that had been ordered by Colonel Sullivan for Sarah. It had been custom made in England and had features that other carriages did not have. In the rear-view mirror attached to the side, I noticed that we had picked up a rider who apparently was following us. He was staying back, but he had been with us too long, and he obviously had focused his attention on us. I would keep watching, and if he stayed there I would take a turn at some point ahead to see if he followed. If he did stay with us, I would have to find out who he was and what he might want.

Sarah obviously was enjoying every minute. She teased me a lot, laughed often, and was as happy as I had seen her in a while. And being with her under those conditions made it a uniquely pleasing time for me.

About twenty minutes after I first saw the rider behind us, I took the turn I had planned. He followed. Why was he there? My greatest concern was Sarah's safety. Normally I would turn and confront him, but with Sarah in the carriage, that would not be an option. I was careful not to let her see my concern. I tried to think of the best way to handle the situation.

"Sarah, would you mind if we stopped by Major Dale's office so I can thank him again for helping us with the bounty hunters? His office is nearby, and I'm sure he would appreciate it. You can stay in the carriage."

"Yes, of course, Alex. He seems like a nice man."

I guided Old Ben in the direction that would take us there. Actually, I had no plans to leave Sarah sitting in the carriage. I believed the rider would disappear as soon as he could see where we had led him. There would be a number of blue clad soldiers on duty out front, and I would be greatly surprised if he did not turn away at that time. And I was right. He got one look at the street ahead and turned away at a gallop. I drove to the front of the building and stopped. I looked around for a minute or so and then spoke to Sarah.

"His horse is not here so it appears we have missed him. I can stop by another time."

We took a different route back to Sarah's, and I didn't see the rider again. It was important, though, for me to find out why he was there in the first place. I wanted to get back to the street where we saw him as quickly as possible. I had to use an excuse with Sarah to get away. I told her I wanted to see a man regarding a business matter. She said it was fine, and I was able to leave quickly without alarming her.

I searched the streets where we had been until it was almost dark. I knew that I would not find him so I went home. It was late in the evening, however, before I went up to bed.

# IV.

"Mista Alex! Mista Alex!"

Was I dreaming? It must have been one or two in the morning, and I was in a deep sleep. Then I heard it again, and this time I recognized the voice of Uncle.

"Mista Alex!"

I got out of bed and ran down the stairs. I had left an oil burning lamp lighted in the entrance hallway, and I could see clearly as I got to the door and opened it.

Uncle was there and he was greatly shaken. He was sweating profusely.

"Mista Alex, law have mercy, they have done come and took Miss Sarah!"

I was stunned.

"Uncle, what do you mean? What happened?"

"The men came, and they pushed me down and they took Miss Sarah!"

"When? How long ago?"

"It was ... I rode as fast as I could to get here ..."

"You mean it was only a short while ago?"

"Yes sir. I heard her scream, and I ran from the buggy house to the big house. They had Miss Sarah, and they was going out the door. It ain't been but about one hour."

"Did you know them, or have you ever seen them before?"

"No sir."

"Did they say anything, leave anything?"

"They ain't said nothing, and they ain't left nothing."

"How many were there?"

"Four or five. Will you come right now and see about her, Mista Alex?"

"Yes! I want you to stay here, Uncle. They may come here, but they won't hurt you. They will come for me, or they will come with a message for me. I'll send help as soon as I can."

"Yes, sir."

I dressed quickly. I got my Colt revolver and a handful of cartridges. I ran to the barn, and in the dark I put the saddle on my horse. In less than five minutes, I was riding hard toward town and Sarah's house. I kept thinking, "I should have known... I should not have left her." I was completely overwhelmed, almost in a panic, and my mind was flooded with anxious questions. Who were they? Was it because she was rich? Would they harm her? There were so many transients in the city, so many different types. It was impossible to understand.

Gradually I was able to calm myself and think more rationally. She had been taken because of me. It was the result of the encounter I had with the bounty hunters. No other person would go into the neighborhood where Sarah lived and commit such a crime, it would be unheard of and too daring.

When I got to Sarah's, nearly all of the rooms in her house were lighted. It was the same with the surrounding homes. There were horses in Sarah's front yard tied to trees, bushes, and other places. Inside there were many people, most of whom seemed to be neighbors. Several men were there who were acting with authority, and they were questioning Armeenia and Tootsie who were sitting in the parlor. I walked past all of the people to the stairs and went up to Sarah's bedroom. Two men were there. One of them looked at me and spoke.

"Who are you, sir?"

"My name is Alexander Fairfield. I am a friend of Missis Sullivan."

"How is it that you happen to be here?"

"I was notified by a servant."

"Well, we must ask you to go back downstairs and wait there."

He spoke with firmness and I turned and did as he asked. Downstairs were men who represented officials of the city, and they were handling the situation in a manner that seemed to be thorough. A very prominent person in the city had been taken, and they would use every possible means to solve the crime. It was obvious there was nothing I could do so I decided to go back home.

I was sure that the abduction of Sarah was related to me, and I wanted to be where I could be found by those who had taken her. I did speak to Armeenia and Tootsie, and I assured them that we would find Sarah and that everything would be all right. I told them that I would send Uncle home and that he should be back within two hours. Then I walked out.

On the way home I considered everything I could think of that would be connected to what had happened. I decided that it was related to the bounty hunters. They knew about Sarah and me, and they would still be very disgruntled about losing the reward for Malcolm. And even though I denied having Malcolm, they must have believed otherwise. Now, I felt that they might try to work out an exchange, Sarah for Malcolm. They were a desperate breed, living in desperate times, and taking a woman from her home in the middle of the night would be simple compared to most other things they likely would be doing.

Early the next morning I rode my horse into town. I went directly to the area where Sarah and I had been the day before. I walked my horse slowly on all of the streets. I wanted to be seen. I stopped occasionally. It allowed me to give the horse a pause, and it placed me in one spot for a few minutes at a time. Nothing happened, and no one approached me. Maybe it was too early in the day. Also I was basing my actions on a guess. My theory that Sarah had been taken as a first step in getting to me could be wrong. In a way it was like a card game in which a person bet everything on a hunch. Fortunately, and sometimes miraculously, my instincts were almost always right.

After several hours I became tired and discouraged. I had slept very little during the night. Before leaving my house, I left a note for Mary Kate telling her that I would be away and that I might not return during the day. I went to Sarah's house but no word had been received about her. I stayed there for several hours.

At three-thirty, I went back to the same area of the city where I had been earlier in the day. There, I decided to go inside a bar, known by some as a saloon. It would be much easier for a person to approach me there than it would outside on my horse. I picked an establishment that seemed to have a little more activity than some of the others. I walked inside and stood at the counter. The other men in the room looked rough, some with hangovers, and others just "down on their luck." Even so, I felt secure. The Colt revolver was hidden under my coat, and I knew it to be a powerful weapon. And, I would have no reluctance to use it.

I ordered whiskey and sipped it slowly. After about twenty minutes, a man who had been in the back of the room walked in my direction. As he passed, he slowed his pace and spoke to me quietly.

"Heavy wants to see you in the alley in the back."

He kept on walking and went out the front door. I looked toward the back of the room and saw a door. It would be the way out to the alley. I didn't rush. I finished the glass of whiskey and paid the amount that was due. I had seen a man go through the door a minute or so earlier, so it would not be out of the ordinary or look unusual for me to do the same.

Outside I saw a heavy-set man standing close by. He had dark hair, a dark beard, and dark eyes. Based on the knowledge I had gained from years of being around men of all types, I judged him to be a dangerous individual. He spoke.

"It's the nigger for the woman, Mister. You try anything else, and you ain't ever going to see her again."

I wanted to be sure to keep him there and keep him talking, try to learn as much as possible.

"What makes you think I have the black man?"

"Aw, I think it's a pretty good guess. If you ain't got him, you know where he's hid."

"I don't have him. Maybe I can find him. But first, I want to know about the woman. Is she all right?"

He frowned and I knew he would respond with a surly and demanding attitude.

"Naw, you don't need to know about that. You tell me, right here and now, when you will bring us that nigger."

I decided on a bold move. I pulled out the Colt revolver and aimed it into his face. The long barrel was about one foot from his nose. I looked hard into his eyes as I spoke firmly.

"If one hair is missing from her head when I find her I will blow your brains out. The same will be true for your friends. I hope I don't have to tell you this again because next time you might not be so lucky. Do we understand each other?"

He was surprised by the revolver. It was large, and with the barrel nearly touching his face, he showed a significant amount of anxiety. When he spoke, it was with a different tone.

"Don't git yourself all worked up, Mister. Just bring us the nigger, and it will turn out all right."

"Tell me about the woman. How is she being treated?"

"Fine, just fine. They ain't nothing for you to worry about. Now, what's yo answer?"

"I need some time to try to locate the black man. Where can I find you?"

"Nawsuh, it ain't gon' work that way. You tell me, right now, what you will do."

I didn't answer immediately. I needed time to think. After a moment or so I asked a question.

"Others came when she was taken. Who runs the outfit?"

He didn't answer, and I don't believe he intended to answer. I was still holding the revolver in his face. I cocked the hammer. It had an immediate effect. I knew by his facial expression that he would give me the name.

"Forest runs things. He likes the woman so he ain't going to hurt her. But, Mister, he can be real mean, and if I was you I would go ahead and settle up quick."

"I'll settle up as quick as I can. In the meantime, you go back and tell Forest if he wants to live, if he wants to avoid getting a forty-four caliber ball from this revolver in his gut and another one through the head, he will send the woman home unharmed. Can you remember that?"

"Yas-suh, I sho can."

"Tell him I will meet him tomorrow. I will come alone. He can name the time and place to work out all other details. You come back to this bar at ten in the morning and give me his answer. Tell him we will discuss the black man and an exchange that can be set up for a later time. Now move out, and be sure nobody makes a mistake."

He turned, got on a horse nearby and headed up the alley at a fast pace. He spurred the horse into a gallop to prevent me from following him. He knew I would have to go back through the bar to get to my horse, and even then there would be a row of buildings between us. It would be hopeless, and I had to accept it.

Then, I realized something else. They were a different group, not connected to Cap and the men we had originally encountered. Malcolm had told me that there were separate bands roving the State, and many of them were now hearing about the large ransom being offered and would become involved. And so, it meant we would be seeing some new faces.

On the way home, it occurred to me that I would need to talk to Malcolm. When I arrived, to save time, I rode my horse to the back of the pasture. At the hedgerow I dismounted and called out to Malcolm. He answered at once.

"Yes, Sir."

"I'm coming in. We need to talk."

After going through the bushes I met him and shook hands. I told him that we had a problem, and as I continued to talk I described everything that had happened. I assured him that I would do nothing to jeopardize his freedom. But, I did warn him.

"You will have to move your shelter from the open area. Can you build something inside the hedgerow?"

He smiled.

"Yes, sir, I can do that. When I am finished no one will be able to see anything."

"Good. I will come again soon and keep you informed."

I pushed my way back through the hedges and got back on my horse. Riding in the pasture in the direction of my house, I thought about Malcolm. He was unique in many ways. He was about thirty years old, lean and muscular, and he had fine facial features that gave him an unusually nice appearance. It probably had contributed to his value when the bidders were attempting to buy him as a slave. The most outstanding feature about him was his deep and melodious voice.

The next morning, at fifteen minutes before ten, I was sitting on my horse in front of the saloon where I had been the day before, at the front rather than in the alley. I was there because I believed that Heavy, or Forest, would be more likely to come there. The alley could be sealed off rather easily, and they would be aware of that so they would not consider it to be safe.

I waited for what seemed like an hour. I was ready to reach for my pocket watch again when I saw a rider approaching on his horse, at a walk, in the middle of the street. He caught my attention because he was continuously turning and looking in all directions, and he seemed to be interested in me. When he was about one hundred feet away, he stopped. Then he used his stirrups to stand up slightly and look carefully in all directions.

After he was satisfied, he looked directly at me and came in my direction. When he was about twenty feet away, he stopped again, and turned in all directions one final time. After that, he looked at me and motioned with his head for me to follow and he turned back in the direction from which he had come. I moved forward on my horse and had soon overtaken him. I rode alongside him, and we were both silent as our horses moved along at a slow trot. Finally he spoke.

"Do you have the revolver with you?"

"Yes."

"Get rid of it."

"No, I won't do that."

There was a long pause. Then he spoke.

"Take it away from your waist and put it in your saddle bag."

I did as he asked, and as he commented further, he seemed more at ease.

"We are going to a location nearby. We will dismount, tie the horses, and walk for a short distance to a spot where we can talk. Don't cause any trouble."

I wanted to know with whom I was dealing.

"Do you know a man named Forest, and a dark haired man who is called Heavy?"

"Yes, they are feeble-minded amateurs, trying to collect a fee from us."

"And so they do not actually have Sarah Sullivan?"

"No. We have her, and I can assure you that she is being well taken care of."

He appeared to be rather young, maybe in his late twenties. He was slender, though not frail. He was wearing a wide brim hat that was pulled down low on his forehead. His facial features gave him a handsome appearance. His coloring, as best I could determine, was blondish. He was light skinned and did not have the markings of a man accustomed to being outdoors. He had a gentleman's likeness, rather than a lowly type. Even his clothing and boots were expensive and were not befitting of a man involved in bounty hunting. Just before we dismounted at the location he had picked, I asked another question.

"How do I know that Sarah Sullivan is safe?"

"You will have to take my word."

After we had tied our horses and walked some twenty-five feet away, he turned and stared into my face.

"Do you have the negro?"

"No, not yet. I'm working on it."

"I can give you twenty-four hours, no more. I have to be absolutely certain that he is returned."

"You don't have to rush. I can arrange for you to be escorted safely away if you return the woman."

"Mister Fairfield, let me explain something. The negro is special. There are critical considerations involved. His value is much more than what has been offered by McCleskey. A great deal of time and money has been spent on this particular negro. He is like one of your thoroughbred horses, and we must have him back."

"If he is so valuable, why was only one thousand dollars posted for his return?"

"To disguise his real value."

I had become somewhat of an expert at determining the location, or part of the country, from which men originated. It was because I had been exposed to people from all parts of the country while gambling, and I was confident that the man standing before me was from New York. The distance from which he had come complicated the present situation with Malcolm, and there were questions I would need to have answered.

"How did you come to believe that I have the black man?"

"All questions we have asked have pointed in your direction. We know you have protection, friends in the military, and it is therefore a situation now that requires negotiations rather than the use of force."

He had become relaxed. He even sounded slightly conciliatory. He obviously believed that I would be his best opportunity to recover Malcolm without creating a major problem. If his efforts with me failed, it might become more complicated. Consequently he would be willing to extend the conversation for as long as he felt safe. I tried a new approach with him.

"I have a great deal of money, and I am willing to pay you for the safe return of the woman."

"No, that won't work, no amount of money will help you. I will give you no further details, Mister Fairfield. You only have one option, and that is to bring us the negro."

"How can I do that if I don't have him?"

"If you actually don't have him, you know where he is. We have talked to other blacks, and we know it was his intent to seek you out."

I paused for a few moments before speaking.

"I can ride to a location ten minutes from here and secure the help of the Union Army. There would be no way for you to escape from Washington. Because of the prominence of the lady you are holding, they will hang you. Do you want that to happen?"

"No, of course not. But if that came about, no one would ever see Missis Sullivan again. And so I will also ask you, sir, do you want that to happen?"

He was holding the best cards in the deck, and he knew it. I had to concede in my mind that he had me backed into a corner. I continued the discussion.

"I need time to locate the black man. There are people I can question who may be able to help me. However, it might not be possible to find him in twenty-four hours."

"It has to be done. Every minute that passes makes it more critical."

"You don't seem like the kind of man who would be responsible for the death of a woman."

"I didn't say she would be killed. I said you would never see her again."

"How is she at the moment?"

"She is fine. Every precaution has been taken to ensure her safety."

"How is she emotionally?"

"Again, she is fine. She is a courageous lady. But we have talked enough, Mister Fairfield, and you must decide if you will pick the woman or the negro. You must act quickly. And forget about money. I already have plenty of money."

"The woman must be returned. I will do my best to find the black man."

He prepared to leave. He spoke as he slowly turned to walk toward his horse.

"Be here at ten tomorrow, and be prepared to take us to the black man. It is the last opportunity you will have."

Then I watched as he walked to his horse. Just before he mounted I called out to him, "One moment, sir!"

He turned to look back at me. I spoke in a firm manner.

"I don't know your name, and I don't know the others. But I will promise you something you can believe. If the woman is not returned, unharmed, I will come for you, and you will live a very short life."

He stared momentarily, and then I could detect a very slight smile.

"I believe you, Mister Fairfield."

He turned, mounted his horse and rode away.

Maybe it was time to go to the City and Federal authorities. My fear in doing that before was based on the possibility of jeopardizing the safety of Sarah. If her captors should panic and run, they might be afraid to leave her as a witness. The only advantage of bringing in the officials, or disclosing information to them that they might not have, would be to have many more people involved in the investigation who would be able to go in the right direction.

But, I was still reluctant. I believed that the safe return of Sarah might be more at risk if others were involved and somehow might make a mistake. I decided against it, at least for the time being.

I began to reason things out. The man from New York was intelligent. He was unlikely to make mistakes. My guess was that he had set up temporary headquarters nearby in Maryland. That would limit the authority of the officials in Washington who would be searching for him. He might even have Sarah there. I believed that he had been truthful in stating that Sarah was being cared for in a safe manner. Also, I believed that he had no intention of seeing her harmed, regardless of the outcome with Malcolm.

Next, I considered his connection to Malcolm and his related statements. He apparently was a part of an organization that was dealing in slave trading with a different twist. Could it be an organization that would secure blacks and train them in such a way that would make them more valuable? It would be a specialized business, offering trained blacks to people not only in the South but the North as well. Mr. Lincoln was concentrating on freeing the slaves in the states of the South that had seceded. It meant that a market might still exist in a more limited way in the North, and other places.

Also, the suave man who had just been there with me had mentioned my thoroughbred horses. Could that have an underlying meaning? Through a selection process that would unite black couples who possessed fine appearances and good physical features, children could be produced that would be a refinement of their qualities. Slavery had been in existence for thousands of years, and it would not be an original thought. It could well be that others, like Malcolm, had been taken from their native lands to places like England where they were given the opportunity to become well-trained and educated. They could then be sold not only in the United States but also in other countries throughout the world.

Although history would portray the South as the culprit in the war now being fought, slavery was still allowed in the North, even though it was more limited. And the slave traders, for the most part, had originated in the North. It brought Malcolm into focus in my thoughts. I would plan to have a detailed discussion with him as soon as possible. I would want to know everything he could remember about his past. Maybe it would tell me if my theory was right.

On my horse, moving slowly along the street, I considered contacting Major Dale. I knew I could trust him, and I needed help quickly. My only reluctance was the question of what he might expect from me in return. I couldn't turn against the South, and I did not want to lie to him about it. I could only hope that he would help me anyway, and decided to take a chance. I turned and rode in the direction of his office. Fortunately, Major Dale was in and immediately received me in his office. I wasted no time in getting to the point of my visit.

"I need help. Can I ask for your assistance without committing myself to anything else?" He knew what kind of help I needed.

"Yes, of course, my friend. I am very much interested in the welfare of Missis Sullivan and any other considerations will not be a factor at this time."

"Thank you, Major."

I proceeded to tell him the details of all contacts I had made with the men who were claiming responsibility for taking and holding Sarah. I told him that they believed that I was protecting the black man they wanted and that they were offering the return of Sarah for the black man. I did not tell Major Dale that Malcolm was hiding on my premises. I simply repeated what the men had said to me, that they were certain that I either had him or knew how to find him.

As I paused, Major Dale gazed deeply into my face and smiled. If was as if he knew that Malcolm was in my care. After a few moments, he spoke.

"What is your feeling, Mister Fairfield? Do you have any thoughts on how we can proceed or what type of help we can give you?"

"No, not really. That is why I came here. They have given me a deadline of ten o'clock tomorrow morning."

"I see. Well, that doesn't give us very much time." And a confident smile appeared on his face. He leaned back in his chair and raised both hands in front of his face, touching his fingertips together. It was a brief gesture, and he then moved his hands downward, back to a normal position by his side. His expression changed, and I could see a distinct look of determination in his eyes.

"Let's get to work."

There was a paper tablet on his desk and he picked up a pencil that was nearby. He began making notes as we talked. I described each individual who had contacted me in relation to Sarah. He was particularly interested in the man who I assumed to be from New York. He was not in complete agreement with my theory that the man had established the point of his operation in Maryland.

"You see, Mister Fairfield, fortifications have been built that circle the city. Even though people are still allowed to travel on the roads it is necessary to pass our sentries. I am not sure he would want to do that and be seen and questioned."

"How about traveling by rail?"

"A better possibility. But, you said he was on a horse. How would he manage that?"

"Maybe he has help here in the city. I know he has at least one man, and probably two, who are helping him. He admitted that when we talked. But, you may be right. He could be somewhere in the city. I know he plans well, and I had just assumed that he would feel it to be too dangerous to stay here."

The Major was quiet and thoughtful. He looked away for a while, then turned back to me.

"We might be able to fool him. If you appear tomorrow with a black man, a man we will disguise, we can arrest him at the meeting place."

"What about Sarah and what he has threatened? She might disappear under those circumstances."

"I know it's a risk, Mister Fairfield, but considering what you have said about him, I believe that no harm will come to her, and I think it may be our only chance to get him. After we are able to question him and impress him with what he will be facing as punishment, I am sure we will have a good chance of finding her. And, if it turns out that there is no other way, we will offer him his freedom in exchange for bringing her back ... under our supervision, of course."

I thought about it and even though it made sense, I still didn't like it. My concern was that something would go wrong, and Sarah would not make it. But the Major was probably right, we didn't have that many other choices, and we didn't have time. I asked him how the plan would work.

"We will disguise a black man and let him ride on a mule behind you. We will try to cover his face with some sort of hat, or something he can wear on his head. You will then lead him to the meeting place. We will have our men hidden, out of sight, surrounding the whole area. It will be impossible for him to get away. How does that sound?"

"It's a good plan, and if he does actually show up, I am sure you will get him. My only concern is Sarah Sullivan. I hope no mistakes are made."

"I hope so, too, but I honestly cannot think of anything that would be better. Time is a factor, and we have to make a move quickly."

I agreed and he continued.

"They may be watching the road at your place, so I think it will be best for you to spend the night here in this building. You can leave from here in the morning and go in a roundabout way with the black man. We will take care of all details. The only thing you will have to do is ride there and let the black man, whose name is Amos, follow you on the mule. Before dawn, I will dispatch a number of cavalry soldiers who will take up their stations surrounding the area, and everything will be in place at ten o'clock."

It was settled. Now would come the difficult part. Waiting.

Major Dale took care of the details needed for me to stay overnight in the building. I was shown to a room on the upper floor and told that breakfast would be served at six o'clock.

During the night I slept very little. In my mind I played out every conceivable thing that could happen the next day. As usual, things always seemed much worse at night.

At nine-thirty the next morning, I was outside standing next to my horse. Everything was in place. Major Dale was with me, and he went over the details of the plan one last time. After that he offered some advice.

"Remember to control yourself, Mister Fairfield. He will not plan to bring Missis Sullivan. He will plan to tell you that he will take you to her. When he realizes that you have brought the wrong man he will run, and that is when we will take him. Good luck."

I smiled and mounted my horse. I was ready to leave when the Major spoke again, "Mister Fairfield!"

"Yes?"

"Be careful with that revolver."

I moved away on my horse. The black man, Amos, was already mounted on the mule and followed closely behind me.

We didn't have far to go, and we moved along well. We were within five minutes of our destination when a rider came up fast from the rear. He had pulled up alongside Amos, almost before I knew he was there. He took a good, hard look at the negro, and then he raised his right arm up high above his head, moving it crosswise as if to signal someone up ahead. Then he came forward for me, yelling.

"You dirty liar, you're a dead man!"

He had a small derringer in his hand, and he stuck it in my face. He pulled the trigger and I heard a metallic snap. It had not fired. He quickly took the pistol in both hands to reset it but it gave me time to bring out my revolver. Just as he was ready to raise the derringer in my direction again, I fired the Colt. The ball struck him in the forehead, just above his eyes. The impact was so great that he was knocked from his horse and landed on the ground three or four feet away.

I immediately looked in all directions to see if there were others. There were none. I then spoke to Amos, who was still close by on the mule.

"It's all right now, Amos. He was not coming for you."

"Yes, sir."

He had remained very calm. And actually, it had happened so quickly it had not greatly affected me. It was over almost before it began, and I had reacted instinctively without having time to think about it.

Soon there were blue-clad soldiers there, both on foot and on horses. By the time I had dismounted and walked over to look at the dead man on the ground, Major Dale was there. He looked at me with concern.

"Are you all right?"

"Yes. He had a pistol that didn't fire. He got here so fast I still don't know where he came from."

A cavalry soldier commented excitedly.

"He came out of that alley over there, sir. I saw him, and had started this way."

Major Dale, standing close to the dead man, picked up the derringer and spoke.

"Well, as I suspected, it is the kind of pistol that is not reliable. Otherwise, Alexander, you might not be here with us."

Major Dale looked through the pockets of the dead man. He found almost one hundred dollars in cash. There was no identification, he had been careful to remove it beforehand. Among the miscellaneous items was the stub of a rail ticket from New York. It might explain how he knew that Amos was not the man he was supposed to be. He had probably seen Malcolm previously in New York when he had been brought in as a slave. Also, in my mind, it confirmed my theory about the man I had met the previous day. He, too, had most likely come from New York. They obviously were working together.

Soon the street was full of people. Major Dale had sent word to the cavalry soldiers in the area of the location where the meeting had been scheduled to take place, and they were instructed to search there thoroughly. Any person who might be suspicious was to be brought in for questioning. After some twenty minutes he turned to me.

"Let's go back to my office and talk. There is nothing further to be done here. The city officials have arrived and they will take over now."

I nodded. Even though I continued talking to him it was a distraction. My mind was full of thoughts of Sarah. What did these new events mean in our efforts to bring her back? It was a very disturbing thought.

A detective with the City of Washington approached and identified himself. He said he had been made aware beforehand of what we were attempting to carry out, and that no charges would be filed against me. He stated that it was unquestionably a case of self-defense. He did ask for the revolver, and requested that I come to his office later in the morning to make a report. He told me that the revolver would be returned at that time. Following my conversation with him, Major Dale and I returned to his office. After we arrived and were settled in chairs, I raised the question that was weighing heavily on my mind.

"What can we do now about Sarah?"

"I don't know. I've been thinking about it, and other than using the best possible means of surveillance we have here in town, we don't have many options."

"I'm sure the man I spoke to yesterday is from New York. Do you think he will head back there now?"

"I believe so. I think he will give it up here. It is too dangerous for him now. Also, you mentioned that he talked about a deadline and that, too, might prompt him to leave."

"What about Sarah, what will he do with her?"

"That's difficult to know. He might keep her with him."

"Can you get any help from New York?"

"Oh, absolutely. I will send a telegram to Major Porter and give him complete details. He has the same job there that I have here, and he is very cooperative. He is thorough, and I should have a response from him in a day or two."

"Will you tell him that there is the possibility that Sarah might be with the man who was here?"

"Yes, I'll give him every detail that we have."

We talked for another thirty minutes. Then I left to go to the detective's office to file a report. I was not there long, and he returned my revolver as promised.

Shortly after one o'clock I was on my horse, riding in the direction of home. Being alone, with only my thoughts to accompany me, I became downcast and remorseful. My instincts and intuition kept telling me, "you will never see her again." It was painful to me, and I could not remember a time when I had felt as upset and sad. She was the one thing in my life that had given me pleasure and happiness that I had never known. I could not give up hope on the only woman I had ever loved.

It seemed I had been grasping for something forever, and when Sarah had come along, she was the answer to everything. It was the reason I had been so jealous when she was with other men, and the thought of losing her was almost unbearable. I knew, beyond the shadow of a doubt, that I wanted to be with her for the rest of my life.

Mary Kate met me at the door when I got home. She knew what had happened. Her husband, Bradford, had gone into town early in the morning after Mary Kate had discovered that I had not come home during the night. She asked me if I would like to come into the kitchen and have coffee. After I was settled, she asked a question.

"Do you want to talk about it?"

"Yes, maybe it would be good to talk about it."

"Do you think she is still in Washington?"

"No. A detective told me this morning that the city has been searched so thoroughly that he is certain she is no longer here."

"Will they continue to look?"

"Yes, he says they never give up. But when I pressed him for an answer, an honest opinion, he admitted he is sure that she is not here."

"Where could she be if she is not here?"

"I've been trying to decide about that. Putting bits and pieces together, I think there is some possibility that the man I met yesterday, the one who seems to be in charge, might have taken her with him."

"How could he manage that? Wouldn't she kick and scream?"

"Probably, unless he had something planned in advance. He seems to be a very well prepared individual."

"Well, don't give up. You don't know anything yet for sure, so there is still room for hope."

"You're right, and I'm sure I will never give up hope."

# V.

Eight days later, while at home in the late morning, I saw Major Dale riding his horse on the long driveway leading up to the front of the house. I walked out to meet him. He smiled as he reached the front yard and dismounted.

"Good morning, Alexander."

"Good morning, Major"

As he tied his horse he responded.

"Call me James. I believe we are friendly enough to use first names."

"All right. Thank you for coming out. Would you like to have some tea or coffee?"

"No thanks, I'm fine."

We each picked a chair, and I looked expectantly into his face. I knew he had information to give me, and after we were settled, he began talking.

"I received a lengthy follow-up telegram this morning from Major Porter in New York. Your thoughts were right. The man you met is from New York, and he owned a slave trading company there. He is using the name of Edward Hawkins. He was about to be shut down and is moving to another place, possibly as far away as England. The man you shot was working for Hawkins as his strong arm man. He was a violent type of individual and a suspect in other crimes. He had come from Ireland originally."

He paused to give me the opportunity to ask a question.

"What was his name?"

"Kip Murphy."

"Can you tell me more about Hawkins?"

"Yes. Major Porter did a thorough investigation, as I knew he would. Hawkins scheduled passage on a ship for himself and others, which most likely included the black man he came here to get. He apparently wanted to leave the United States to establish himself in another country. Major Porter could not learn the name of the country, or the departure date, but he assumes it was within recent days because he seems to have disappeared."

"So there is no way to trace him to the port he would have used?"

"No. But that does explain the deadline Hawkins used with you. He had to be somewhere in time to board a ship."

"Did Major Porter mention Sarah Sullivan?"

"He did, but there was not too much he could say about her. He speculated that Hawkins may have taken her with him."

"Why would he do that?"

"I don't know. We can only guess. We do know that Hawkins is not married and has no family. And, because Missis Sullivan is quite a beautiful lady, he might take her for that reason. But, that could be totally wrong, Alexander. It is simply the first thing that comes to mind."

What he had said had given me quite a jolt, and I let my anger pour out as I spoke.

"I wish I had shot the bastard instead of the Irishman."

A very slight smile came over his face although he was clearly in sympathy with me.

"I know, I know. But just keep up your investigation and you will find her."

We talked another twenty minutes. It was mainly about the war. James, during that time, very politely and diplomatically, let me know that he would have to concentrate his future efforts in that direction. He stood to leave, and I expressed my appreciation as he moved toward the steps.

"Thank you, James, for all you have done. I'll come in to see you soon"

He smiled.

"I'll look forward to it."

The days passed slowly. Sometimes I went out several hours for a ride. I stopped in to see Phillip twice, and as always, he was pleasant to be with. We moved Malcolm into the barn in a room we added there for him. Mary Kate and Bradford knew about him, but I was very confident that both would keep his presence confidential. I didn't gamble much; I didn't feel like it. I did play in the game with the two men from Illinois although my heart was not in it, and I only won eight hundred dollars.

One day when Bradford returned from town with the mail, he came hurriedly in my direction. He had a serious look on his face as he handed me a letter. I looked at it immediately and could see that it had originated in Canada. Then, as I looked closer, I recognized the handwriting of Sarah. I was stunned. It was like a bolt of lightning had hit me.

With my heart racing, I carefully broke the seal, took out the letter and began reading:

*Dear Alex:*

*I wanted to let you know that I am all right. I have not been harmed and have been treated respectfully. I am no longer close by.*

*Please do not worry about me. I was taken by a person who is not unkind, but I will not be released. This will have to be brief because I am doing it secretly. I hope I can get it posted, and I pray that you will receive it.*

*I want you to know something that I should have told you when I had the opportunity. I love you. I always did. I always will. I am deeply sorry that we are now separated, and I cannot say these words to you.*

*We are still traveling and I do not know our final destination.*

*All of my love,*
*Sarah*

I felt exuberant. Just to know that she was still all right was a great relief. I had imagined everything, including the thought that I would never hear from her again. And the best part of her letter, of course, was her expression of love.

I knew that she had been reluctant to say such things in the past, for various reasons, but I could never be sure about her true feeling as long as she did not actually express it. Now, she had finally said what I had wanted to hear.

The troubling part of her letter was the deepening mystery of where she might be - she obviously was in Canada when the letter was sent, however she had said, "I do not know our final destination." That could mean anything and would give me nothing to go on in my effort to search for her. Even so, I knew that I would never give up, and I would look for her for as long as it would take.

As for Hawkins, I would make him regret that he ever came to Washington. Maybe there would be another letter later that would give me the location where she had settled. Major Dale was right; Hawkins had taken her because she was a beautiful woman.

I would keep the letter from Sarah a secret. If others should become aware of it, and if that information became known to Hawkins, it would become much more difficult for her to send another letter in the future. Although I would guard the letter carefully, I felt an urge to talk to someone. It always happened when I received news similar to the contents that had come in Sarah's letter.

Who could I trust in discussing Sarah? After considering others, I thought of Malcolm. He would be perfect. We had completed a nice room for him within the barn. It was in a part of the large structure near the rooms where feed was stored, across a large middle aisle that separated it from the animals. We had finished the room in such a way as to make it comfortable and pleasant. He told me that he was highly pleased with it. I had spent time there with him previously. I enjoyed our conversations because he gave deep considerations to the subjects we discussed, and he had an amazing kind of perception and instinct. Mary Kate and Bradford knew he was there, and both approved of my decision to provide a safe haven for him. Malcolm insisted on doing some of the work, things that could be done inside of the barn. It was still dangerous for him to venture outside during daylight hours.

I walked back to the barn and found Malcolm occupied in repairing a saddle. After a friendly greeting, I told him that I would like to talk, and that I felt it would be best if we could go into his room for privacy. He was puzzled, and I could see a hint of anxiety in his expression. I quickly reassured him.

"It's nothing for you to worry about. In fact, it's about me."

He smiled and we walked into his room. I closed the door, and we were seated. He was looking at me with anticipation as I began.

"I have just received some news that has to remain confidential. I want to tell you about it and get your opinion on what it means, or how it can be considered."

His rare intelligence achieved by the tutoring in England was the reason for my question.

"Yes, indeed, I would like to hear what you have to say. Thank you for thinking of me."

I took the letter out and read it aloud. Then I looked up at him.

"Can you tell me what you think about everything she has said?"

"It sounds like she has no chance to leave the person who is restricting her. She is being treated well which might indicate that the person has a great admiration for her. Or, it could mean that her wealth is a factor. In either case, I do not believe she is in danger. I am more inclined to believe that she is being held by a man who finds her to be very appealing. He is kind to her because he wants to cultivate her affection, or attraction to him. He guards her carefully, and he knows that she would run away if she had the chance. I feel sure that you will get another letter from her. It's just a matter of time."

"And that is what makes it very difficult. Waiting. It is going to be a maddening situation."

"I know my dear friend, how well I know. You must prepare yourself to be patient. Your chance of success will be much better."

His statement reminded me once again about his past. He had lived almost all of his life with constant anxiety. After he was taken from his native land, he had lived day to day wondering what would come next. Neither I, nor anyone like me, could understand the fear and insecurity that would have been his constant companion. He spoke again, and what he said was a surprise.

"Would you mind, sir, if we consider some words from my Bible?"

"No, I don't mind. But tell me, where did you get a Bible?"

"From Miss Mary Kate. She is a kind lady."

He walked over to a shelf, picked up a Bible and returned to his seat. Before opening the book he looked at me.

"I was told by Miss Mary Kate that you attend church and that is why I made the suggestion. I hope to find just a few words that will be meaningful to you."

He turned some of the pages for a few moments, then stopped and began reading. "...that the trying of your faith worketh patience ... Let patience have her perfect work, that ye may be perfect and entire, wanting nothing." He paused and looked at me. "Maybe that will give you some thoughts that will be helpful."

"Thank you, Malcolm. I know that the book you hold in your hands has helped you through some difficult times."

"That is quite true. And it can help you as well."


Every day I hoped there would be another letter, and every day I was disappointed. What did it mean? If she was able to get one letter to me, why couldn't she do it again? Perhaps there had been a change in the conditions of how and where she was being held. After all, there was speculation, reported by Major Porter in his message to Major Dale, that Hawkins was planning to go to England. If he had done that, and if he had taken Sarah, there would be a long sea voyage in progress, and she would have no chance to post a letter.

I thought of her almost constantly. I could remember every detail about her, and I relived every occasion that I had been with her over and over. It was happening to me because she had become the opposite of everything I had known previously. I didn't realize that I could be as emotionally involved with anyone to this extent until I met her. As I became deeply in love with her, my life changed, and a totally new world evolved for me.

Time passed and winter was coming. An officer with the Union Army had come and taken a count of my horses. He said they would most likely be requisitioned by the Union Army. Major Dale helped to get that delayed although I knew it would only be a matter of time before they would be gone. The war had become serious in the minds of everyone. The armies of the North and the South were maneuvering for good positions nearby, and we knew that another major battle would take place soon.

Sarah's father had come from South Carolina, and although not sympathetic to the Union, he had arranged for Sarah's home to be used as a hospital for wounded Union soldiers. Uncle, Armeenia, and Tootsie stayed and helped with the care of the recovering soldiers. Sarah's assets were placed in trust and remained intact. Sarah's father, on my recommendation, had allowed Phillip to act as attorney in establishing and administering the trust. Sarah's father was allowed by Union officials to return to South Carolina.

Food and many other items became more difficult to find. Fortunately, with the land I had, we were able to have a better than average amount of food. Mary Kate, Bradford, and Malcolm stayed put, and we were more secure than many others. Some of the people who had the means moved to New York, Philadelphia, and other locations in the north. There was talk that Lee was planning a campaign to take the city of Washington, and with the successes he was having, it was more likely than many of the residents liked to consider. Both sides recognized Lee and Jackson as perhaps the most brilliant battlefield leaders in the history of warfare.

In November, General Burnside replaced McClellan as Commander of the Union Army. With one hundred and twenty thousand well-equipped men, he moved to a position near Warrenton, Virginia. Lee, Jackson, and Longstreet, with seventy eight thousand men, were opposing him on the West side of the Rappahannock River.

By December eleventh, Union forces were poised to cross the river directly across from the small city of Fredericksburg. Initial investigation by the Federals revealed that a river crossing, with the Confederates occupying the city, would be disastrous. Consequently, an artillery bombardment of the city was ordered, and it was so fierce that the Confederates withdrew to the higher ground in the rear. The city sustained heavy damage and was almost reduced to rubble. Pontoon bridges were built and put in place, and the Union Army advanced across the river.

On the thirteenth of December, the Union Army attacked the Confederate positions which were located on higher ground. Charge after charge, wave after wave, of Union soldiers moved courageously across open fields to try to reach the Confederate positions. Each time they failed. Although it was a day of significant and memorable American military courage, the result would be a tragic defeat for the Union. Lee and Jackson had won again. It was later reported that the Union had thirteen thousand casualties, the Confederates five thousand. The Union Army withdrew.

I had not been into town for several weeks. Three days before Christmas, I decided to ride in to see a few friends, including Phillip and Major Dale. Phillip was his usual self. Nothing seemed to bother him much, and I could always get a lift in spirits by going to see him. After we had talked for a while in his office, I asked a question about a matter that I had been considering.

"I want to make Malcolm a freed man. Can you draw up papers to do that?"

He smiled.

"Of course I can, my good friend. I can draw up papers that you might need for anything." And then he laughed. I laughed too.

"You're a real crook, you know that?"

Still grinning, he replied.

"Of course I know that. How else would I be able to keep all of my clients?"

He said he would have it done within a few days. We visited a while longer, I wished him 'Merry Christmas' and left his office to make my final stop. I wanted to thank Major Dale again for all of his help. Also, I planned to say that my wish for him was that the coming year, 1863, would be one of his best.

When I arrived and went inside the office where Major Dale was located, I noticed there were several new faces among the men working there. Also, I noticed a slight difference in the young corporal who sat near the entrance and received the visitors. He became a little uneasy when he recognized me. I asked to see Major Dale.

"Sir, I guess you haven't heard about Major Dale."

"No, I haven't heard anything. Has he been transferred?"

"No, sir. Major Dale ... he was trained at West Point as an army engineer. He was called to battle duty three weeks ago to help with the pontoons at Fredericksburg." He paused for a moment, then continued. "He was killed on December eleventh by Rebel artillery fire."

I couldn't believe it. The words of the corporal were the most shocking I had heard since Sarah had been taken. Once again I was greatly stunned by sorrowful news. I needed to move on, get out of the office and be back on the street. I said, "I'm very sorry. Thank you for telling me." And then I turned to leave. At that moment I heard a loud voice.

"Fairfield!"

I looked across the room and standing in the doorway of what had been Major Dale's office, there was a young man with the insignia of captain on his uniform. He walked in my direction with a stern look on his face.

"You are Alexander Fairfield?"

"Yes."

"Come into my office. Follow me."

He turned and walked away. My grief turned quickly to anger, and I answered loudly.

"I don't have time to come into your office!"

He turned immediately, and I could see anger and contempt in his expression.

"I have given you an order. If you do not comply I will have you arrested."

I returned his hard stare and again spoke loudly.

"Go to hell."

I turned and walked out of the building. Before I could get to my horse, I heard footsteps coming out of the doorway behind me. I proceeded to mount my horse. By then, the young captain and two enlisted men had come up within a few feet of where I sat on my horse. The captain was fuming.

"You damned no good Rebel, you're not leaving here."

I moved my coat and placed my hand near the handle of the Colt revolver that was stuck inside my waistband. I spoke calmly.

"Captain, I advise you to be very careful right now."

He was very angry. I could see it progressing further into frustration and embarrassment as well. His face was actually turning red, and he shuffled his body some to ease the awkward situation.

He suddenly turned to the two enlisted men and told them to go back into the office. I had seen his type before. Young and bursting with pride because of his rank, he had intended to impose his power in front of an audience of subordinates. He would demand great respect from all who served under him. And to be denied that respect by me, in front of his men, would bring about ridicule. His pride would be damaged beyond description. After the two men were back inside the office, he spoke.

"You're on government property, Fairfield. Get off immediately! And if you ever come back, you will be prosecuted."

"You won't have to worry about that, I am finished here."

Back home, Mary Kate recognized at a glance, even before I spoke, that something was wrong. She could read my mind, it seemed, like a newspaper. I sat in a chair in the kitchen where she was working. She stopped and sat down near me.

"What has happened?"

"I've just learned that I have lost a very good friend."

"Who?"

"Major Dale."

"Oh my, that is terrible. What happened?"

"He was killed in the battle at Fredericksburg."

"Dear, dear, this terrible war! When will it end?"

"Not for a long time, I'm afraid."

"I'm so sorry about Major Dale. He was always very polite and nice during his visits."

"Yes, he was that way. He was one of the best men I have ever known. I will miss him."

On the last day of the year, Phillip rode out to see us. It was cold and Mary Kate invited him inside and gave him a cup of coffee. Then she came out to the barn where I was with Bradford and Malcolm. She told me Phillip had come, smiling slightly, and she winked as she talked. I knew what her signal meant. We had kept it secret about the papers for Malcolm, I wanted to surprise him after it was done. I told Mary Kate that we would all come inside. Bradford knew what was taking place but Malcolm was puzzled.

"Did you want me to come too, Mister Alex?"

"Yes, Malcolm, I want you to come, too."

We went into the kitchen, which was the warmest room in the house. After we had greeted Phillip and talked to him briefly, he handed me an envelope. We were all seated, and as I had glanced at Malcolm while we talked, I could see that he was unsure of what to expect. He knew it was unusual for him to be out of the barn and in a gathering with all of us.

Once again, the same feelings of uncertainty that had consumed him during his entire life were returning, although he did not show great anxiety. I took the papers out of the envelope and quickly read them. Everything was in order. I put the papers back inside the envelope, stood, and handed them to Malcolm. When I spoke, I felt a sense of great pleasure.

"Malcolm, I am pleased to tell you that you are a free man."

He was greatly affected and momentarily speechless. I reached across and shook his hand, and the others in the room did likewise. Malcolm was reacting in a way that none of us could feel or understand. Still unable to speak, he took the papers out of the envelope and read what was written on the documents.

We all remained silent as he finished reading the papers and carefully put them back inside the envelope. He was standing, and looked around at each of us slowly, acknowledging his appreciation. As he continued to stand, I saw small tears form in his eyes. A time had come for him that he believed to be out of reach, and his life had suddenly taken a dramatic change. After a few more moments, he spoke.

"Thank you, thank you all my good friends. I cannot begin to describe, I cannot find the words at this moment, to tell you what this means. It is, of course, the greatest day of my life."

After that, talk began among all of us, and it was a cheerful time. Mary Kate brought out her fruit cake and gave each of us a serving. Malcolm regained his composure and laughed along with the rest of us as Phillip provided most of the humor. I watched Malcolm some, not in a way to attract his attention, and his new manner was heart warming. It was clearly the best day of his life.

Phillip became serious as he talked about the war. Being in the city of Washington each day, he was privileged to learn from many different sources about the actual events that were occurring. He heard descriptions from both sides. Washington, before the war, as well as southern Maryland, was predominately sympathetic to the South. Many of those people were still there, living side by side with the people who supported the North. It gave Phillip a view of facts that otherwise would not have been so easily obtained. We learned for the first time about the brutality of war. Northern troops, releasing some of their anger and seeking revenge for the loss of some of their companions, had literally torn apart homes and furnishings in Fredericksburg while occupying the city, deliberately destroying property needlessly as a means of retaliation.

Later in the day, when I saw Malcolm again out in the barn, I teased him.

"Have you come down out of the clouds yet?"

He laughed.

"No sir, not really. I think it might take another day or two."

"I understand. Well, I'm sure you know we are all happy for you."

"Yes, sir, indeed, I do know that." Then he was more serious. "I've been wondering, sir, if you have had any other thoughts, or plans, about Miss Sarah?"

"I've had a lot of thoughts, but I haven't been able to make any plans that would be rational. I hope there will be another letter soon."

"Do you think it is possible that McCleskey might know something about Hawkins, the man who took her?"

"No, I don't think so. At first I considered going to see McCleskey. But after realizing how clever Hawkins is, and how well he covered his tracks in New York, I felt it would be useless. And trying to question a man who would not be willing to give me information in the first place, in his own surroundings, would be difficult. I think my best opportunity to find her will occur if she is able to send another letter."

He was thoughtful and then formed a kind expression on his face.

"I will continue to pray that she will be kept safe and that you will find her."

"Thank you, Malcolm."

Later in the evening, I considered what Malcolm had said about McCleskey. If another letter did not come soon, I would pay him a visit. And it might not be a pleasant visit.

Within a week I had made a decision. I wouldn't wait for another letter. I would go immediately to see McCleskey. I rode into town to see Phillip and get some paperwork done that I anticipated I would need. He was astounded.

"Alex, my friend, I have never given you bad advice. Listen to me now. Give up this wild notion of a trip. You will get your ass shot off in a hurry."

"No, it has to be done. McCleskey might give me some hint about how, or where, I can find Hawkins. He could have heard something when he went to New York to get Malcolm. It could be anything, something that Hawkins could have said without realizing it."

"Do you know what is out there? Scavengers of all kinds. Army deserters. Desperate men who will kill you at the drop of a hat just to take a dollar out of your pants."

"I know, but I will have to deal with it. I have the Colt revolver and a large supply of cartridges. I learned a few things the hard way when I was on the streets in New Orleans."

"What do you plan to tell the Union Army, or the Confederate Army? My guess is you won't make it twenty miles. They will probably take your horse and tell you to go home."

"That's where you come in. I need papers stating that I am on official business, looking for horses and mules for the army. Who is going to take time to check that out?"

"Horses for who, the Yankees or the Rebels?"

"It depends on who stops me. I will need two sets of papers, one for the Yankees, and the other one for the Rebels."

He shook his head and obviously was not convinced it would work.

"Would you go alone?"

"No. I will take Malcolm."

"Alex, are you totally mad? There are people out there who would see two horses and a black man they could sell, and you would be left somewhere lying face down in a ditch. You better think that over."

I smiled at him.

"Phillip, just draw up two sets of papers. Describe Malcolm as my manservant. I've got to do something, I can't just give up on Sarah."

When I mentioned Sarah, he changed.

"All right, I'll do it. But this is something I don't feel good about. Don't say I didn't warn you. I'll bring the papers out to you in a day or so."

"Good. I will need some fake script forms that will appear to be promissory notes for payments for the purchase of a horse or a mule. Make it look convincing, and again, give me one for the Union and one for the Confederate government."

"Okay. And you know what Alex? I'm going to be praying for you in church on Sunday."

Later in the day I talked to Malcolm. We had already discussed the plan to go, and he wanted to be a part of it. I decided to go over everything with him again so he could repeat what he knew about McCleskey, and what we could expect.

"As I said before, Mister Alex, he is not a bad man. His reason for having me was to help the slaves who were already there, teach them to reach a higher level. He was going to search for other blacks, people he would carefully select to be in his possession while I was present. He did not own me outright. I was to be there for only a certain length of time. I believe it was to be a year. He is not the abusive type, and I feel there is a possibility that he will cooperate with you now that the war is serious. He knows there is a good chance that the slaves will be freed anyway."

On a cold, late date in February, Malcolm and I made our way out of Washington. Heading westward on the route that would take us to the McCleskey farm, I used papers given to me by Phillip to pass by the Union soldiers and checkpoint locations. We had no problems, and my mission was not questioned. It was surprising because I had anticipated more of a problem due to the tightened security around the city. I believed we could reach our destination in two days if not stopped.

As dusk was descending on the first day, we were on a lonely road about fifty miles outside the city. We were in an area where large pine trees formed a thick forest on each side of the road. Suddenly from the right, horsemen came from the woods. Moving at a gallop, they were upon us quickly, and I was able to distinguish that they were military men. We stopped immediately. Looking closely at the lead horseman I could see that he was wearing what appeared to be a grey military uniform, and I recognized him to be a Confederate officer. There were six riders and when they reached us they pulled up and formed a circle around us. The officer looked at me in a no-nonsense way.

"Who are you, Mister?"

"My name is Alexander Fairfield."

"What is your business here?"

"I am procuring horses and mules for the army."

"Which army?"

"General Lee's army."

"Let me see some proof."

I withdrew the papers made out by Phillip and handed them to him. He read the documents carefully and seemed to be at least partially satisfied. He handed them back to me.

"Why is the black man with you?"

"He is my manservant."

"He is your slave?"

"No, he is not my personal slave. He has been furnished by the Confederate Army to assist me."

He thought for a few moments, and I believe he was still somewhat suspicious.

"How much are you paying for horses?"

"One hundred, to as much as one hundred and ten dollars, in script."

"Script? What do you mean by script?"

"It is a promissory note. I am carrying no money, it would be too dangerous."

Still not completely sure of me, he wanted more information.

"Describe the kind of horses you will buy."

"They must be sound in all particulars, well broken, in full flesh and in good condition, from fifteen to sixteen hands high, from five to nine years old, and well adapted in every way to cavalry purposes. I will pay one hundred and ten dollars for dark colored horses that are strong, quick, and active."

That seemed to satisfy him about the horses. Next he wanted to know about me.

"Where were you born?"

"Savannah, Georgia."

"Is this your first trip to buy horses?"

"Yes."

"I thought so. Let me advise you about a few things. Yankee patrols are in this area. Cavalry. They are probing to see what is happening with Lee and Jackson. If they come across you, they will treat you rough and might take you prisoner. How far are you going?"

"To Merritt Springs. I have heard that the McCleskey farm near there might have horses for sale."

There was a temporary lull in talk. Then a man on a horse near the officer spoke, looking at me.

"Yeah, you better be careful, Cap. I think Uncle Bobby and Stonewall has got them blue-bellies a little worried right now."

And then he and several others laughed. The officer spoke again.

"You can join our camp for the night, Mister, but not the black man."

"Thank you sir, but I cannot leave the black man on his own. We will find another place."

"I understand. There is a farm five miles ahead where they might let you stay in the barn. Ask for Missis Mason. It's a two story house on the right, at the top of a hill."

"Thank you, sir."

With his reins he turned his horse back toward the woods and gave the men a command. "Okay boys, let's go kill some Yankees!"

There were loud yells in unison and they were off, galloping away as quickly as they had come. Only the officer was wearing clothing that resembled a uniform. The others were in faded and worn-looking coats, trousers of various descriptions, and old hats.

If I had seen them on the streets of Washington I would have believed them to be common laborers. But I could see an unusual look of confidence and determination in their faces, and a distinct impression about them was formed in my mind. They would be very dangerous if encountered by Northern troops.

They were men who were most likely typical of Lee's army. Although poorly equipped and always outnumbered in battles, they had been victorious almost every time they had been engaged in combat. I could see, too, that a new kind of resentment was building toward the blacks. The Negroes were being blamed for the war more predominately, and it would compound the problems for the blacks who were already the victims of slavery. The attitudes of many people in the South who had been kind to the blacks might now change. People would blame them wrongly, hold them responsible simply because of their existence, for the loss of friends and loved ones.

Malcolm and I rode on in the direction of the Mason home. We pushed our horses at a slow gallop. I wanted to reach the house before dark. And we did. The house was located in the place described by the Confederate officer. We stopped in the road and I dismounted. I asked Malcolm to remain with the two horses and the pack mule then I walked toward the front of the house. Suddenly the front door was opened, and a woman appeared, holding a shotgun. She raised the weapon toward me and spoke firmly.

"Stop where you are, Mister! What do you want?"

"Only to talk, ma'am. We will cause you no harm."

"Who are you?"

"My name is Fairfield. I am traveling in this area to buy horses for the army. I am looking for shelter for the night."

"Why is the black man with you?"

"He is my manservant."

"We don't have horses to sell. It will be best for you to move on."

She had lowered the shotgun and was a little more at ease. I felt that she might give me further consideration.

"I can pay if you will help us."

She thought for a long while before answering.

"How do I know you are speaking the truth?"

"I can show you papers."

"All right, show me."

I did. During the time she was holding the papers she occasionally looked up at me. Finally she became more relaxed and put the shotgun down. She appeared to be about thirty years old, and I could read a mix of fear and anxiety on her face. She was rather pretty, and I felt that she must have a husband. I asked her about him. "Is your husband away in the army?"

She stared back at me for a long time. I knew that she had decided that she could trust me, or I would not have asked such a question. She still didn't know whether to answer so I spoke again.

"It's all right, you need not answer that question. It just seems that you have a heavy load right now, and I was wondering if you have any support."

"Thank you, Mister Fairfield. So many people come, I don't know who to trust. The Yankees came once and took nearly everything. It is so fearful at times. My sister will be here soon, and it will be better. You asked about my husband ... he was wounded and died in December. It has been like a bad dream since then."

"I'm very sorry. The war is beginning to have an effect on all of us. I, too, lost a very dear friend last fall although I have not been told that she is dead."

She agreed to let us stay in the barn for the night. She gave us food and provided feed for our animals. I wondered about her later. Was she like hundreds of thousands of others in our country? Were we just in the beginning stages of the worst of all times?

Malcolm and I arrived at Merritt Springs late the next day. There was a church located on the square of the city with a sign in the yard that said, "Shelter For Needy." I knew before going inside that Malcolm would probably not be given a room, or shelter, although I also knew that I would have to find some way to protect us from the freezing weather during the night. The front door was unlocked, and I walked into the sanctuary. Near the altar at the front, there was a pot-belly stove with two men sitting close by. They saw me and came to meet me. One was older, probably seventy, and the other one turned out to be a young boy, possibly sixteen or seventeen years old. They greeted me, and we shook hands. The elderly man was the pastor of the church. I told him that I had seen the sign and that I needed shelter for the night. He readily agreed for me to stay inside the church. Then, I told him about Malcolm. The young boy spoke at once.

"Grandpa! A black man cannot stay here!"

Reverend Gregory remained calm.

"Son, we will turn away no man." And he turned to me.

"You can go out and bring in the black man, Mister Fairfield. In the meantime I will go and tell my wife to prepare two meals. There are outhouses in the back, and a fenced area for your horses."

"Thank you, Reverend. You are very kind."

"Not really, Mister Fairfield, I am simply doing what God expects me to do."

When the Reverend returned later with our food and saw Malcolm, his expression became one of surprise, but he made no comment. He told us he would return later to pick up the dishes.

He came back in about an hour. He pulled up a chair, and the three of us sat near the stove. Malcolm and I had finished the meal, and the warmth of the stove had provided us with a pleasant feeling of comfort. I looked forward to talking to the Reverend. His first remark, however, was quite a surprise. He looked at Malcolm and then turned back in my direction.

"Mister Fairfield, I know about Malcolm. Vernon McCleskey is a member of this church. I have had a few visits with Vernon during the past year, and he told me about Malcolm. Vernon has been struggling with the thought of holding slaves, he knows it is wrong. But like others, he is financially dependent on them, and he can not maintain the large orchards or his livestock without them. And he has hundreds of acres of corn and other vegetables, and he is unable to bring in his crops without his slaves.

"We talked, and the only way he could halfway justify it was that most of the blacks could not take care of themselves if free. Most are illiterate. That was the main reason he brought Malcolm here: to teach the others and, in future generations, make them more independent. His attitude changed to an even greater degree after his only son was killed in the war last year. He came in and cried like a baby, saying that the problem brought about by slavery had also brought about the death of his son. He felt that he had been punished by God." He paused and looked directly at Malcolm as he continued.

"Malcolm, were you by chance aware of any of the things I have said?"

"Somewhat, although most of my contacts were with Mister Breedlove, the overseer. Mister Breedlove, or the master as some called him, had an entirely different philosophy. He hid it from Mister McCleskey. He believed, and now I am speaking about Mister Breedlove, that fear would accomplish more than anything else, and he used it sometimes with the slaves to be sure that he accomplished the assignments he had to complete. I will say that I know of no abuse. I do not believe Mister McCleskey would have allowed it."

The Reverend responded.

"No, I am sure that Vernon would not have allowed it."

I was eager to bring up the question that had brought me there.

"Reverend Gregory, do you believe Mister McCleskey will be agreeable to meet with me tomorrow to discuss Malcolm? I am searching for the man who placed Malcolm with Mister McCleskey."

"Oh, I am sure he will meet with you, Mister Fairfield. I'll have my grandson ride out to his farm early, and you can meet here in a room at the church."

"Very good, sir. I appreciate your help."

We talked for about another hour. Reverend Gregory left for a short while after that and returned with bedding items suitable for pallets. Following that, he said "goodnight." Malcolm and I arranged our bedrolls close to the stove and huddled up near it during the night. I discovered that I could easily stay warm on one side when facing the stove, however, my backside soon became cold when I was in the wrong position. As a result, I turned myself about every thirty minutes. Even so, we were very grateful to be inside and near a stove. During the night, Malcolm and I alternated adding wood to the stove to keep the fire going well.

# VI.

At seven the next morning, Reverend Gregory brought us coffee along with scrambled eggs, cured ham, and biscuits. It was delicious. After breakfast I offered to pay him for all he had done. He would not accept it so I gave him twenty dollars as a donation to the church, which he did take. He told me that his grandson had left at seven-thirty for a twenty-minute ride to the McCleskey farm, and he anticipated that Vernon McCleskey would be at the church between nine and ten o'clock.

Malcolm and I talked to Reverend Gregory while waiting for McCleskey to arrive. We were sitting beside the pot-belly stove, and most of our conversations were about the war. I had been calm up to that point, but then I began to feel tension. The memory of the night Uncle came to my door to tell me that Sarah had been taken kept coming back into my thoughts, and that progressed into many other concerns. I would be very happy to talk to McCleskey and get a few of my questions resolved.

At approximately ten minutes past ten, he arrived. He came in through the front door and walked toward us. Reverend Gregory immediately went forward to meet him. They shook hands and had a brief conversation. Malcolm and I remained by the stove.

Mister McCleskey appeared to be in his late sixties. Slightly heavy-set, his face was that of an honest and kind man. He had a slightly eager expression as he looked beyond Reverend Gregory and settled a stare on Malcolm. He spoke softly to the Reverend who turned and walked back to where we were and spoke to Malcolm.

"Mister McCleskey has asked for the opportunity to speak to you alone if you are willing."

Malcolm answered.

"Of course." He walked to where McCleskey was standing. McCleskey reached out and shook hands with Malcolm. Then he surprised me. He reached around Malcolm and hugged him. After that they talked for about another five minutes, each man smiling broadly. Finally their conversation was concluded and McCleskey came toward me.

For the next fifteen minutes, I gave him every detail I could recall about Edward Hawkins, as well as all facts relating to Sarah and her disappearance. He listened patiently, and I could tell by his attitude that he was eager to remember all he could to help when given the opportunity. Finally, I asked if he would tell me everything that he could recall about Hawkins. He said he would and began.

"I dined with him in New York on the occasion of our first meeting. He told me he could furnish what I was looking for, a black man who was educated and could teach other blacks. He recommended Malcolm. He said that Malcolm had been educated by in-home tutors in England. We agreed that I would keep Malcolm for one year for which I would pay him ten thousand dollars. The plan was for Malcolm to teach the colony of black people on my farm. I felt it would be a good investment for me and for them. But, to get around to your interest in Hawkins, I cannot imagine why he would have taken Missis Sullivan to Canada.

"As for the rumor you mentioned, I do not believe he would have returned to England. In fact, there was trouble there for his parents, and he felt they would leave and go to another country. Edward Hawkins had no desire to leave for another country. He wanted to remain in the United States. However, he was fearful of staying in New York because he had become known there, and he was afraid he might be arrested. After Lincoln had been in office a while, he made definite plans to move. He was very wealthy, and had no money problems. Of course I am telling you his plans before he met with you in Washington.

"My guess is he had been planning to relocate somewhere in this country away from New York, and if he had been able to take Malcolm with him, it would have given him the opportunity to make a new start in another city."

He paused and I was ready with several questions. I started with the one that was most important to me.

"Knowing him as you did, what is your best guess regarding his whereabouts, where would he have gone after he passed through Canada? Or do you believe he is still in Canada?"

"No, I do not believe he is in Canada. There are things he wanted that he could only have in the United States. So, to answer your question, I believe he would be somewhere in the southern part of the United States."

"Why would he go there?"

"He would hope that the war would be won by the Confederacy, which would allow him to resume the business that made him rich. Slave trading."

That was a surprise, and it was a possibility that I had not considered. My next question was a follow-up to his speculation.

"Where in the South would he go?"

"Well, I can only guess, of course, but I believe it would be a port city. Maybe Charleston or Savannah, or a city near a port."

I had to think for a while about the new possibilities he had mentioned. I let a minute or so go by before resuming my questions. He understood, and it was obvious that he was trying to help me. It was during this time that I realized that he, too, felt a resentment toward Hawkins. I thought of a problem that Hawkins might have had with Sarah.

"How would he be able to travel in public, let's say in a rail car, with a woman who was unwilling to go with him?"

"If your relationship with Missis Sullivan was as you say, he might have told her he would have you killed if she caused trouble or did not cooperate. She might have done it to protect you."

For the next ten or fifteen minutes we discussed the circumstances that involved Sarah and how she might be able to handle it. It brought about many unpleasant thoughts for me, and it culminated in a question I had for him to sum things up.

"Sir, if you will be kind enough to think carefully for a moment, I would like for you to give me your very best guess concerning Hawkins and his intent to pick a location where he might settle. I ask you this because you know more about him than anyone else, his tendencies, future plans, and his habits."

"All right, I can do that. I think he would pick a city reasonably well-developed that would afford him a nice lifestyle. It definitely would be a city somewhere in the South because at this point he is betting on the South to win the war. It would be a port city on the East Coast, or not too far from a port and in a warm climate. Even Atlanta would work nicely for him, at least until the war is over. Of course, Mister Fairfield, you must realize that we are only making guesses, at best."

"I know. But even guesses are helpful to me. Now, let me ask you to make one final guess. What will he do with Missis Sullivan?"

"If she is as beautiful as you say, he might keep her with him for a long time, possibly permanently."

That was an answer that I did not wish to hear. Being realistic, however, I knew it to be correctly stated. Sarah not only had physical beauty, she also had an unusual appeal which was seen more easily by men. It was a sort of hidden or underlying attraction that could be detected very soon after spending a short amount of time with her. I responded to his statement.

"Well, as you know, I hope that does not happen. At least Hawkins does not seem to be like a tramp, so in that regard I suppose it could have been worse for her. He is apparently treating her respectfully."

"I believe that would be true. As a matter of fact, he can be a very charming individual."

I thanked him for his time and the information. Then I told him and the others that Malcolm and I would leave within the hour to return to Washington.

When Malcolm and I were ready to mount our horses just before noon, there were some "goodbyes" and "best wishes" expressed by all. The wife and grandson of Reverend Gregory had joined us, and we had the opportunity to state our appreciation to them. After we were mounted, the last person to speak was Vernon McCleskey. He looked directly at Malcom

"I am glad you are a free man."

We nudged our horses and moved away. I thought about what McCleskey had said, and for the first time since leaving Washington,

I realized what it meant. I turned in my saddle enough to look directly into the eyes of Malcolm.

"You know, if you rode as the crow flies, you could easily be in Pennsylvania tomorrow, or maybe sooner."

He smiled slightly.

"I know."

"I have been so pre-occupied with thoughts of Sarah I had not realized it until this moment."

"Oh, I realized it. After we were out in the countryside I knew it could be done."

I waited a few moments to respond.

"And you didn't consider it?"

"No, I didn't consider it."

The sun was shining brightly, and it warmed us. Even though we had spent the night inside the church near the stove, we had not felt relaxed or at ease. I had thought several times during the night that it would be nice to be in my kitchen at home with its large black cooking stove and open fireplace.

Riding steadily, we covered a lot of ground, making good progress. Missis Gregory had prepared food for us, so we were not slowed by searching for nourishment. During the afternoon, we passed people walking on the road; there were men, women, and some who were together seemed to make up entire families. Many were apparently being uprooted by the war, and I suspected that the raids by the Northern cavalry were becoming more frequent. We learned from some of the people that the Yankee troops were becoming more vengeful, and on some occasions they had burned homes and barns. It was obvious that a hatred was being born that would be long lasting, and the people of Northern Virginia were undoubtedly facing very difficult times. As we rode along, I discussed it with Malcolm.

"What is going to happen to these people?"

"I don't know. I have thought about it and only one thing seems certain. A great amount of fear and hatred is going to spread quickly over the land."

He was right. He had a keen sense of perception, and his ability to analyze a situation was very reliable.

"That's true. It is an unprecedented time in our history. Wounds are going to be opened that will not heal during our lifetimes. A new day has come, and it has brought bad news."

We rode hard for the rest of the day. We had decided that we would try to make it back to the home of Missis Mason where we had stayed the first night of the trip. She would remember us, and would probably let us stay in the barn again.

The number of people on the road grew larger later in the day. All seemed to be refugees from the area where the Union cavalry raids were taking place. I noticed that some were beginning to stare more closely at Malcolm and I could see a stern look in their eyes. I became concerned about his safety, and I thought it would be wise to warn him.

"You may not be safe, Malcolm. Be sure to keep your horse close to mine."

"I will."

Again, I thought about the plight of the blacks. Through no fault of their own, they were becoming the center of the wartime controversy. People who were losing loved ones and their homes and possessions were seeking revenge. And many, despite never having owned a slave or having had any meaningful encounters with blacks, were, in their desperation to strike back at something, beginning to look more in the direction of the blacks. A resentment of the blacks was coming about that had not existed previously. None of the blacks would be safe in the South in the future. Even if freed they would need to cling to what they had and remain where they were, because an angry and frustrated white population would otherwise do them great harm.

And regretfully, the Union had no organized plan to provide for the hundreds of thousands that would be set free. It was said that Mr. Lincoln had shown a slight interest at one time in a project that would return the blacks to their native homes. However, the logistics and other considerations were not feasible. In any event, if the North should become victorious, the future of the black people would be placed in the hands of the Federal government, and there would be astronomical problems involved in creating a good life for them.

It was dark when we reached the home of Missis Mason. She remembered me, and although reluctant, she agreed for us to stay in the barn. She advised me to be careful with Malcolm, and said it would be best if he could be hidden inside, toward the back of the barn. I knew she could use money, and I gave her twenty dollars. Other people came into the barn seeking shelter during the night, but we had found a small place behind stacks of hay for Malcolm and were able to pass through the night safely.

After the others had cleared out the next morning, Malcolm and I saddled our horses and were soon under way on the last leg of our trip. Late in the day we arrived at the outlying approach to Washington, and by six o'clock we had reached home. It was a good feeling.

The next morning, following a good night of rest, I began thinking of how I would try to find Hawkins. Mary Kate was with me in the kitchen, and I described every detail that had been given to me by McCleskey. She wanted to help me by making suggestions.

"Do you think you can travel to some of the port cities he named and ask questions?"

"Yes, I can, and I will if I decide that his theory is correct."

"You don't have many other things to go on. I am wondering..."

"What?"

"It's just a thought, but, if she didn't get on a ship, it's been a long time since you got the letter..."

She didn't want to finish the sentence. I needed an explanation.

"What are you thinking?"

She paused for what seemed like a long time, then spoke.

"I hope she hasn't been sick."

I knew that was not what she was actually thinking, but I didn't want to push her, so I simply agreed with her.

"Yes, hopefully she has not been sick."

I wanted to get other opinions about Hawkins before taking any action, and on Saturday I rode into town to see Phillip. He was jovial and appeared genuinely pleased to see me.

"I'm glad you made it, Alex. I hear it is getting worse out there every day."

"Yes, it is. We saw a lot of people who have been displaced because of Yankee raids. And you were right, it's no place for a black man."

"I think we are going to see another big battle soon, and if Lee wins again he may head for Washington. But tell me, how did it go with McCleskey?"

I described everything to him, being careful not to leave out any details. He listened carefully, and I was sure that all of my statements were being carefully stored in his resourceful mind. When I was finished, he thought for a while before speaking. His first statement was somewhat surprising.

"Alex, he's been with her for four or five months, and you haven't heard anything from her for about three months. I am wondering what that means? Do you feel that there is some kind of explanation for that?"

"I don't know. I wish I did know. I don't have an answer."

"Well, let's think about it on the positive side. You know damn well she hates everything he has done, and she despises all he represents. How in hell could she feel anything but hatred for the man?"

I couldn't think of an answer and didn't speak. He continued.

"Okay, let's assume he likes her. Let's assume, too, that he is right about the war. If Lee is still winning at the end of this year, he will get help from England or France. Or both. I think at that point there will be a negotiated peace. So if Hawkins, in the meantime, heads south and bides his time, he will be all set. And that will take care of him and what he wants.

Now, let's think about Sarah. She told you plainly in the letter how she feels, she will love you forever, my friend, so don't ever have doubts about that. There must be something else involved, and I can't think, at this moment, what it would be. For some reason, she is cutting you off, and I don't know why she would do that. We know she could have slipped you another letter by now, but for whatever reason, she has not. Why? Has he threatened her in such a way that she is too afraid to take a chance?"

"Could be. But, I can't really be sure about anything."

"And neither can I. And to leave here looking for somebody who might be anywhere in the country would be crazy. Let me think about it, and maybe I can come up with an idea. In the meantime, keep your chin up. You know how much she loves you."

He had made me feel better, and as I got up to leave I let him know how I felt about our friendship.

"You've been standing by me for a long time, Phillip, and I appreciate it. I sure hope the Yankees don't get you."

He grinned as he uttered his last words.

"Me, too."

On the street, there were three Union cavalry soldiers and an officer standing near my horse. As I approached them I recognized the officer. It was the young Captain who had replaced Major Dale. He spoke in a loud and commanding manner.

"Fairfield, you are under arrest."

"For what reason?"

"For having government property in your possession."

"What property?"

"An army six-shot Colt revolver."

"I have no Colt revolver."

Fortunately I had not brought it with me.

"Oh yes, you do most certainly have one. There is a record of it." And he pulled out a paper from his coat pocket. "I have here a report that was made on the day that you shot a man dead on a street here in Washington. The weapon you used is described in the report. It was a U.S. Army Colt revolver, with the complete identification of the weapon included in the report. Do you deny the facts I have stated?"

While he had been talking, I had time to think of a way to avoid his accusation.

"Oh, that revolver. It was loaned to me by Major Dale. It was returned later."

"I don't believe you." He turned to one of the enlisted men. "Search him, McGraw."

I smiled and walked forward to meet the man. I took off my coat and handed it to him. I told him when he was finished looking through it he would be welcome to go through the pockets of my pants. Several people had stopped near us, and I heard one lady remark, "Why this is absolutely ridiculous. It seems a person can no longer walk on the streets in Washington without being harassed."

McGraw finished his search, and finding no revolver, he looked at the Captain for further instructions. The Captain was embarrassed and quite angry at the same time. He made an attempt to overcome his mistake while showing his authority.

"You are released, Fairfield. You may now leave."

I smiled at him.

"Why thank you, Captain, that is very kind."

The people dispersed, and I climbed onto my horse. The Captain was still in the same spot nearby. I looked him straight in the face with a serious expression.

"Captain, I advise you not to approach me again unless you are prepared to bring your complaint to a final settlement."

Riding in the direction of home, I explored in my mind many of the recent developments. The preponderance of questionable activities by some of the Northern troops was beginning to be disturbing to me. I gave thought to Major Dale and our wonderful friendship. He had come and dined with me on several occasions. I remembered how he had enjoyed the fried chicken that was prepared by Mary Kate. He said chicken was not cooked that way back home in Ohio.

Usually we would take a stroll over the grounds after a meal, and our conversations were enjoyable. We were in agreement on nearly all things. I could not remember a man I respected more. In my mind, he represented the Union, and he was the Union. Fair, honest, reliable, and very humble, yet steadfast and strong. Now he was gone, and in a sense his passing was more than the loss of a friend. It might also be the passing of my close ties to the Union.

In the early evening on Monday, I was alone in the kitchen at home, reading a book. As usual at that hour, Mary Kate and Bradford had gone home, and Malcolm was in his room in the barn. I heard a slight noise that came from the side porch next to the kitchen. I looked over at the window, and there on the outside looking in, was Ed Jenkins. He grinned, and so did I. I got up immediately and walked to the door. As he came in, I teased him.

"Ed, you old rascal, how were you able to sneak up on me like a possum?"

He laughed.

"Well, that's my trade, Alex, and I have to be good at it."

I showed him to a chair and poured him a glass of whiskey. He began talking, telling me what had been taking place in his life. He said that spying activities in Washington were going well.

"I have four operatives now, Alex, and we are getting good information."

"I know you are pleased, Ed, and I am happy that you are having success."

"Me too. But that is not why I am here. I have some news for you."

I knew what it had to be, and my heart jumped.

"It's about Sarah, isn't it?"

"Yes. But before you get too excited let me explain a few things. The information I will give you came to me indirectly. In other words, it came through a second party. I cannot verify what was said, and neither can you. You have to understand that."

"Okay, okay, I understand. What can you tell me?"

"Some months ago you got a letter from Sarah that came from Canada, right?"

"Yes. "

"Sarah was never in Canada."

"What do you mean?"

"She never left the Washington area. She was being held here. The letter was sent as a ploy."

"Who sent it, or who mailed it from Canada?"

"A young man who goes there occasionally. He agreed to take it there and mail it."

"Where is she now?"

"She is no longer here. I am told that she has been taken south by the man named Hawkins."

"Where? Where was she taken?"

"I don't know. The information given to me was very limited."

"Ed ...try to think and remember everything that you were told. I am desperate to find her. Where were they here in Washington?"

"Actually, it was Baltimore. Hawkins had help. He has plenty of money, and he can buy people who will do anything for him. He had learned that he was going to be arrested if he returned to New York. That is the reason he had to stay hidden and continue to be on the move. In fact, he had to move in a hurry."

"Tell me the name of the man who mailed the letter from Canada."

"I can't because I don't know. Remember what I told you in the beginning. I have had no contact with anyone except my operative here in Washington."

"Tell me the name of that person."

"I cannot. I would violate a solemn promise I made to him. He is leaving Washington, anyway. In fact, he has already left."

"Why did he leave?"

"The Federals were on to him, and he found out about it. He believed they would hang him if they caught him."

"Where was he going?"

Ed thought for a long while before speaking.

"I will tell you on one condition. If you should ever be questioned you must not reveal where he went under any circumstances."

"I give you my word, I will never tell anyone."

"California."

"Why would he go so far?"

"He felt he would be safe there."

There was a lull in the conversation. Many thoughts were crowding into my mind. I wanted to find out more about the man who mailed the letter.

"Why was the man in Canada, the one who mailed the letter?"

"He is a southern sympathizer and it seems there is a plan to use a town in Canada that is near the New York state line as a base for something. I don't know the details because I am not a part of his group."

"How did Hawkins meet him?"

"I can only guess. With the kind of money Hawkins has, I believe he can find people who will do anything. And with the information about big money floating around, he could probably line up an army of undesirables very easily."

I still needed information that would help me track Hawkins.

"Okay Ed, let's say he was in Baltimore with Sarah, and he wanted to go south into the Confederate states. How, in your opinion, would he go about it? How would he travel?"

"He would rent a closed coach and hire a driver. He would take a southern route through the Maryland countryside to a point where he could ferry across the river. Or, he might stay on the ferry and go down the river. Either way, once he arrived in Virginia, his problems would be solved, and he would then most likely travel by rail."

"Where would he take her, what city?"

"I don't know except it would not be Charleston or Savannah. Because of her reputation of being very beautiful, Sarah would have been well-known in both cities. That is how her husband, Colonel Sullivan met her. He heard about her while visiting Charleston. Hawkins is wise enough to know that she would be recognized there."

"How about a city like Atlanta?"

"Well, yes, he could go there. But, as you well know, it could be any number of places."

"You've been in the business of investigating people for over two years now, and I know you have become experienced with the habits and tendencies of men like Hawkins. If you had to find him, where would you begin looking?"

"I don't know simply because he is a moving target. Also, making it more difficult, he has the means to do many things. You've got a real problem, Alex, and there is no doubt about that."

"All right, Ed, let's try something else. Put yourself in his place. What would you do?"

"Okay, I can make a guess on that basis. We know he has lived high-on-the-hog all of his life, and he will want to continue to do that. He will stay in the South for only a short while. Right now it is the best place for him because he can avoid being arrested by police in the North. If the South should lose the war, he will go to some distant place, maybe California, or even a foreign country. I can't even guess where he might be at present, except that it would be a place where he could set himself up in a nice lifestyle. So, your best bet is to find him as soon as possible because he will be gone in the future."

"What about Sarah?"

"Apparently he has been swept away by her. He has taken on a lot of extra baggage by keeping her with him while he is on the run. It means, in my opinion, he will hold on to her for a long time. She is young and she will remain a beautiful woman for many years."

"But, I know her well, and I am sure that she must hate him. Why would he keep her under those circumstances?"

"He will probably try to change the way she feels."

"How?"

"He will be very kind to her. But, in the beginning at least, he will convince her that it is hopeless to try to get away from him."

What he said was discouraging. Ed saw it in my face.

"Alex, many tragic things are happening now. People are saying goodbye to loved ones every day with the full knowledge that they may never meet again. I think that kind of situation might have come to you. Unfortunately, we are living in a time like no other we have known. I am sorry, and I wish I could give you a more encouraging outlook."

"Yes, so do I. Thank you for being honest. All you have said makes sense, but even so, I will never stop looking for her."

"I know, and you have my sincere best wishes for success."

He said he would stay the night, and a short while later, I led the way to a room upstairs that would be suitable for him. As we climbed the stairs, I made one final request.

"Ed, when you return to Savannah, please be sure to keep your eyes and ears open just in case Hawkins might have taken a chance and settled there."

"I certainly will."

The next morning Ed was preparing to leave, and was sitting astride his horse. I was standing close by. I wanted to convey to him new thoughts that I was feeling.

"Ed, my thinking is beginning to change. If I should have the opportunity to help you, how could it be done?"

He was pleasantly surprised, and it showed on his face. He didn't answer immediately. Instead, he raised his right hand upward and let his fingers come to rest under his chin. He waited, and obviously was giving careful consideration to what I had said. Moments later he responded.

"There is something that might fit you well. We know the North has sent spies into the South. If you would help by searching for these men it might serve two purposes. You could look for Sarah at the same time. There may be other considerations to be made, however at this moment, I can see no reason why it would not work."

"Very good! How can I get in touch with you?"

"I'll be back in the near future. Let me talk to some other people, and I will plan to meet with you when I return. Be sure you keep it a secret."

"I will, and I will expect to see you again soon."

He nodded, turned his horse in the direction of the road, and was off.

I felt good. I might have fallen upon an answer that would solve the most important question in my mind ... how to go about the search for Sarah. If I could travel far and wide in the South with the authority given to me by the Confederate government, it would be much easier to find her. And I would certainly feel no remorse in looking for men who were there to carry out assignments that would result in turmoil and grief similar to what I had already seen in Northern Virginia. It would be different than firing a weapon at a man in a blue uniform, something that I had decided I could never do.

It was an exciting moment in time for me. I wanted to share it with someone. Not too surprisingly, I thought of Malcolm, and I realized that I was invariably turning to him more often. An unusual bond had formed between us, and I knew that he felt the same. It explained why he did not make a run for Pennsylvania when he had the chance. He had realized, when I was not willing to give him up to Hawkins even though Sarah was in danger, he had a loyal friend. He was safe at last.

I found him working in the barn. I asked him to put aside his tools and come inside his room. I closed the door, and we were seated. He no longer became anxious when I would come because I came frequently to visit him. He had become secure and comfortable, and I believe he had formed a sentimental attachment to the room. I looked at him and smiled.

"Are you ready to saddle up again?"

"Absolutely."

"I might be headed south this time. Are you willing to go there?"

"Yes."

"It hasn't been worked out yet, so it is too early to make plans. If approved I will have authority to travel extensively throughout the South, and I will be allowed to spend part of my time searching for Sarah. My primary duty would be highly secret and cannot be discussed, however it could be combined with personal business."

We talked another fifteen minutes. I told him that we would travel as a "gentleman" and "manservant," something seen quite common in the past. He seemed to be pleased to be included in my plans, and as I left he appeared to be in a good mood.

Weeks went by, and I heard nothing from Ed Jenkins. I became restless. A thought occurred to me about Hawkins. He had fooled us once by making it appear that Sarah was in Canada. Could he have tricked us in other ways? How could I find out? Should I at least trace the route I thought the men had used the night Sarah had been taken from her home? There might be a clue of some sort, or I might happen upon some person who would remember. I decided it was worth a try.

Two days later, on a rather warm morning with spring in the air, I saddled up and rode into town. I knew that Sarah had been taken into Maryland, so I made my way to 11th Street and on out to the Navy Yard bridge. I no longer carried the Colt revolver because of the problem with the impertinent young Captain in the Union Army who had confronted me on two occasions. I replaced it with a Sharps breech loading pistol. That particular pistol had an advantage that others did not have – in operation the falling breech cut off the rear of the linen cartridge when it was returned to battery.

When I arrived at the bridge, I stopped and paused to take in the view. The span of the river appeared to be some six or seven hundred feet. The bridge had a solid plank surface and was wide enough so that approximately six feet of space was marked off for the people who would be walking. There were others on the bridge, both riders and walkers. I proceeded to cross, moving my horse at a walk, and after arriving on the opposite side, I continued up Good Hope Hill. After about another mile, I saw a house on the right with a hand-painted message on a short wooden plank nailed to a post in the yard. It stated, "Rooms For Rent." I saw a man chopping wood at the side of the house and decided to stop. I dismounted, tied my horse to a tree, and walked toward him. He greeted me.

"Looking for a room, mister?"

"No, I'm looking for someone who might have stayed here."

He was disappointed and was ready to pick up his ax.

"What name? And when was it?"

"I don't know the name for sure, and it might have been more than one man. It would have been last fall."

"Lord have mercy, mister, I couldn't begin to remember that far back. So many people come and go it would be impossible."

"It would be worth ten dollars if you could help me."

He dropped the ax and became much more interested.

"What did he look like?"

"Heavy-set with dark hair. He had a friend named Forest."

"Yes! Those two did stay here. About two weeks. Said they had been in the Rebel army but got tired of it and quit."

"Can you remember anything else? Where they were going or where they had come from?"

"Let's see. They said they were a long ways from home – oh, I remember, the big one said his home was a place that stuck in my mind because it sounded different. Big Shanty."

"What state was it?"

"I don't know. I don't believe he ever mentioned it."

"Which unit in the Rebel army was he in?"

"I don't know that either. Him and the other man had just walked off and left the army, and they came here because they were afraid to go straight back home. They wanted to wait a while, I guess, and hope they were not caught. I'm sure they were deserters, and they didn't want to talk too much."

I paid him and left. I spent about another hour riding through the area and talked to several people. They were unable to help me and I learned nothing in addition to what I already knew. Strangely enough, it was just the opposite of what usually happened, and the first person I had talked to had been the only one who could help me.

I rode back into town and went to Phillip's office. He was busy, so I told him I only had one quick question.

"Have you ever heard of a town in the South called Big Shanty?"

"No, I don't think so. Oh, wait a minute! That was the name of the town where the Andrews raid took place last April. Andrews and his men stole a locomotive there."

"Where was it, what state?"

"Georgia. Not very far north of Atlanta."

"Thank you, Phillip. It's connected to Sarah. I'll explain later when you have more time."

I turned to walk out of his office and he spoke again.

"Alex, I've got a favor to ask. Polly has invited me to come to her home and dine on Sunday. Her cousin, Martha, is visiting from Alexandria, and Polly asked me to bring a friend. Will you go with me?"

"Phillip, you know that I have absolutely no interest in any woman other than Sarah."

"Yeah, I know, but you may have to get over that some day. Besides, I'm not asking you to marry her. Just come and sit and grin and say something occasionally."

"Who is Martha?"

"She's twenty-one years old with no husband. Polly says she is very pretty."

"And looking for a husband?"

"I don't know, maybe so. But who isn't?"

"I'm not a good prospect for her."

"Forget that and help me out. Be at my house at eleven-thirty on Sunday, and we will go from there."

I shook my head and turned to go. I didn't have to speak. He knew I would be there.

Riding home I continued to feel the excitement that had consumed me when the man in Maryland had informed me about Big Shanty. It was the first good lead that had come to me in the search for Hawkins. The man I had described, the one called Heavy, would have been in contact with Hawkins over a period of several days, maybe even on that last day when Hawkins apparently left Baltimore.

And then a thought occurred to me that was even more exciting. Possibly the man from Big Shanty, Heavy, could have guided Hawkins southward through Maryland and beyond. He and Hawkins could have been accommodating each other. Both were on the run, and both had a desire to be in the South. I would wait a little longer for Ed Jenkins, but very soon I would be going to Georgia. If I could find Heavy, I might also find Hawkins and Sarah.

Sunday morning, as I rode into town to meet Phillip, my thoughts turned to the war. I wondered how many others had been like me and had been caught, undecided, in the middle? I remembered all of the things I had been told, or had heard, about Mr. Lincoln. Maybe I had felt a nearness to him because of his background, a humble beginning, somewhat similar to my own. Even though during the period that followed we had traveled a different kind of road, I could easily relate to the early years of his life. He was a good man and a kind man, and I believed in what he was trying to accomplish.

It was pleasant, too, to think of his great sense of humor and his enjoyment in bringing it to others around him. It was said that he looked forward to receiving a particular newspaper that included articles written by David R. Locke, who wrote under the name of 'Petroleum Vesuvius Nasby'. Locke almost always poked good-natured fun at Mr. Lincoln, using a method that amused the President so much he would oftentimes come out of his room in the middle of the night searching for someone with whom he could share the contents of the articles.

But, I thought, too, of my birthplace and my home, including the early beginnings there in a good family environment. And others like Sarah had been born there with friends and family who were still a part of her life, so when the war began, I could not see myself fighting against either side. I think I had come to realize only after the death of Major Dale that I would have to take a stand. It resulted in what I had come to identify as *The Decision*.

Phillip was ready and waiting when I arrived. He obviously was relieved to see me, knowing that I might easily default on making an appearance. We talked as we made the ten-minute ride to the home of Polly. Just as we got there, he offered some final advice.

"Now don't sit there like a knot-on-a-log. Say something nice to the young lady, and laugh a little. Who knows? You might enjoy yourself."

"Okay, for you I will do it. But, remember, you owe me one."

He had been right, Martha was a pretty young woman. She appeared at first to be a dark haired brunette. After a closer look, I could see that she had deep blue eyes. We had a nice meal after which we settled into the parlor for conversations. Invariably, talk turned to the war. Phillip, always well informed, said we could expect another big battle within weeks. 'Fighting Joe Hooker' had gathered a Union Army of one hundred and thirty thousand well-equipped soldiers near Fredericksburg. He had vowed to push Lee backwards and destroy his Rebel army. Lee, with approximately seventy thousand men, was positioned nearby, just south and west of where the Federals were located. A clash was inevitable and imminent.

The ladies were soon tired of such talk and we turned to the discussion of other things. Being in the company of another woman, a very nice young lady, once again gave me the knowledge that Sarah was the only woman I could ever truly love. Martha was a sweet and compatible young lady, and I enjoyed being in her presence, but it just confirmed what I already knew: I had to find Sarah.

Later, while riding in the direction of home, I considered the letter I had received from Sarah. It had been written, undoubtedly, with the full knowledge of Hawkins. In fact, he would have told her to include some hint that she was far away and still on the move. However, knowing Sarah as I did, I believe that she would have agreed on one condition. She would have demanded that she be allowed to include a personal comment of her own choosing, and thus she had been able to express her love for me.

Ed Jenkins appeared at my home five days later. He arrived at the door a short while after dawn, which was in keeping with his usual practice of coming at an unexpected time. We had a brief conversation about things in general before settling in chairs in the kitchen. It was too early for Mary Kate to be there, so we were alone. He smiled in a relaxed manner while holding a cup of coffee. He kept a pleasant expression on his face as he looked across a table at me.

"I am happy to inform you that you are now working for the Confederate States of America."

"Well it's about time! I was beginning to wonder about it."

"We have to be careful who we pick, Alex, and other people are involved in making final decisions."

"I understand. When do I head south?"

"Not immediately. Something else has come up close by. We've got a serious problem here, and we believe you are best suited to handle it."

"But, Ed, you said yourself that I would have to move fast to find Sarah."

"I know but the war comes first. We have a very serious situation that involves Jackson's army. We have to root out a spy before another battle takes place."

"What is he doing?"

"He is operating within our quartermaster department. We discovered it by accident. He drives a wagon back and forth from the depot to the army in the field. He delivers loads of food. While he is in the area with the army, he makes notes on movements, supplies, and other pertinent information and passes it on to the Yankees. He has to be stopped."

"How?"

"We know what he is doing and when he does it. We have a good idea about how you can find him."

"And then what?"

"Bring him in if you can, otherwise shoot him."

"Wait a minute, Ed. I didn't take this job to go around shooting people."

"I know. But remember, he is not a soldier, he is a spy. He is a man who is willing to take his chances in an effort to get a great many of our people killed. He deserves no better. And if you are caught, my friend, you will face the same consequences."

"Yes, I am sure you are right. I had not previously considered it in that way."

"It's a part of war, Alex. Before it is over there will be violence and hatred like nothing we have ever seen in this country. Part of what happens will depend on the individual commanders in the field and what they will allow. In any event, it will be a nightmare that will not soon be forgotten."

Ed explained that he would set me up to deliver mail. I would be driving a wagon from a depot to where the men of Jackson's army were located. I would be taking the same route that was being used by the spy. Ed told me that I would be able to take Malcolm because the men, in the excitement of receiving letters from home, would pay no attention to him. He said other blacks were being used anyway so it would not be unusual. Malcolm had already told me that he wanted to be a part of whatever I did so it was settled. All that remained was working out specific details.

# VII.

Over the next twenty-four hours, I made preparations to be away for a while. I talked to Mary Kate and Bradford, and told them to take over as they had in the past when I was not there. Mary Kate questioned me.

"What if the Yankee soldiers come out here?"

"Tell them I am away buying horses for the Union Army. If it is necessary, send them to see Phillip Anderson in town. He has a copy of papers that were drawn up originally for me."

Malcolm and I created some humor about the forthcoming adventure. I told him that he should begin calling me "Marse Alec," and I advised him to practice a new way of pronouncing his words, forget about what he had been taught in England. He had told me that he wanted to go with me, and I realized once again that he was a deeply committed friend. I knew he felt that I not only had brought about his new status as a freed man, but had turned his life around completely and given him a vibrant new hope.

Following a final meeting with Ed Jenkins, Malcolm, and I left Washington, passing the Union Army sentries much the same as when we had gone to Merritt Springs. We had no delays as we headed across the Northern Virginia countryside in the general direction of Fredericksburg.

On Thursday, April twenty-third, we reached Guiney's Station, traveling on the Virginia Central Railroad. There we found much activity among the Confederate troops occupying the station. An air of excitement could be felt immediately as we departed the rail car. Men in grey uniforms were moving about at a rapid pace, and all seemed to have some important job to carry out.

The platform adjoining the station building was completely covered with wooden boxes and barrels, and there were many large bags filled with either soft goods or items of food. Oddly enough, we had stepped out of the rail car directly onto the very spot we were told to conduct the search, the location where the supplies were assembled for distribution. It would be the place where the Northern spy would be carrying out his assignment.

I had been told by Ed to find a Captain Hale who was in charge of the quartermaster operations involving the large supply dump. He would be expecting us and would know about our mission. We paused to get oriented, and I thought carefully about my new role and the appearance I would make being accompanied by Malcolm. I made sure that he was carrying our two bags, as would a manservant. Then, I realized it didn't matter. The men who were there were so well occupied that they had no time to stare at others. Also, I noticed that other blacks were there, working side by side with the whites who were mostly soldiers. It verified a fact. A very big battle was in the making, and there was little time for people to think about other things.

I stopped a young soldier and asked if he could tell me where to find Captain Hale. He looked around briefly and then pointed to an officer some fifty feet away who was directing a group of men lifting large boxes. I told Malcolm to stay with our bags, and walked hurriedly over to meet Captain Hale. He was busy, but he seemed happy to see me.

"Welcome, Mister Fairfield. I'm glad to see you. How much have you been told about our problem?"

He moved along with me as I turned and walked back in the direction where Malcolm was standing.

"I was told that a young soldier discovered a note left by the spy. It is my understanding that he was not seen well enough to be identified and that the spy is unaware that he has been discovered."

"That is correct. I have the soldier here with me on temporary duty waiting for you to arrive. His name is James Parker. He's a private in the Georgia 23rd, a unit of Colonel Colquitt's Brigade."

"Very good. I will go to work at once. Can you tell me about provisions and where we should go for shelter?"

"There is no shelter, Mister Fairfield. You will have to place your bedroll in whatever space you can find. There is a separate area for the darkies. You can take necessary provisions from our supplies here. Now, sir, if you will wait, I will go and find Private Parker."

Suddenly, a soldier standing about ten feet away let out a loud and long-lasting yell. It was immediately taken up by all of the soldiers. It was a nearly ear-bursting noise. The men were all looking at an officer who had stepped down from the rail car. They greeted him with a tremendously loud cheer. Captain Hale had stopped, and when the cheering died down some, he looked at me and grinned as he spoke.

"In case you are wondering, Mister Fairfield, you have just heard the Rebel yell."

I smiled.

"I'm glad you told me. I was about to evacuate the area."

"Well, they are just getting warmed up. That's what the Yankees will be hearing pretty soon. Our boys know they are outnumbered two to one, but they are still itching for a fight. Stay put, Mister Fairfield, I'll be right back."

He was away for only a few minutes. When he returned he was accompanied by Private Parker. Captain Hale introduced me to the young soldier.

"Mister Fairfield, I will have to leave you on your own now, I have a great deal to do. Private Parker will stay with you as long as he is needed. We have to get ready for Hooker. We know he has over one hundred and thirty thousand well-equipped men and over four hundred artillery pieces. And we are told that he is a fighter, so we have to be prepared. Good luck."

He left, and I turned to Private Parker.

"Thank you, Private Parker, for helping. Your keen eye turned out to be very helpful. Can you tell me about it?"

"Yes, sir. I was assigned to be here for a few days to help with supplies. I got in the habit of getting up on top of one of the rail cars each evening to eat my provisions. It was cool and quiet there.

The first time I saw the man he was acting kind of strange. He kept looking all around to see who was watching him, but he never saw me. He took a piece of paper out of his coat and put it under a rock and left.

The next night he did the same thing. I thought it was odd, and after he left, I went and got it and took it to Captain Hale. He knew right away it was not right and he went to some other officers. They knew it was information for the Yankees. He had marked it with a pencil and the officers changed it and told me to put it back where I found it. They watched that rock all night, but it was never picked up, I guess the other man realized they were there. So they never caught either one."

"Can you describe the man"

"No sir, it was too late in the day and getting dark. But Captain Hale says he knows he is a driver of one of the supply wagons, and he believes we can find him, maybe tomorrow."

So it meant that we would be searching for two men, the one who left the note and the one who retrieved it and took it to the Union Army. And they would be back even though they would know that the job had become more risky. But the battle was drawing near and the information would be needed quickly. I spoke to Parker.

"You say that the Captain believes the man is a driver. How does he know that?"

"Because of the arm bands. The drivers wear different colors depending on what they are to pick up. The man I saw had on an arm band."

"I see. All right, we will meet in the morning at the loading dock. Be there early, Parker. I will be there with the black man who is with me. We will load wagons and hope that somehow you will be able to identify him."

"Yes, sir."

The next morning, Malcolm, Private Parker, and I took positions on the platform and began working together. We loaded provisions into the slowly moving wagons that were backed up and waiting in a long line. After each wagon stopped, was loaded, and pulled away, I spoke briefly to Parker to find out if he could remember any of the drivers. He could not.

There was the same sense of urgency that we had seen the previous day, and each person on the dock was working steadily. We had worked for about four hours, and I was beginning to wonder if the man had been scared off when Parker came over and whispered to me just as another wagon pulled up.

"That's him, Mister Fairfield. I remember his hat."

I turned and winked at Malcolm who nodded slightly. Then we began loading the wagon as we had the others. We had decided that we would not attempt to take him at the dock in case the other man we wanted was watching. When we had his wagon ready to go, I spoke to the man.

"This darkie is going with you to help unload. We have been told to speed up the turn around time."

He replied abruptly.

"No, he aint going with me, I don't need no darkie."

I spoke quickly.

"Parker, get down there and hold the reins of this man's horses."

Parker jumped off of the platform and did as I had asked. Then I looked straight at the man.

"Mister, we don't have time to argue. If this black man does not ride with you, I will call an officer from the inside and have you arrested."

He changed immediately.

"All right, all right. Tell him to get on the wagon, in the back."

Malcolm quickly jumped on top of the large bags in the back of the wagon, and the man popped the horses with the long reins. After they pulled away I turned to Parker.

"Are you sure that was the man you saw?"

"Yes, sir, I am sure because of the hat, I remember it. And the man is the same size and shape."

"Good. It looks like we've got one of them."

"What will your darkie do?"

"Stay with him and watch him closely."

I found Captain Hale and told him that we apparently had one of the men. He was elated and said that there would be no need for me to pose as the mail courier as originally planned.

In about two hours, I saw Malcolm returning in the wagon, handling the reins. Looking closer, I could see the man who had come in the wagon earlier was tied and riding in the back. When he pulled up, Malcolm explained.

"He tried to run. I caught him, and with the help of some of the infantry soldiers, we tied him with the rope you gave me. He didn't seem to enjoy the ride back too much."

We both laughed. Then I wanted to know about his reaction when he was caught.

"What did he have to say during the ride back?"

"Not too much. But the sash sure came in handy."

He was talking about a yellow sash he was wearing around his waist. It was identification given to him by Captain Hale that let the soldiers know that he was authorized to be there to carry out an important mission, and they quickly helped him.

I found Hale close by. He brought four soldiers with him, and they took the man from the wagon. Hale turned to me and spoke hurriedly.

"Mister Fairfield, I think your work has been completed. Thank you, sir, and I believe you are free to leave the area, and it may be wise to do so. The Yankees are beginning to make contact along the edge of the wilderness. We will soon be fully engaged."

"All right, we will take your advice and leave in the next rail cars headed east. And I wish you well, Captain."

"And the same to you, sir, and your darkie."

Before we walked away, he made it a point to shake hands with Malcolm. It was rare and almost unbelievable to see a Confederate officer shake the hand of a black man.

When we were finally on the rail car and pulling away from Guiney Station, I looked at the soldiers on the platform. Some would soon be dead. Others would be maimed or lose legs or arms. But none seemed to think of those things. Instead, they were confident and eager to enter into the fighting.

This was due to the influence of their commander, Stonewall Jackson. It was said that his troops would walk straight into hell if he gave the command. No other leader had as much respect and admiration as "Old Jack." He was a fearless commander, possessing a level of military skill that perhaps no other man had attained. He was more daring than others and would take great risks that had brought his army many successes, and he was truly idolized by both his soldiers and the people who were waiting back home. In addition, he was known to be a devoutly religious man.

We reached Washington the next day. A short while later we arrived at home. It was early afternoon, and Mary Kate was still there. She met us on the outside, and we followed her into the kitchen. She put water on the stove to make coffee and then she brought out her fruitcake. I asked how things were going.

"All right, except we had one visitor who was not so nice."

She very quickly got my attention with that remark.

"Who?"

"A Yankee Colonel and his aide. He's going to take your horses."

"You mean the four thoroughbreds?"

"Yes, that's what he said."

"He can't do that, they are the last I have."

"I don't think he cares about that. He said something about us being Rebel sympathizers anyway."

"Those horses are worth thousands of dollars."

"He said he will pay one hundred dollars each, otherwise he will just requisition them and pay you nothing."

Malcolm had a smile on his face and spoke.

"Marse Alec, I noticed a hole in the fence in the back pasture."

Mary Kate grinned, as did I as I responded.

"You know, you're right, Malcolm. I'm surprised those horses haven't already escaped."

"You suppose," and he paused as if giving serious thought to the matter, "that those horses could get loose tonight?"

I tried to look serious.

"Yes, I believe there is a good possibility that they will get loose tonight."

I told Mary Kate what we would do. Bradford was to come after dark, put ropes on the horses and lead them three miles down the road to Jimmy Young's place. Jimmy was an avowed Southern supporter, and he would take them in for the night. After that I would plan to get them to the farm of a friend in southern Maryland where they would be safe. So far the Yankees had not spent much time in that particular area. Those horses were too rare to give them up without trying to save them. I thought while we were together it would be a good time to discuss a plan. Mary Kate was to tell Bradford to let Jimmy Young know that Malcolm and I would come and get the horses within the next day or so. Continuing, I turned to Malcolm.

"It will be best not to try to take those horses across the Navy Yard Bridge. Instead, we can ride north in Maryland and go around that bridge. It will take longer, but it will be safer. I am wondering what I can tell the Union sentries we will encounter?"

He thought for a few moments before speaking.

"I believe you can tell them a convincing story by saying that you are delivering the horses to high-ranking Union cavalry officers. I think you can be vague or evasive about a meeting place. And you have the papers to show them that allow you to travel."

"Yes. It will work. I will wait to see Ed Jenkins tomorrow, and then we can go."

Ed had moved to Richmond and was coming to Washington each week. He had devised a scheme that made it easy for him to pass by the sentries. He had a set of papers that identified him as a courier, a non-dangerous person who was acceptable to both sides. Once inside the city, he would meet with his four operatives and collect the information they had accumulated. My purpose in meeting with him was to finalize my plans to go to Georgia. Finding the man called Heavy would be my top priority.

I was planning to tell Ed that I would like to set up my headquarters initially in Atlanta or one of the smaller towns nearby. Malcolm would go with me. He had already stated a desire to do so. And it gave me a good feeling, having him with me. He was wise, strong physically, a good conversationalist, and he was intensely loyal. My only concern was what we might find regarding the attitude of the people toward blacks in Georgia. Also, before leaving the Washington area, I was planning one final investigation to verify that Hawkins had taken Sarah south through Maryland. On the return trip, I would stop in Baltimore and stay long enough to check a number of the livery stables. If Hawkins had rented a closed carriage, or barouche, I might be able to find the driver. If so, he most likely would be able to identify Hawkins and Sarah, and he might remember where he had taken them.

Malcolm and I arrived in Baltimore at ten in the morning, four days after our return from Guiney Station. We had just completed our trip to deliver my horses to Reynolds Plantation, which was owned by a good friend and located in an isolated area of Southern Maryland.

There were sixteen hundred acres of land, most of which was used for grazing by horses and mules. The plantation was located in a place with a big advantage: it was not easily reached by others and was known to exist by only a few people. It was a good spot for my horses, and I was happy with my decision to put them there.

After making a few inquiries in Baltimore, I learned that many of the livery stables were concentrated on the streets around the rail station. And so it was there that Malcolm and I began looking about, and I starting asking questions at each stable we found. At one o'clock I walked into a building that had an overhead sign that read, "Horses and Carriages For Rent." Only one man was there. He was large and appeared to be about fifty years old.

He spoke with a slight accent as he gave me his name, Kurt Mekker. He was not busy, and it seemed that I had caught him at a good time. I explained the purpose of my visit, describing in the process both Hawkins and Sarah. He listened carefully without interrupting until I paused. Then he spoke.

"I can tell you, sir, that I remember the man you described. He is easy to remember because he paid me a great deal of money, much more than I would have normally charged. He said he would pay a bonus for me to leave immediately. It happened about the same time last fall that you mentioned."

"Who was with him?"

"A woman and a man. And there was a lot of baggage. Two or three trunks and many carpetbags. He said that they preferred to travel in a closed coach. The load was so great that I used four horses. He said that he wanted to move along quickly, and it seems that he was in a great rush to get to his destination."

"Can you describe the woman?"

He thought for a few moments.

"She was young. And I believe she had dark hair. I do not remember her very well."

"Are you sure she had dark hair?"

"Yes, I am reasonably sure that she had dark hair."

Malcolm was listening, and he spoke quietly to me.

"It could have been a wig."

That would have explained it. I looked back to Mekker.

"How about the second man, do you remember him?"

"No, not very well. I remember that he seemed to have been hired by the first man to lift the trunks and do other things."

"Do you know their names?"

"No, I do not know their names."

"Sir, if you will please, try to remember a name."

I took a twenty dollar bill out of my pocket and let him see it. He immediately began thinking more deeply and I felt he would now give it his very best effort. After half a minute the look on his face changed to a pleased expression and he spoke.

"Smith! And I believe the first name was Gerald. Yes, his name was Gerald Smith."

Hawkins would have used a fake identification. I should have known that before asking the question. I thought of something else.

"Can you remember anything about the second man?"

"Well, let's see. He was strong. He could lift the trunks without assistance."

"He must have been large."

"He was. Big in his middle. Larger than me, or you, or your manservant."

It was Heavy. I was almost certain that Hawkins, Sarah, and Heavy had been driven south by Mekker. I withdrew another twenty dollar bill and questioned him further.

"Now, please sir, if you will, try to remember anything that was said about their destination during the time you were with them. And I mean by that, their final destination, not just the point at which they would have boarded the ferry."

He had glanced at the forty dollars several times. He turned slightly and looked outward toward the street. I knew that he was giving careful consideration to what I had asked. Finally he spoke.

"I am trying my best, sir, to remember, but I cannot. He was rather quiet, or maybe even secretive. He only wanted to make sure that he was on the ferry."

"How about the other man, did he sit beside you as you drove the coach?"

"Yes. Let me think a moment or so about him. He talked about food, he wanted to get back home and have some fried chicken and turnip greens. He said he had lived on a farm." He paused, deeply in thought, then continued. "And was there something else? Oh, yes, he said that he had been wounded in the war and was going home."

"Did he say anything about where it was, or how long it would take to get there?"

"It seems he was planning to be there in about two days."

"Did he say that the man and woman who were with him would go to the same place? That is, the same place where his home was located?"

Again he thought carefully.

"He did say that the man was going to pay him for his work, and it seemed that he might have had a job that was to continue."

"Can you think of anything at all that would make you believe that they were all three going to the same place?"

"Ah, I will try to think of that for a moment. We talked some about the war and how it would turn out. He believed the South would win. Oh! Yes! He did say that the other man would buy a large plantation, and he would let him, the big man, become the master of the slaves."

"Where? Where would that be?"

"I don't know. He did not say. The only thing he did say was that he would go home first. I assumed that the man and woman would go to that place as well."

"Thank you, sir. You have helped me. You have earned this money."

He smiled and took the money. I said, "goodbye," and Malcolm and I left.

On the first day of May, a Friday, Mary Kate, Bradford, Malcolm, and I gathered in the kitchen. I had originally planned to leave for Georgia on Saturday or Sunday. I decided to delay the trip for several days. I knew that a battle was getting under way near

Guiney Station, and I wanted to learn what had happened there before leaving Washington.

Mary Kate commented on it.

"From what we have heard, I don't see how the Yankees can be stopped this time."

I answered.

"I don't either. They have a new commander, "Fighting Joe Hooker," and at least sixty thousand more men than Lee. It appears to be an overpowering force."

Malcolm spoke.

"I just hope the war will come to an end."

Bradford added his observations.

"I agree with you, Malcolm. There is absolutely nothing good about a war. And I believe Mr. Lincoln will see to it that things are settled in the right way. All of this hatred and revenge should be stopped before it ruins the whole country. We just need to continue our lives in a normal way. Perhaps people will have a chance to live and work side by side."

Reports on Saturday about the battle were inconclusive. Then, late Sunday, the third of May, sensational news hit Washington. The Union Army had been routed and had suffered a major defeat. It was at a place called Chancellorsville. Jackson had devised a plan to secretly bypass the main body of the Federal troops to spring a surprise attack at their rear. It had created chaos. The Union Army leaders, fearing that they would be cut off, retreated in a great rush back across the Rappahannock River.

But, shockingly for the Confederacy, bad news accompanied the good. Jackson had been wounded. The severity of his condition was unclear. Mixed reports were being received, and specific details were not included. People in Washington and Southern Maryland, predominately sympathetic to the South, were stunned, and were more distraught than joyful. One noted person, perhaps typical of most southerners, had been heard to say, "As long as we have Jackson, we cannot lose the war." Most people had become very confident based on the past victories of Lee and Jackson, and now, to realize that half of that leadership might be taken away was devastating.

Finally, news came that Jackson had been hit in the right hand and in two places in his left arm. He was being attended by Doctor Hunter McGuire, the chief surgeon on his staff and his personal friend. It was reported initially that his wound was serious but not mortal. Even though it was necessary for Doctor McGuire to amputate the left arm of Jackson, the people breathed a sigh of relief.

The events that were being reported gave me an uncertain feeling about leaving Washington. I decided to delay my original plans a few days. On Wednesday, I rode into town hoping to see Phillip. Fortunately, I arrived at his office just as he was preparing to leave for a noontime meal. He agreed to be my guest for a visit to Mary Carroll's Tea Shop. After we were seated and had ordered, I asked Phillip a serious question.

"What is your best prediction now regarding the outcome of the war? And before you answer, let me explain something. I believe Hawkins will remain in the South as long as the Confederate Army is winning. That, of course, will give me more time to find him. Should the situation be reversed, he will most likely leave and take Sarah with him. So, I want your opinion on what may happen next?"

"You want my short answer?"

"Yes."

"It depends on what happens to Jackson. If he returns, the South will most likely win. If he does not return, the South will lose. It's just that simple."

"How can it possibly be that simple?"

"Because there is not a commander in the Army of the Potomac who can defeat Lee and Jackson when they are making decisions together during a battle. Think about it. Consider what they have accomplished with much less than what the Yankees have. Tell me who can stop them? Nobody. But, at this point, it's hard to speculate because we don't know about Jackson."

Although Phillip's opinion differed from the one put forth by Ed Jenkins, he had been accurate about results in the war so far. Later in the day I told Malcolm that we would leave for Georgia the next morning. Earlier, while visiting with Phillip at noon, I had made the decision to go. In meetings with him previously I had "put my house in order." Two acres of my land were to go to Malcolm, as well as ten thousand dollars in cash. In the event that I did not return, my home and the rest of my land and possessions thereon, would go to Mary Kate and Bradford. I had all of my money, except fifty thousand dollars, transferred from a bank in Washington to a "sister" bank in St. Louis, where I already had an account.

On Friday, Malcolm and I went by rail to Baltimore. The latest reports concerning Jackson's recovery were optimistic. He had been wounded at a late hour on the previous Saturday, and almost six days had passed. The only problem in considering the reports was the obvious delay involved. Reports of his condition would arrive a day or two after being posted by the army. He was the subject, sooner or later, of almost all discussions. It was as if the war was being decided by Jackson's condition, and Philip's analysis appeared more accurate than I thought.

From Baltimore, Malcolm and I took the route used by others and went southward through Maryland. Following that, we were able to go by ferry to a location in Virginia from which we made our way to Richmond, and beyond. As we traveled by rail, I used the papers prepared for me by Phillip, and as the buyer of horses for the Confederacy, I encountered no problems.

The people in the rail cars were downtrodden and seemed to be shouldering heavy burdens. There was little gaiety or light-hearted talk. It was a first hand look at the population of a new nation struggling with the stark realities of war. Some of the women were able to bring their black "nannies" with them in the cars. There were no black males allowed, however, so Malcolm was in a separate car toward the back with the other manservants.

We were in the rail cars for two days. Many times we stopped for several hours, sitting and waiting, and at other times we were stalled in the stations. On Monday, we finally reached our destination, Atlanta. It was the eleventh day of May, ten o'clock in the morning. We had been in the railcars for the last nine hours with only three short stopovers.

As people stepped down onto the platform, we all heard the same thing: a young boy of fifteen or sixteen, standing beside a foot-high stack of newspapers, calling out loudly, "Jackson is dead!"

Everyone was shocked. There was silence at first, and then there were comments of disbelief. Some of the ladies, already tired from spending a lengthy time in the rail cars, began crying. It was, indeed, a tragic bit of news that would spread quickly over the South.

Like others standing nearby, I was greatly saddened by the death of Jackson, No other man, with the exception of General Lee, had given the people of the South as much hope. Jackson's ability to plan a battle and then make the adjustments needed as the plan was executed, was unparalleled. His capability in anticipating enemy objectives, preceding and during a battle, was unique. And during the battles, he was always close to the fighting men, showing great courage on numerous occasions by exposing himself to enemy fire. His assessment of action needed at critical moments during a battle had resulted in many successes, and to his soldiers it had brought about an unyielding confidence. We had lost an endearing warrior and none of us would be able to pass through the coming days without sorrowful thoughts and memories of him. Already a legend in the South, he would undoubtedly be considered in the future as one of the most skillful military leaders of all time.

Other thoughts began to enter my mind that were disturbing in a different way. Hawkins would realize the significance of the loss of Jackson and it could have an immediate effect on his future plans. It was a regrettable addition to the sad news about Jackson.

I walked back to find Malcolm. Near the very back, I saw him standing alone some one hundred feet from the baggage car. I smiled as I greeted him.

"Well, I'm sure you had a pleasant ride and enjoyed the journey."

He managed a smile as he responded. I had finally convinced him that it was all right to use my first name when we were together privately.

"Alexander I must give you credit. You are certainly an expert in creating grand tours."

We both laughed. Momentarily it lessened the great remorse I was feeling about Jackson. Malcolm told me that he had little to eat or drink since our last stop and that he had slept no longer than ten minutes at a time during the ride. I told him that I, too, was tired and that we would get under way as soon as possible. I asked him to stand by with our baggage while I looked to rent a rig or a buggy for our trip to the home of my contact in Atlanta. It was a man named John B. Dabney. He had been sent a coded message by Ed Jenkins, using the telegraph system. It said, "A gentleman will be arriving soon, accompanied by his manservant. His purpose will be to procure horses for the army."

Later, driving on Peachtree Road, we found the home of Dabney. I left Malcolm in the buggy and walked to the front door. Just before I raised my hand to knock, the door opened and a large man stood before me. He spoke.

"You are Alexander Fairfield?"

"Yes. And you are John Dabney?"

"I am. Come in, and we will talk."

"Sir, if agreeable, I would like to suggest a meeting at a later time. At present I need rest."

"I understand. I have arranged for you to have access to a small house located a few miles from here. It sits back from the main road and is hidden among a thick growth of trees. You and the nigra will be safe there. You will find provisions in the house. I will give you directions on how to go there. We will talk in the morning. How does that sound?"

"Very good. Thank you, sir."

"Did you hear about Jackson?"

"Yes. It's a sad day for the people of the South."

"And for Christian people in all places. I am told that he showed quite openly a great faith in God."

"I heard that as well. Well, Mister Dabney, I will plan to see you in the morning."

We found the house easily. It was small, although adequate for our purposes. There were fresh provisions, placed there undoubtedly in anticipation of our arrival.

John Dabney came early the next morning. I invited him inside and we sat in a front room. The house had two bedrooms, as well as the front room and a kitchen. Four rooms in all. In the back, some one hundred feet away, there was an outhouse. Also in the back, there was a fenced area approximately forty feet square that could be used as an enclosure for horses or livestock. The furnishings in the house were rough but good enough to accommodate our needs.

Mister Dabney was seated with me in the front room and Malcolm could be seen through the open doorway to the kitchen, moving about as he was performing simple duties there. I noticed that Dabney glanced in that direction several times with a slightly uncomfortable expression. I knew what it meant, and I spoke out in a slightly louder tone.

"Malcolm, would you go out and see if there is water in the horse trough? Also, you might need to clean up some around the outhouse."

Malcolm came to the door and looked at me in a puzzled way. Then he understood, and replied.

"Yes sir, Mister Fairfield, I will take care of it right away."

After he turned and walked to the outside, Dabney commented.

"Your darkie seems to be well spoken. Where did you acquire him?"

"In Washington. He has been well trained in the past. Now, if you will, sir, tell me what you need here?"

"We are very concerned about any further acts of sabotage. After the Andrews raid we realized that even here, this far south, we are not entirely safe from the Yankees. We are alerting people in all parts of the country to watch for suspicious strangers and report them to us. We will then investigate them. You may be called upon to do that."

"And that I can do. What is done with people who are caught in these acts?"

"We hang them. Just like they will do to our people if caught in the North. But I am wondering, sir, if you can tell me about your immediate plans? It is my understanding that you have a personal matter to settle before you become involved in anything else."

"That is correct."

Then I gave him a limited amount of information about Hawkins. I did not mention Sarah. I did use the opportunity to follow up on his comment about the Andrews raid.

"You mentioned Andrews. I believe the raid took place at Big Shanty. Are you familiar with that area?"

"Yes, very much. My original home is a few miles north of there at Acworth. I know many of the people in that area."

"That is interesting! I have reason to believe that Hawkins might have been traveling with a man from that area. Unfortunately, I do not have his name, but I do have a very good description of him. In fact, I have seen and talked to him. He is approximately twenty to twenty five years old, with dark hair and dark eyes. He is large through his middle and upper body. He claims to have been in the Confederate Army, and when I last heard about him, he was apparently on the way back home. Can you think of anyone who might fit this description?"

"I'm not sure. It could be one of the Perkins boys. Sam Perkins has a small cotton farm four miles west of Big Shanty. One of his boys joined a unit that was formed in Acworth in March of sixty-two, however, that unit went to the west. I do not see how he could end up in the Washington area unless he had deserted."

"The man I am looking for may be a deserter, although I am not looking for him for that reason. My only purpose in finding him would be to question him about Hawkins. And I would like to ask you, sir, at this point, to be very careful to keep the information confidential. If Hawkins is alerted before I can get to him, he will move on quickly. I will lose any chance that I might have to get him. Do I have your solemn promise that the information will be kept secret?"

"By all means, Mister Fairfield. You can depend on it because I have given you my word. Also, the sooner you find Hawkins and wind up your personal business, the better off we will be with you in our services."

I wanted to get more information about "the Perkins boy," or as I would know him, Heavy. I looked at Dabney.

"I need help from someone to investigate Perkins. I cannot go because he would know me. Do you know anyone who can help?"

"I can help you. I have authority to ride in the rail cars and I can go in the early morning. I can ask questions."

"Very good! But remember, it has to be done in such a way that people will not think you are searching for Perkins as a deserter. If he thinks you have come for that reason, I doubt you will gain any knowledge. And worse, he will most likely tell the man I really want, and he, too, would slip away. Do you think you can handle it under those circumstances?"

"Absolutely. I have been in similar situations. I have actually brought in two deserters in the past. You may be surprised to know, Mister Fairfield, that deserters are not shielded. They are considered cowards and are quickly disposed of by local citizens."

"Perkins must know that because he is claiming to have been wounded. He made that statement to a man in Baltimore."

"All right, we will find out. I will go early tomorrow and most likely will return on the south bound rail cars late in the day. I will contact you on Thursday."

"Thank you, Mister Dabney. I feel fortunate to have your help. If I can resolve the problems that may involve Perkins, I can work with you on other matters much sooner."

"Well, all I can say is, if he is actually a deserter, you won't need my help anyway. He will be dealt with by others who will probably make him feel like he would rather be facing the Yankees again."

Dabney was a no-nonsense type of individual. Even though perhaps fifty-five years of age, he appeared to be capable of handling himself well. Standing well above six feet and weighing some two hundred fifty pounds, he was an intimidating figure. He commanded respect, and it was understandable that he would have a considerable advantage when questioning other people.

On Wednesday, Malcolm and I spent most of the day inside the small house. Being unaware of general conditions in Atlanta, I felt safer avoiding people. During the day as Malcolm and I talked, I learned more about the philosophy and reasoning of black people. Their instincts and perceptions were possibly more keenly developed than that of other races. I believed it to be because of the history of their existence, which included a need for awareness

# George McGuire

as well as an ability to quickly identify dangers that would almost always be close by.

# VIII.

At mid-afternoon on Thursday, John Dabney appeared at the door. He came inside, and when he was seated in the front room, he began talking.

"At Big Shanty I had a visit with the Kemp family. I have known them for many years. We spoke about the death of Jackson and other things related to the war. Finally, I asked in a casual way what news had been received about our local boys who were away serving in the army. We exchanged information about various young men. Then I raised a question, as would a person inquiring in a general fashion, about one of the Perkins boys. I said, 'Didn't a letter come some time ago from Harold? It seems that he had been wounded.' And Henry Kemp responded. 'Yes, he wrote a letter home last fall saying that he had been wounded and would be confined to a place in Tennessee while recovering.' I said that I had heard the same and that I supposed him to now be at home. Henry said, no, he had not come home, and it was believed that he returned to his regiment to continue with his duty."

As I heard the words of Dabney, I formed a strong belief that the man I knew as Heavy was actually Harold Perkins. I continued the conversation with Dabney.

"It sounds as though you handled your questions well. Now, I am reasonably sure that Perkins is the man who is traveling with Hawkins. As I told you, I am only interested in Hawkins, and based on what you have just told me, I feel there is a good chance that Hawkins may be nearby. Even so, I don't know how to proceed. Both will run if they learn that I am in the area. Do you have any suggestions?"

"Not at the moment. Let me give it some thought. I can discuss it, in general, with others that I trust to try to set up a plan."

Then I realized that I was flirting with danger. Time could easily run out on me. I decided to tell Dabney everything, including all of the information about Sarah and my relationship with her. He was not too surprised.

"I knew some of the details of that, Mister Fairfield. Ed told me. And I have already given it some thought. You may wish to ride about in your buggy, just looking around in Atlanta. And you might want to check in two towns close by, Marietta and Roswell. Many times we can learn things by just poking around and asking a few innocent questions. Roswell should be investigated. It is a place where many fine families have settled, and based on what you have told me about Hawkins, he would look for such a place. In the meantime, I will check deeds and recent transfers of property and new depositors in the banks. I have authority to do those things. If he is here, we will find him."

"Thank you, Mister Dabney, you have certainly encouraged me with your help."

A week passed. Malcolm and I rode in the buggy some each day as John Dabney had suggested, all to no avail. During those times we were careful to dress so that we would appear to be a gentleman being driven by his manservant. We had no problems.

At mid-morning on a Saturday, John Dabney paid me a visit. I was glad to see him and invited him into the front room where we engaged in small talk as he got settled in a chair. After several minutes he got to the point of his visit.

"I'm sorry to say that I don't have much. I have checked all possible places, and I do not have any real encouragement. I inquired again, with a different person, and the Perkins boy has not been seen in or about Big Shanty. I am sorry that I do not have better news."

"We are dealing with a very clever man, Mr. Dabney, so don't feel bad."

"There was one thing that was slightly puzzling, but I feel it has no connection to the man you described."

"What was it?"

"An officer of the bank in Marietta told me that a man came in about five months ago and arranged for the transfer of a large sum of money from a bank in Richmond to his bank. But he was using a different name and it seems he could not have been Hawkins."

"How much did he deposit?"

"The bank officer said that he could not disclose the exact amount. He could only tell me that it was in excess of ten thousand dollars."

"What was his name?"

Dabney reached into his coat pocket and withdrew a piece of paper. He read the name aloud.

"Michael J. DeAngelo. And I have the feeling it is his real name."

"But after being Edward Hawkins for so long, why would he now begin using his real name?"

"He feels he is so far removed from his previous locations he is now safe in a remotely located place. He most likely has a great deal of money deposited in his real name, in London or Paris, and it will make it much easier to carry out financial transactions by using the name of DeAngelo."

"Has he been back to the bank and made other deposits or withdrawals?"

"He has not been back. At least the bank officer has not seen him. He has issued bank drafts from the account."

"For how much?"

"The officer would not divulge the amounts."

I paused to think for a few moments before speaking.

"Yes, as you say, this is somewhat puzzling. How often does the bank get other new accounts of this kind?"

"Not often. And based on the reaction of the bank officer as we talked, I believe it could have been a very large sum of money."

"Did DeAngelo give an address?"

"Only an address in Richmond. He said that he was not settled here yet."

"It sounds odd, and possibly suspicious. How can we check further?"

"I had thought about how to go about that and I am not sure. It is difficult because you can easily arouse the suspect's suspicion if you use his name. I will try to track him through the people that I can trust and let you know what I learn."

"Fine. And we must remember now that we are looking for DeAngelo, not a man using the name of Hawkins."

He left, but I continued to think about DeAngelo. I knew that he had been planning to leave New York and move to the South, and as a first step, he could have transferred money to Richmond. And because he was very clever, he could have possibly set up a method of using people in various places to accomplish his goal without leaving an obvious trail. Now, I would give priority to DeAngelo on the list of people that I would try to find. Also, I wanted to know exactly when he first began transferring money to Richmond.

During the following days as I considered everything, I questioned whether it was right for me to be in Atlanta. Every reason I had for making the decision to come to the city was based on assumptions. Sarah could be a thousand miles from Atlanta. This doubt had always been in my mind, and to place myself in a distant place without having a more valid cause might be pure folly. I mentioned it to Malcolm.

"Do you think I was wrong to come here?"

"No. I don't. You had good reason to come here."

"But nothing is here, at least we have found nothing."

"You are very discouraged, my friend, and it is understandable. But I am wondering, did you raise the question to get my advice?"

"Yes."

"Stay here. It is the best opportunity you have. I think your reasoning about DeAngelo is right. I know it is difficult for you, but you must try to be patient."

"But nothing is happening, and time keeps going by."

"All right, let's do something. Why don't we go to Roswell tomorrow? If we find nothing, we can wait a few days and go there again."

His idea sounded good, and I thought of something else that could be done.

"Okay, we will go tomorrow. And when we get there you can be the one to ask questions."

He was puzzled momentarily, and then he knew what I meant.

"So, you intend for your manservant to talk to other manservants?"

"Exactly."

The next morning, in the buggy riding in the direction of Roswell, Malcolm looked at me and grinned.

"You know, Marse, you're an unusual man."

"Why?"

"What other white man would form a close friendship with his manservant? How did you come to be like you are?"

It was a good question, and I gave it some thought before answering.

"I believe it happened when I was very young and starting out in New Orleans."

"What made you go to New Orleans?

"I think I might have been a little like the Prodigal Son."

"Did you have trouble at home?"

"No. Everything was fine. I just wanted to go to the "far country" and have a good time."

"And what happened in the far country?"

"I soon learned that a sixteen year old boy with no money has got a real problem on the streets of New Orleans. Right away I found out that others will kill you for a dollar or less. There is a broad mix of people there, and that was when I came to realize that the color of a man's skin makes no difference. Many times I was in desperate situations and sometimes I would be helped by a black man, other times by a white man. Even though it was a dangerous kind of lifestyle, to a young boy it was exciting. Also, I wanted to stay on long enough to see the cream rise to the top."

"And you did, of course."

"Yes. I was determined that I would make it, and I did." I looked into his face. "And that is when I learned that a manservant can be a good friend."

He smiled and looked back to the road ahead.

In Roswell we found that Dabney was right; there were more than the usual number of mansions normally seen in a town of that size. We spent several hours traveling over the city, but we were never able to come upon a situation that would allow Malcolm to speak to another black man. All were with their masters, or other people which did not afford the opportunity to talk to them in private. By mid-afternoon we decided to return to Atlanta. As we passed, I saw a young woman walking on the grounds of one of the mansions. She was at least two or three hundred feet away. At first glance my heart jumped. She looked exactly like Sarah. Then, I could see that she was "with child," and pretty far advanced at that, so I turned away quickly before she could see me. The ladies were very sensitive about being seen in public while in waiting. And, I knew it could not be Sarah anyway because she would not have been in that condition. It did, however, create some excitement for me, and I mentioned it to Malcolm.

"Did you see that lady walking in the rear of the large home we just passed on the right side of the road?"

"No. Why?"

"She looked a lot like Sarah."

"Do you want to go back?"

"No. It was not her. The woman I saw was going to have a baby."

He looked at me in a way that I had come to know. It was a silent means of questioning the reasoning of my judgment. I let it go. I knew it could not be her. We continued on our way and arrived back in Atlanta in the early evening.

By reading the newspaper, I stayed abreast of the happenings in the war. The day after we were in Roswell, the paper reported that Lee was moving northward, and if he was victorious there, Washington would be put in jeopardy. In the west it was not as encouraging. The Union Army, under the command of Grant, had a stranglehold on Vicksburg. If the city should fall into the hands of the Yankees, the Union would have control of the Mississippi River. For Mr. Lincoln, such an event could not happen too quickly. He would be seeking a second term in the fall, and already some of the newspapers in the North were expressing discontentment with him. Consequently, his approval ratings were in a downward trend.

The day after our trip to Roswell, Malcolm asked a question that was related to our visit.

"The woman you saw yesterday who was with child, how well did you see her?"

"Not well. Why do you ask?"

"Do you believe there is absolutely no chance it could have been her?"

I waited long enough to give considerable consideration to the question before answering.

"Yes, I am sure it was not her."

"Why are you sure?"

"Because Sarah would not be having a baby."

He waited to respond. He looked out the window for a few moments and turned back to face me.

"She is a woman, Alexander. She could be with child, the same as any other woman."

He was suggesting a possibility that I had already considered. I simply had not been willing to admit it. I answered him.

"Yes, I know. I just didn't want to talk about it."

"I can understand that. You don't want to think it could be possible, but you might have to face it. How long has it been since she was taken?"

"Since early October. Now it is the middle of June, so it has been eight months."

"And the woman you saw, how big was she?"

"Big. Probably not too far from delivering a baby. At least she appeared to be in the last month."

He looked into my face without speaking. He didn't have to say anything, his thoughts were obvious. And mine were the same. Finally, he made a remark.

"I think we need to go back to Roswell."

"So do I. And this time I am going to talk to somebody."

We began making plans for the next day. We would go in high style. I told Malcolm that I wanted us to look like a gentleman of wealth being accompanied by his finely-dressed manservant. I was sure that it would increase my chances of being able to start a conversation with a resident of the city.

We were up early the next morning. Malcolm put on a black coat and vest with a white shirt showing neatly just below his chin. His pants and boots were immaculate. He would draw attention immediately as the servant of a gentleman of unquestionable wealth. I wore a long black coat with a grey vest, and my remaining attire was composed of expensive garments and boots. Our hats were suited to the status we represented. And so it was that we rode into Roswell at approximately eleven o'clock with a feeling of great confidence.

We passed by the large home where I had seen the woman with child, this time on our left. There was no one out and about. We continued on to an area that had many large trees on each side of the roadway. We stopped there to give our horse a pause, and it turned out to be an excellent decision. An elderly gentleman, who appeared to be sixty-five or older, was coming toward us along the pathway adjacent to the road, some one hundred feet away. He was accompanied by a lady who was about his age. They were moving along well. Not only did they appear to be alert, they were looking eagerly in my direction as if they wished to speak.

I had prepared myself with an explanation of why I was there, and now, it seemed that I would soon have the chance to use it. Malcolm stood by the horse, in front of the buggy as would normally be done, and I stood in the pathway next to the street.

The couple arrived at the spot where I stood, and we smiled and exchanged polite greetings. The woman indicated early on that she was interested in knowing details about me, and I made most of my initial comments to her. I said that I was involved with raising thoroughbred horses in the Washington area. However, I was giving consideration to a move to the south to remove myself from the turmoil of the great battles that were now taking place there. It was then that she asked me a question, and she repeated the false name I had used to protect my identity.

"Are you thinking about moving to Roswell, Mister Jacobs?"

"Possibly, Missis Farnsworth. It depends on the availability of land and facilities."

We talked further about horses. Finally, I brought up the subject of how to go about locating a home of good quality. I managed to bring into the conversation an observation about the home of the woman who reminded me of Sarah.

"I noticed a particularly nice home as we rode into the city from the south. It was on the left, and has twin magnolias in the front yard."

The elderly man responded.

"Yes, that is the Harrison home place. Mister Harrison died last year."

"It appears to be occupied."

"I believe it has been leased to a young couple until the estate can be settled."

"Then possibly it will be put up for sale. I am wondering how I can find out."

"The only person I know is his son who lives in Monroe where the large cotton farm is located."

"Do you think the young couple would allow me to come in to look at the house?"

"No, I don't think so. He is not friendly, and they usually stay away from others."

I paused for a moment. If it was DeAngelo, as I suspected it could be, he was still carefully covering his tracks. Maybe the elderly man could give me their name.

"Do you know the name of the young couple in the house?"

"It is an unusual name and I cannot recall it at the moment. My wife and I are here in Roswell only a few days each month to visit our daughter and her children. Her husband is away in the Confederate army. I'm sorry that I cannot be more helpful."

"Oh, that's fine, sir, and I understand. The only reason I asked is because there is some slight possibility that I might know them. Is the name DeAngelo?"

"Yes! That is it. I remember it now."

"Thank you, sir. You have been helpful. I will not keep you from your walk. Good day to you both."

They both smiled and walked away. I turned to Malcolm.

"Did you hear what was said?"

"Yes."

I walked in his direction as I spoke again.

"I believe Sarah is in that house, and I am going in there right now and find out."

"Slow down, slow down. We have a few things to talk about first."

"Okay, we can talk some, but I am not leaving here today until I go in that house."

"Alexander, did you bring a pistol?"

"No."

"Thank the Good Lord."

I looked at him and smiled.

"Don't worry, I'm not going to shoot DeAngelo. I just want to be sure that I have found her."

"And if you have, what will you do?"

"Talk to her. Let her tell me everything that has happened since the night she was taken out of her home in Washington."

"And if DeAngelo is there?"

"He will have to stay out of our way."

"And that is what we have to talk about. Have you considered that she may be staying with him of her own free will?"

"No, I haven't thought about that because I don't think it's a possibility."

"Well think about it for a minute. If she was out in the yard walking around, couldn't she very easily have walked away? And couldn't she very easily have sent you a letter?"

"She's going to have a baby. She will need a doctor, or mid-wife, at any moment, and she couldn't be on the run at a time like that. I think she is just trying to get through this time as best she can."

"How did she get to be in that condition, having his baby?"

"He forced himself on her."

"And now? How does she feel about him now?"

"She has to hate him, as she has from the beginning."

"Are you sure?"

I stopped talking to try to think carefully about the things Malcolm had said. I couldn't be sure about anything. It was easy to know how I wanted her to feel, but Malcolm had been talking sensibly, and some of his comments had to be considered. I spoke to him again.

"All right, tell me what you think I should do."

"Talk to her. And let her do most of the talking. In other words, you don't tell her how it should be or how you want it to be. She has to tell you. And if DeAngelo is there, don't lose your temper. It may actually be up to her to settle things."

His words and the thoughts they provoked were hard to swallow. How could it be possible that I might lose her? She had become the one thing in my life that I could not give up. And now, if Malcolm was right, I could no longer be sure that I would have her. I resigned myself as best I could to what he had said and looked back into the eyes of Malcolm.

"How could she ever care for a man who would take her out of her home and do what he has done to her?"

"Do you remember what Vernon McCleskey said about him?"

"He said that DeAngelo could be very charming."

"And he also said that DeAngelo would be very kind to her to try to influence her feelings for him."

"That may be right, but you have to consider that he is a questionable kind of individual. I believe he gave the Irishman the order to shoot me. How could such a man have any appeal to her?"

"She might not know everything he has done. And he has been with her day in and day out for eight months. He has had plenty of time to use his charm."

I thought about Hawkins, or, as we now knew him, DeAngelo. He was a handsome man. The day I had talked to him I had formed the opinion that he was out of place. He had seemed more like a respectful gentleman than a type to be involved in activities that were wrong. And, thinking of Sarah, I remembered some of the comments she had made about Alan, misjudging him in the beginning. And then there was the impulsive behavior that came to the surface with Jennings. I had to admit that Malcolm was right. Even though she had said emphatically that she loved me, I was not convinced now that I would stand alone as the only man in Sarah's life. Malcolm spoke again, with a kindness in his tone.

"I am not trying to discourage you. I only want you to be prepared for anything that may happen."

"Yes, I know. What do you think I should do?"

"Go there and walk straight up to the front door. Talk to both of them and put everything on the table. Don't threaten him. If she makes a decision on that basis, you may never know how she really feels."

I finally managed a slight smile.

"How did you get to be so smart?"

"Well, maybe I had something similar to your New Orleans kind of education while I was living in London."

"How old are you, Malcolm?"

"Actually, I don't know. I think I am somewhere close to your age."

"Well, I think the day you came to my farm turned out pretty well for me."

"Likewise, my friend."

We got in the buggy, and Malcolm guided the horse back in the direction of the house where we would most likely find DeAngelo and Sarah. We rode along in silence. I was committed to carrying out Malcolm's plan, and I believed that very soon I would see Sarah again.

Malcolm stopped the buggy directly in front of the house, which was back from the street some two hundred feet. I turned to look at him just before stepping down out of the buggy, and he smiled as he spoke.

"Good luck."

"Thank you."

The walk from the street to the house was long. It was not so much the distance as it was the time that it gave me to think. I had lost some of my confidence, and I had what amounted to almost a slightly dreaded feeling. Even though my great hatred for DeAngelo was coming back more predominately, I knew I would have to keep myself under control. Anything else, as Malcolm had pointed out, could have a detrimental effect on Sarah at the wrong time. It would be very difficult for me, my anger and resentment having reached a peak, and even facing him in a conversation was going to be a challenge. But the safety of Sarah, and her baby, would have to be put before all other things. Therefore, I would use my very best efforts to be pleasant with him.

Just before I reached the door, it was opened. Standing before me was DeAngelo. He stepped out onto the portico, closed the door behind him, and spoke.

"Well, Mister Fairfield, I see that you have found me."

"Yes. And I trust that I have found Sarah as well."

"You have. Sir, I hope that we can have a reasonable conversation."

"So do I. I would like to see Sarah first."

"And so you shall. But at the moment she is resting in an upstairs bedroom. In fact, she is asleep."

"All right, we can talk here for a while. How is she?"

"Fine. She will soon be having a baby, but somehow, I believe you may already know that."

"Yes, I know about it. Will she have all of the assistance needed during the birth of her child?"

"Absolutely. I have been assured that it will be provided."

"That is very good. And now I would like to ask about your name. Is it DeAngelo?"

He appeared to become slightly uncomfortable, although he managed a slight smile.

"I must admit, Mister Fairfield, that I underestimated you. Yes, my name is DeAngelo."

"Why did you force Sarah from her home?"

"Because, as I told you that day in Washington, I planned to use her to bargain for Malcolm."

"And you were willing to have me shot as well to get him back?"

"No, that was a mistake by the crazy Irishman. I told him to fire across the front of your face, hoping it would scare you and change your intent. I only wanted to get Malcolm as quickly as possible and leave through southern Maryland."

"Why did you take Sarah with you?"

He hesitated and thought for a few moments. I wondered if his answer would be truthful. After the pause, he spoke.

"I am not sure, and you may find that hard to believe. I think it might have been a combination of things. Maybe I felt I could still bargain for Malcolm."

"And what were the other things?"

He hesitated again, and it obviously was a sore spot. He suggested at that time that we go to some chairs that were nearby on the portico and be seated, which we did. After we were settled, he replied to my question.

"It was Sarah, and I hope my comments do not provoke you. She is perhaps the most appealing woman I have ever known. I wanted to keep her with me because I admired her so much. Her beauty, both inside and out, is unique. I hoped to be able to keep her long enough to gain her respect and admiration."

"You allowed her to send me a letter. In the letter she expressed her sincere love for me. I am sure you must have read that letter before it was sent. And so you knew that she was in love with another man."

"I did read the letter. She insisted that she be allowed to include the statement you refer to, or, she said that she would not write a letter."

"And knowing how she felt, you continued to keep her with you. Why?"

"It's like anything else in life, Mister Fairfield. We never give up on the things we want. I am sure that is the reason you are here today."

"That's true. And that is the reason she must be allowed to return to her home in Washington."

"Mister Fairfield . . .this is a complicated matter. I know it is going to be a shock to her to see you. At this late date, as the time approaches for the birth of the baby, I believe it would be unwise for her to suddenly see you or have you appear without some advance knowledge. Can you understand that, sir?"

"Yes, I can understand it. What do you suggest?"

"Can you return tomorrow? I will discuss it with her later today, so she will be at least somewhat prepared."

I thought about it. I didn't know whether to trust him. Although, in thinking about her and her best interests, I believed him to be right. I responded accordingly.

"I will agree on one condition. Do not attempt to leave this house with her."

"Oh, I can readily agree to that. Even if I was inclined to do so, it would be impossible for her to travel."

"All right, I will take you at your word. What time of day will be best for her tomorrow?"

"One-thirty or two in the afternoon."

"I will be here at that time. And just so you will know, I now have a position with the government of the Confederate States that provides me with connections all across the South. I can alert men quickly who are located in port cities, and other locations, by use of telegrams."

"That will hardly be necessary. I can assure you I will make no attempt to leave the City of Roswell. And now – about tomorrow, you can come up the driveway in your buggy. If it is a pleasant day, Sarah can plan to see you on the back grounds, near the big oak tree. She sits in the chairs there quite often. I will not be there, so you can talk privately. Perhaps later I can join you. Does that sound agreeable?"

"Yes."

We stood, and although it was difficult for me, I reached out as he motioned that we should shake hands. I then turned and walked away.

At exactly one-thirty the next day, Malcolm pulled left with the reins, and our horse turned from the main road onto the long driveway where I had been the day before, at the home where I was to find Sarah sitting near an oak tree in the back. I was tense and emotional. And I was worried. Something about the manner of DeAngelo the previous day, an underlying air of confidence, had convinced me that he had reason to believe that he would be able to keep Sarah. He had shown no reluctance to have me talk to her in private, in fact, he had suggested it.

As we pulled up abreast of the house, our view of the back was extended, and I saw her. She was sitting in a chair near the big tree. At about the same moment, she saw us and immediately smiled and waved excitedly. I waved back. As Malcolm brought the buggy to a halt, I stepped down and walked toward her. She remained in the chair, as would be expected. But then, as I reached her, she stood and spoke.

"Oh, Alex! How wonderful it is to see you!"

"It's wonderful for me, too, Sarah!"

I embraced her gently and kissed her on the cheek, and then I held her arm as she sat down again. I told her about my thoughts as we had traveled to get there.

"I've been trying to think of what to say, and the only thing I can think of is that I love you."

"And Alex, my dear Alex, I love you. Things have changed so much, but my love for you has not changed. It is the same and it will always be that way. I wanted to say that to you before anything else because I know you must have doubts, and I knew that you would need to hear me say it."

"Thank you, Sarah, you can't imagine how much that means to me."

"Did you get the letter I wrote?"

"Yes, and I appreciated what you said more than you will ever be able to realize."

"I meant every word, and I still do. I was so afraid I would never have the chance to tell you in person. I am now very thankful that you have come and I can say it."

"You know, Sarah, I have always heard that a woman is more beautiful when she is with child than at any other time. And now I can understand how that saying came about. I have never seen you as beautiful as you are at this moment."

She smiled slightly and looked downward as she replied.

"Thank you, Alex."

Then she looked up as she spoke again.

"There is something that I have to tell you, and I don't know how."

I knew it involved details of what happened after she had been taken from her home in Washington. I was eager to know about everything, but I did not want to see her become upset so soon just after we had become reunited.

"You don't have to tell me, Sarah, if it will be difficult for you."

"It is difficult. And it is something I have to tell you, something you have to know."

"Maybe you would rather discuss it at a later time."

"I don't know. I've thought about this moment a thousand times and what I would say if the time ever came."

"Sarah, I know it has to do with the baby and DeAngelo. It can wait. By the way, is his first name Michael?"

"Yes. How did you know?"

"I found out as I was looking for him, and you, of course. Is he planning to stay in Roswell?"

"He says it depends on the war. If the South begins to lose we will have to move."

"Sarah, you just said 'we'. Did you mean to say that?"

She raised both hands and covered her face. I stayed silent, and she, too, was silent. In a few moments she began crying softly. I waited a few seconds and then reached over and very gently pulled her hands away from her face and held her hands in mine. She had raised her head up, and she looked away, off to the right.

I released her hands and reached up to the pocket of my coat and withdrew a handkerchief for her. She used it to dab at her eyes and then placed her hands together in her lap, holding on to the handkerchief. I didn't try to rush her into talking, and after a minute or so, she regained some of her composure. Finally she started speaking.

"That first week, while we were in Baltimore, he forced me, and… he created my baby. I didn't know it until later, of course. After we were in Virginia, and he felt safe, he became very kind. He has a great deal of money, and he did everything possible to make me happy. Even so, I still hated him."

"I am so sorry, Sarah, but now I am here. You will no longer have to stay with him."

Her facial expression didn't change.

"That is the difficult part I have to tell you . . .we . . ."

I tried to reason it out, and then the worst sort of question came into my mind.

"Sarah, are you trying to tell me that you are married?"

She couldn't answer. After a moment she nodded, raising her head up and down affirmatively. And again, tears were forming in her eyes. My first reaction was a feeling of anger toward DeAngelo. Then, I thought, he could not have forced her to marry him. I would just have to wait and let her explain it. And in a short while, she did.

"After I realized that I was going to have a baby I became depressed. I knew how disgraceful it would be to come back to Washington. I didn't even want to go home to South Carolina. Michael could see what was happening to me, and he became very supportive. He told me that he loved me and that he would try to make me happy for the rest of my life. He said that he wanted to marry me and that it would be best for the child. I was alone, Alex, and I felt so helpless I didn't know what else I could do."

I was concerned that she might be getting too upset. I tried to smooth things over some.

"Maybe it can be worked out somehow and changed. Try not to worry. I am here now, and I will not leave you."

"I know, and I am so thankful."

"I think it will be best if I try to form an amiable relationship with Michael, at least at present. He told me yesterday that he would let us talk first and then he would join us, so I will make an effort to be friendly."

"Thank you, Alex, I am sure it is not easy for you."

I remembered a comment I had made to her in Washington and I thought it might help her mood.

"You may not remember, but you asked me once if I would try to take another man's wife, and I told you that if it happened to be you, I would. Well, I would like to inform you at this time that my intent remains the same."

She smiled, and we both felt better. While we talked further, a large black woman, obviously a servant, came out of the back door of the house and walked across the yard to the spot where Malcolm was standing. After speaking briefly, they walked together across the yard to the veranda in the back of the house. He sat in a chair that was near a table and I saw him pick up a glass and drink from it. I commented to Sarah.

"I see that Malcolm has been invited in for a drink of some sort. That's nice."

"Yes, it was Lula, the woman who is going to be with me in the future. It's lemonade. She will bring some out to us shortly."

"And so you already have someone to help you. That is good."

"It was done by Michael. We have another black woman who helps. She cleans and prepares meals. Michael has done everything to make it easy for me."

"I'm glad. Do you like it here in Roswell... I mean, as much as could be expected, under the circumstances?"

"Yes, I suppose. I have no friends or visitors, and I miss that. Although even in Washington most women go into hiding while waiting for their babies to be born. I have tried to think of it like that."

"I will look for a house in Roswell so that I can be close to you. Do you think there might be a house here that I could rent?"

"I don't know. But the two black women might know or be able to find out. I will mention it to them. Sometimes I think they know more than the whites."

She smiled, and I was happy to see it. And I realized, too, that being with her was creating as much happiness as I had known in ages. Even the problem with Michael faded from my thoughts temporarily, and she was once again the center of my attention. She was feeling better. Her mood had improved since she had told me about her marriage. It had obviously been a worrisome ordeal, a nagging thorn that was finally removed.

Sarah had been right when she had said that Lula would be out soon with lemonade. She was now coming across the yard toward us with a tray in her hands. Sarah introduced me, and Lula responded good-naturedly.

"How you do, Mister Alexander? Miss Sarah say she has known you for a long time."

"That's right, Lula. We're old friends." I could tell by the wide grin on her face that she would welcome some teasing. "Now, Lula, you watch yourself around my man on the veranda, he might just try to get a little rowdy."

She laughed heartily as she turned to go back inside, and she responded merrily.

"All right, Mister Alexander, I sho will remember that."

After she had walked away, Sarah poured the lemonade and handed me a glass. She gazed tenderly into my eyes.

"It's so good to have you here, Alex. I hope we can always be near each other."

"We will. I promise. You have your baby and then we will talk. All right?"

"Yes, all right. And I feel so much better about the baby. At first I was mortified, and resented it. As time went by, I changed, and I found that I wanted it."

"That is sweet, Sarah."

I glanced toward the veranda and saw DeAngelo standing near Malcolm. They were talking. I knew that Michael would come out to sit with us as he had told me he planned to do. I regretted that my visit with Sarah, being alone with her, would be over in a few minutes. I wanted her to know about my plans for future visits.

"I see that Michael will soon join us. I plan to let him know that I am expecting to see you often, and I don't know how he will take it. I think I can handle it in a way that will be acceptable to him. I will choose my words carefully so that nothing unpleasant will happen."

"I know you will. You were always so careful not to step on toes." And then she smiled. "Except, of course, when you were jealous."

Her facial expression changed as she seemed to suddenly have an important thought. "Alex, before Michael comes out, there is something important I want you to know… Oh, it's too late, he's on the way. I'll have to tell you later."

Just at the moment, Michael walked to within a few feet of our chairs. He spoke.

"Well, it seems that you two are having a nice visit."

I stood and spoke.

"How are you today, Mister DeAngelo?"

We shook hands and he responded.

"I'm fine. And you, sir, I hope you are well."

"Yes. Thank you. Maybe we should dispense with formalities and use first names. Call me Alexander."

"I will. And as you know my name is Michael."

Although it was almost impossible for me, I was holding on to my original intent to create a friendly environment with DeAngelo for the sake of Sarah. As long as she would be kept in his care, and considering her situation with the baby, I knew that my personal feelings would have to be set aside. Otherwise, I might have killed him. After we were seated, Michael asked about the war, looking in my direction.

"What do you hear about Lee, is he still moving northward?"

"I believe so. His strategy might involve a plan to cut off the Army of the Potomac from Washington. If he can do that, it will more than offset what Grant is doing at Vicksburg."

"I agree."

We talked for about twenty minutes, mostly in general. I noticed that Sarah appeared to be getting tired, and I told them that it was time for me to be leaving. I stood and looked at Michael.

"It may be of interest to you to know that I am considering buying land here to set up a thoroughbred horse farm. So, I will be here in Roswell quite often in the coming days."

And then I looked down at Sarah. "When I am here I will stop by to see how you are progressing . . . if you feel it will be convenient for you."

"Of course it will be convenient, and you are welcome to come by on any day."

I looked back to Michael, and he had a look of disbelief and frustration on his face. He made a half-hearted attempt to recover and shook hands with me. I said "goodbye" to Sarah and turned away.

Malcolm, who had been watching from the veranda, had come out and was walking toward our buggy. I joined him in the buggy, and as we rode down the drive, I had a question for Malcolm.

"Well, you spent some time talking to him, what is your verdict?"

"I don't trust him. He is as big a liar as he ever was. I hope you can get her away from there after the baby is born."

"Don't worry about that, I will take her away in the middle of the night if I have to. He goes to Marietta on Thursdays and is there all day, so I know there is at least one day of the week when I can be alone with her."

"Good. How much will she tell you about him?"

"I don't know yet. But there is something else you and I need to keep in mind."

"What?"

"He is still a dangerous man."

"That had already occurred to me."

"He told me he gave the Irishman orders to fire the pistol in front of me to scare me. That is ridiculous. If ever a man tried to kill me, it was that Irishman. He had the pistol aimed straight at my face."

"And if not by the grace of God, you would no longer be here."

"Right. And you, he is going to resent deeply that you are walking around as a free man rather than performing duties for him. Did you tell him that you are legally free?"

"No."

"That's good. I can assure you that he would have come after you in any case."

"You may be right." And then he chuckled. "Now I know how a couple of bank robbers might feel while they are on the run. I think we're both in trouble."

Each of us laughed. I thought of one advantage we might have, and I told Malcolm.

"At least we know what he is capable of, and that will help. In any event, we should try to think of everything he might try, and because he is clever, that will cover a broad range of possibilities."

My statement didn't seem to bother Malcolm. He smiled.

"But we're clever, too, Marse."

I grinned at him. He enjoyed calling me Marse when it could be used with humor. But I did have a concern for him. Being a free black man in white country might cause him problems. There was still a loyalty, and an attitude of kindness between many blacks and whites. Although it was beginning to fade, there was no question that a new way of thinking by both races was developing.

# IX.

The next morning I went to see John Dabney. I gave him the good news first. I told him that I had found Sarah, and that it had happened sooner than I had considered possible. He was delighted and eager to hear the details. I explained that the unusual name "DeAngelo" was the key to my success.

Even so, he said, it was like finding a needle in a haystack with no more information than I had in the beginning. He asked if Sarah would be returning to Washington. I told him that she would not in the near future, and explained the reason. I told him about how she had come to be with child, then later, in a desperate and forlorn state of mind, she had married the man who was the child's father. She knew she would need his help. Dabney questioned if she would have any manner of recourse or if she might somehow be able to revoke the marriage.

I had not considered that because she had made the decision of her own free will. However, I would consult with Phillip, or send him a letter, and ask about such a possibility. With Phillip, all things were possible. Next, I told John about DeAngelo, describing his history of activities in detail. I described him as conniving, distrustful, and quite dangerous. I asked John if he could assist me with surveillance beginning with an investigation of the trips to Marietta each Thursday by DeAngelo.

"By all means, Alexander. I don't like what I have heard from you about his past activity. We usually try to take a good look at any person coming from the North these days anyway, and I already have other reasons to find out about him."

I gave him a very detailed physical description of DeAngelo, and he said he would pass it along to his men immediately. He added one final comment.

"Actually, my man in Marietta has been watching him on a limited basis already."

During the conversation I had told him that I would be moving to Roswell. It seemed that things had taken a good turn for me in the last two days.

Back at the house with Malcolm, I began a conversation about DeAngelo and the current circumstances.

"I think the thing we have to consider is the fact that he is capable of doing something that will be totally unexpected."

"You are right. And it might be very difficult to figure out."

"I know. Maybe we should begin by eliminating some of the things we feel he will not do. As an example, I do not feel that he will try to move Sarah until after she has the baby. Even though I hate to admit it, I believe he does care enough about her not to jeopardize her situation with the baby."

"I agree."

"So we can be reasonably sure that he and Sarah will stay put for a month or so. Also, I don't believe he can find anybody in Roswell to do his dirty work. It doesn't seem like the kind of community where people like that are around. So, what does that leave?"

"How about the man, Perkins? Do you think he might still have contact with him?"

"Possibly. That might be the reason he goes to Marietta. He might already have something in the works. He seems to plan well. John Dabney has agreed to watch him in Marietta, so maybe we have got that covered."

He was not quite as talkative as usual, and I continued.

"Maybe you and I should go to Big Shanty and look around for Perkins. We might get lucky again."

"What kind of story would you use?"

"Same thing as Roswell, I'm looking for land for a horse farm. What do you think?"

"It should be all right."

I noticed there was a slight change in his attitude.

"Have you run into anything around here that you haven't told me about?"

"Nothing too important."

I could see that I was going to have to pull it out of him.

"Malcolm, has anybody come up to the house while I was away?"

"Some riders came this morning."

"How many?"

"Three."

"What did they want?"

"Just looking around. They didn't get down off their horses."

"Did they say anything?"

"One of them asked me what I was doing in this house."

"What did you say?"

"I told him that I worked for Marse Alexander."

"And that was all? They left?"

"Yes."

"Do you think there is any possibility that they were connected to DeAngelo?"

"No. It's too soon, he couldn't have found people that quick."

I didn't like it. Malcolm had been affected more than he was willing to tell me. I knew him to be courageous, but he had been shaken some by the three men. John Dabney had told me that some problems were developing due to the shortage of food and other items. Men were becoming bolder, especially the ones who were more adversely affected by the war, and reports of thefts and other crimes were being heard more often. In the back of my mind I already had an uneasy feeling about Malcolm, and I decided that it would be best if he was with me at all times in the future. And in thinking about the overall situation, another possibility came into my mind.

If the same type of men who had come to our house should approach DeAngelo, it would give him a chance to hire devious types, men who would probably do anything for money. I decided that the Colt revolver would now go with me, wherever I might go.

In two days it would be Thursday, and I would go back to see Sarah. We had agreed on a time that I could come during my initial visit. I could hardly wait. She was, as she had been in the past, the most exciting person in my life, and her presence with me now was a vivid reality, no longer a frustrating dream. I just wanted to sit near her, talk to her, and touch her.

News about the war filtered into Atlanta more slowly than it had in Washington. It was understandable. Reports were received in Washington only hours after the action had taken place, mainly because it was required by the War Department and the President. That same information was usually relayed to Atlanta a day later. Current reports concerning the action in the north indicated that a major battle was about to take place.

Lee had crossed over into Pennsylvania, and the Army of the Potomac was moving in a direction to be in a position to block him. Now, there could be no doubt that they would soon collide. If Lee was successful again, as he had been at Chanscellorsville two months earlier, it would be a staggering blow to the North. But I remembered the words of Phillip the day we had dined together in Washington: "If Jackson does not come back, the South will lose."

Was he right or wrong? Jackson was gone, so we would soon have an early indication of whether Phillip's prediction would turn out to be accurate.

On Thursday it was warm, and as we rode toward Roswell, I thought about Sarah and how well she might hold up sitting outside in the heat. I decided that I would not keep her outside too long. We arrived right on time and she was there, sitting near the oak tree as she had promised. She smiled when she saw me, and when I had walked near to her I thought again that she was more beautiful than I had ever seen her.

"Well, Mister Fairfield, I see that you are still very prompt. You have arrived just when you said you would."

"And I see that you are still the most beautiful woman I have ever known."

"Oh, thank you, what a delightful compliment at a time when I am as big as a cow."

"How are you today?"

"I'm all right except for the heat, of course. If we didn't have that little breeze it really would be hot."

"I know, and I will not keep you out too long. Is Michael in Marietta?"

"Yes. He never fails to ride over there on Thursdays. I think he might pick up letters and other things. It seems he has an important reason to be there."

"It doesn't matter. I just wanted to know if we could be alone for a while."

She had a sweet expression as she spoke again.

"This week, after you left, I just kept thinking about you. I couldn't stop because it was so wonderful to be with you again."

"And it was the same for me. I wish it could be like it was in Washington again."

"So do I. I have thought about it so often, being there with you. I never dreamed that anything could happen the way it did to change my life so quickly and drastically."

"We're going to change it back. But let's don't worry about it today, we have too many other things to talk about."

She smiled and agreed. We began a pleasant conversation in which we discussed a wide range of things. Lula came out and brought refreshments for us, and then she walked over and asked Malcolm to go with her to the back veranda. I was careful not to ask too much about Michael, although I did want to find out everything I could about him.

"Do you think Michael will be disturbed by my visits to see you?"

"Yes, some. But he doesn't say much. He is a rather secretive person."

"He hasn't told you too much about his past?"

"No. He prefers it that way, and actually it doesn't matter to me."

I changed the subject. I remembered to ask her if there was a way she could get a message to me, and I told her one of the reasons for my question.

"I might not even know when your baby arrives."

"Yes, there is a way. A courier rides to Atlanta each day. I could send a note in that way. Lula could send it off, and you could pick it up at the depot. They would notify you if it was urgent."

"That's good to know, and I am glad you told me."

She was beginning to look a little tired and uncomfortable. Even though I was reluctant to leave her, I knew it would be best for her to go inside and rest. I told her.

"I can see that the heat is effecting you, so I better go. It has been a wonderful visit."

"And for me, too."

She was ready to stand up, and I helped her. Then she spoke.

"When can you come again?"

"Any time. Tell me a day, and I will be here."

"Saturday might be good. Many times Michael goes out for a while on Saturdays."

"Good. I'll see you on Saturday."

I reached down and took hold of her hand. I glanced toward the house and looked back to her.

"Sarah . . ."

She knew what I was going to ask. She held on to my hand and guided me up close to the back side of the house where we were out of view, then she stopped and turned toward me with a look of anticipation. I very carefully and gently embraced her, and then we kissed. It was a kiss that consummated our passionate dreams once again. We held on for a long while before pulling apart.

As we backed away, she was smiling, and so was I. Then we walked together to the back entrance of the house, and there we separated. Malcolm saw me and came forward, I said goodbye to Sarah, and we walked to the buggy.

After we were underway in the buggy, Malcolm looked at me and grinned.

"That man is going to split your head open if he catches you."

"You saw us?"

"No, but I know why you were hiding."

We both laughed. After he had turned onto the main road, I asked him about the two black women.

"Have you learned anything from Lula, or the other woman?"

"You mean what goes on in the house?"

"Yes."

"Not much. The other woman, Arbedella, has been there longer. Neither one is willing to say much, and I believe it is because they are afraid of DeAngelo."

"How do they react to each other, Sarah and DeAngelo?"

"All I know from what little the two women say is that they stay apart most of the time. Lula did say it was a strange marriage, that the master and Miss Sarah are so different."

"In what way?"

"Lula can sense he is the way you and I know him to be. On the other hand, she says she loves Miss Sarah. They talk a lot, and Miss Sarah looks to her for companionship. If I had to guess, Alex, I would say that Sarah hates him with a silent passion even though he has done everything he can to change the way she feels."

I could feel the anger coming back in the same way I had felt it when I first learned that DeAngelo had taken Sarah.

"I might decide to change things someday with my Colt. I think it might give me great pleasure."

"Hold it now, don't get all stirred up."

"No, I won't really do it. I just don't know how long I can stand by and watch him with Sarah."

He was quiet for a while and then I continued.

"You know, Malcolm, I have enough money in the bank in St. Louis to go anywhere in the world. Maybe you and I should take Sarah and her baby to California. What do you think?"

"I would be happy to go wherever you go."

After I acknowledged his comment with a smile, he continued.

"What about DeAngelo?"

"To hell with him. I'll get some help from Phillip. We will make it legal for her to leave him."

July had just arrived and with it came the heat. Fortunately, the small house where Malcolm and I were staying was among trees, which helped some. Insects were a problem, mainly flies and ants. We were still able to get enough food to maintain a reasonably good diet. It was the season when the farmers would load their wagons with fresh vegetables, before dawn, and head for Atlanta where the produce could easily be sold. I found out that Malcolm, among the other things he had learned while in England, had become a good cook.

The people had gradually learned that they could do without some of the things that were available before the war, not only items of food but other things as well. The conditions during the past two years had created a unity among the people, a spirited determination of cohesiveness, and, a resentment toward the North was building each day.

People who had supported anti-slavery views were being blamed more openly for the problems that were beginning to take a severe toll on the South. Men who were the most vocal were convincing others that the South, under the Union, would not only no longer have slaves but would have their States Rights removed as well.

Consequently, nothing was too much to ask for what had come to be known commonly as "The Cause." Unfortunately, in my opinion, people would be willing to fight until there was nothing left. Then with the North having a huge advantage with resources and manpower, the South would be facing almost total destruction.

On Saturday, while heading to Roswell, I thought about Sarah and whether it might be too warm for her to sit outside. I would suggest to her that we move to the back veranda if the heat appeared to make her uncomfortable. Malcolm was handling the buggy. When we arrived, he guided the horse with slight pulls on the lines into the driveway and up to the spot where we had stopped previously during our visits. Sarah was not in thc chair under the large oak tree. My first thought was the baby. Could she be having the baby? Malcolm said he thought it was the heat.

"It's too hot for her out here today. She might faint."

I wasn't so sure it was the heat. We sat for a minute or so and then saw Lula coming from the back of the house in our direction. I stepped down from the buggy and walked around in front of the horse to meet her. She had a serious expression on her face.

"Mista Michael say that Miss Sarah is not feeling well today, and she can't spend no time out here in the heat."

"Thank you, Lula. What did Miss Sarah say?"

"She ain't said nothing."

"So, Mister Michael decided not to leave today?"

"Yes sir, he is right in that house."

"Lula, will you please tell Mister Michael that I would like to talk to him? I will walk around and meet him at the front entrance."

"Yes sir, I will go right in and tell him."

I turned to walk to the front of the house. I looked at Malcolm, and he was shaking his head from side to side. His intent was to warn me to remain calm.

On the front portico I waited for Michael for several minutes. During that time I was trying to decide if what Lula had said was true. Was Sarah feeling bad or was it Michael?

Michael came out, and we shook hands. He spoke first.

"It seems you have come on a bad day. Sarah is not feeling well."

"I'm sorry. Could it be time for the baby?"

"No, it's not that. The baby is not due for another month. It's probably an upset stomach."

"Have you notified the doctor?"

"Oh no, it's not necessary to do that."

I wanted to be sure about whether he might be trying to prevent me from seeing her.

"I assume she must be in bed."

"Yes."

"I have come quite a distance to see her. I would like to stick my head in her doorway briefly and speak to her."

"No, that would not be appropriate."

He was either being evasive, or he was lying. I needed a few moments to think about what I should do. I looked away from him as he continued to stand silently. If he could successfully stop me now, he would do the same in the future. It was a delicate situation, and I would have to handle it with care. As I was ready to speak, Lula opened the door and stepped out through the opening. She handed Michael a small piece of paper as she spoke.

"Excuse me, sir, Miss Sarah has sent this down."

He took it and didn't speak. Lula returned to the inside. He opened the folded piece of paper and read the message. He then handed it to me. The note on the paper was addressed to me:

*"Dear Alex: I am sorry but I cannot come down to see you. I am really feeling bad today. I hope to see you soon. Sarah."*

I recognized her handwriting and knew that she had written the note. Therefore, it seemed that Michael had told me the truth. I let him know that I was willing to accept his explanation.

"Well, it appears to be just as you said. Will you please tell Sarah that I am sorry she is not feeling well?"

"Yes, of course, I will tell her."

"Thank you. By the way, what is the name of her doctor?"

His initial reaction made me think he would not tell me, however, I knew that he wanted to get rid of me. And I was right. After several moments he answered.

"John Stiles. I believe he is the most notable doctor in town."

We shook hands, and I turned and walked to the buggy. DeAngelo went inside. Malcolm was curious, and did not immediately urge the horse to get underway.

"What happened?"

"Apparently he was telling me the truth. She sent a note down telling me that she really is feeling bad today."

Malcolm still had doubts. I could tell by the look on his face. I questioned him.

"You don't believe him?"

"No, I guess it's because I don't trust him. Also, I just remembered something that Lula said the other day. He takes breakfast up to her sometimes on Fridays. It's the only day of the week he does that. It didn't seem important at the time Lula told me, and I forgot about it later."

"What are you saying, Malcolm?"

"He takes her breakfast on Friday and she feels bad on Saturday. I guess that's what I am saying."

"That's pretty strong stuff. Do you really think the two things are connected?"

"I think it could be connected. Have you forgotten who we are dealing with?"

His remark gave me cause to consider it further. It was odd, I had to admit, although it had to be unrelated.

"But he likes her. Why would he do anything to cause her to feel bad?"

"Lula put out some hints the other day that made me think he might not be all that happy about having a baby in the house. And if you will think about it for a minute it makes sense, a baby would be excess baggage for him."

"So he wants to keep Sarah, but he doesn't need a baby to go along with her?"

"That's right. That's what I am saying."

Had we uncovered something that we speculated about earlier, his capability to do the unexpected? Or, were we assuming too much? I couldn't convince myself that he would try anything that would be harmful to Sarah or the baby. He seemed to care for her too much. Nonetheless, I decided that I would make an attempt to talk to her doctor, even if I had to stretch the truth about myself to get information from him. I mentioned it to Malcolm to get his opinion.

"I might try to see her doctor while we are here. I have his name. What do you think?"

"I think it's a good idea. What will you tell the doctor?"

"I don't know right now, but let's get going. Turn left toward town when you leave the driveway."

A short distance away there was a man walking along the road. We stopped long enough for me to talk to him and get directions to the doctor's home. Ten minutes later Malcolm pulled up in front of the house. I walked from the buggy to the front where I tapped on the door several times. After a minute or so a woman opened the door. I smiled at her.

"Good afternoon. My name is Alexander Fairfield, and I presume you to be Missis Stiles."

She smiled slightly.

"Yes, I am Missis Stiles."

"I am pleased to meet you. I would like to see Doctor Stiles if he is available."

"Ah . . .what sort of ailment do you have, Mister Fairfield?"

"None at all, Missis Stiles. I am in the process of moving to the city and I simply wanted to introduce myself to the doctor."

She glanced beyond me and saw Malcolm. I felt certain that she would be impressed favorably, believing that I was being driven by a manservant. She looked back to me.

"Yes, I am sure he will see you. Please come in."

She guided me into a parlor where I was seated. She walked away to another part of the house, and a few minutes later a pleasant looking man appeared, smiling as he came into the room. I stood to greet him. He spoke as we shook hands.

"Mister Fairfield?"

"Yes. And you are Doctor Stiles?"

"I am."

We were seated and began a discussion in which I told him that I was experienced with thoroughbred horses and would soon set up facilities in the nearby countryside to raise horses. We moved on from that to other subjects, including the battle that was believed to be in progress in Pennsylvania, a matter being discussed by all at present. After about fifteen minutes, I shifted my body slightly to get up to leave, and I spoke as if I had just remembered something.

"Oh, by the way, Doctor, I am very well acquainted with Missis DeAngelo. We come from the same coastal area near Savannah. I stopped by to see her today and was told by her husband that she is not feeling well. Is she your patient?"

"Why yes, she is, but I had no knowledge that she is ill today."

"Her husband advised me that it was not severe enough to notify you. I merely mentioned it because we are like family and naturally I am interested in her well being. How is she progressing with the baby? I believe she told me in a previous conversation that it is due in about four weeks."

"Four weeks at most, maybe sooner."

"And is she doing well?"

He paused, and it seemed as if he might be trying to decide whether to answer.

"Mister Fairfield, did you say that you are a member of her family?"

"We are not related, Doctor, but yes, we consider ourselves family."

"I have a slight concern about her. And sir, I am sure you will keep that confidential."

"Absolutely. What is your concern?"

"Well, I cannot be absolutely sure, but I believe she is no longer gaining weight or getting larger. And if that is correct, it might suggest a problem."

Doctor Stiles appeared to be about sixty-five years old. I would guess that he had delivered hundreds of babies, and his concern about Sarah was alarming to me.

"What sort of problem?"

I think at that moment he decided that he had gone far enough in disclosing information about a patient. It was reflected in his answer.

"Well, maybe I am getting the cart before the horse. I probably should not have mentioned it. My wife tells me I am a worrier. We will just consider that she will do well and everything will be fine."

I wanted to ask more questions, although to do so might be out of order and might give him reason to wonder why I would be expressing an unusual amount of interest. I stood and thanked him, and we walked together to the door. He made one last comment.

"Mister Fairfield, we must all pray for General Lee and his men. They are most likely engaged in battle at this moment."

"I will do that, sir. And I just remembered. It will be best if you do not mention to Mister or Missis DeAngelo that I was here inquiring about her, they might believe that I came out of fear about her condition, and I would not want to alarm her."

"I assure you it will be kept confidential."

In the buggy Malcolm looked at me with inquisitiveness.

"Well?"

"The doctor says he is concerned because she might not be getting larger or gaining weight."

"What does that mean?"

"He didn't tell me, and he is not sure about it anyway. What I would like to do next is find a mature woman to talk to, somebody who has seen a lot of babies come into the world."

"Like a midwife?"

"Yes, exactly. She might know as much, or more, than the doctor."

Malcolm tapped the horse gently with the long reins, and we moved out in a southward direction to start the three hour ride back to north Atlanta. I continued to think of Sarah, and I decided to have a discussion with John Dabney and seek advice. He always came to our house late on Monday afternoons. I would tell him that I needed information from a midwife, or if possible another doctor, who could further explain the comments of Doctor Stiles.

On Sunday, Malcolm drove me six or seven miles south in the direction of Atlanta to a church. It was overflowing with people. The pastor dedicated the service to "the gallant men in the Army of Northern Virginia," asking that all would be sustained throughout the battle in Gettysburg. I thought of them, and for some reason I remembered Major Dale and others who might be like him. In my silent prayers I asked that all who were fighting there, men on both sides, would be given the same comfort and support.

On Monday, late in the afternoon, Malcolm and I were sitting in chairs outside of the house when John Dabney rode up. He dismounted and approached us with a serious look on his face.

"Have you heard what happened?"

I was not sure what he meant.

"No, I don't think so. What can you tell me?"

"Lee has lost in Pennsylvania. At least he was turned back and lost a great number of men."

I was surprised because it had not been expected. We all had come to believe that Lee could never be turned back in a battle. I asked John about it.

"What happened?"

"I don't know the details of the battle. The reports say that Lee is retreating back toward Virginia."

"Does this mean that the end will come soon?"

"No! Oh, hell no. It just means that the war will be prolonged, and a new strategy will have to be established. We will never give up our land and homes to those bastards, and we will not let them defeat us." He turned toward Malcolm. "And Malcolm, my good man, we will set your people free, but we will damn well do it in our own way."

Malcolm nodded and responded.

"Yes sir, I hope that will happen."

We continued to talk about the war for a while. Then I told John that I had two requests to make. First, I told him about Sarah and the need I had for information. And taking it one step further, I asked if we could intercept the letters that DeAngelo was apparently receiving in Marietta, the ones that he was picking up on Thursdays. John said he could have the man assigned to the case in Marietta do that very easily because some letters were already being opened and re-sealed by a censor. He said that DeAngelo most likely knew about the procedure and he would not become suspicious. We talked for a few more minutes and then he left.

I located the office of the courier service early the next morning. It was crowded, and the people working there were busy. When I finally got my letter for Sarah to the proper person, he spoke as he took my money.

"You got here just in time. We have a full load going to Roswell and beyond, and we will most likely have to send a second rider later in the day. It's all because of Gettysburg, you know."

In my note to Sarah, I said that I would be at her home on Thursday at one-thirty. Since talking to John Dabney the day before, I considered how the news of the Union victory at Gettysburg would affect the thinking of DeAngelo. I was certain that he would plan to leave as soon as possible. He had stated that he would stay put only as long as the South was winning. Now, he would begin planning to move on, and it could be to any number of places, even a location outside of the country. But, at least one aspect of Sarah's pregnancy was good. It would likely delay a movement by DeAngelo for at least six or seven weeks, assuming he planned to take her with him.

When I got back to our house, I was surprised to see that John Dabney had returned. After a greeting he told me that he had some interesting but puzzling news. His man in Marietta who was assigned to track DeAngelo had reported earlier in the day that two letters addressed to DeAngelo had already been opened by the censor due to his own suspicions. In each letter there were two small, flat packets that contained a substance that could not be identified. The censor had taken one packet from one of the letters and opened it, and he described the contents as being granular, as sugar, with the smell of chocolate. He re-sealed the letter with only one packet inside and passed it on for pick up by the addressee. No written information was included in the letters, only the packets. Dabney asked the same question that had occurred to me.

"What would make a man ride his horse all day to get something like that? And what was the substance in the packet?"

"He goes to Marietta because he does not want to be traced to Roswell. But the packet…you say it is not chocolate?"

"No. The consistency was different."

"Who has the packet?"

"The censor. He will keep it and try to identify the contents."

"But if he knows for sure it is not chocolate why does it have a chocolate smell?"

"I don't know. I'll follow up on it and let you know. Regarding the other matter, I talked to a lady who has worked with women during their confinement when they are with child. She feels the doctor might just be cautious. If he can hear the heartbeat of the baby and if it is still active, it is probably not significant if the doctor cannot be sure about weight gain. She says there are times when the mother may change her eating habits and that will be a factor in a slow down of gaining pounds. That's the best I could do for you, Alexander. I hope it helps."

"Yes, it does, and thank you."

After John had ridden off, I remembered what Doctor Stiles had said, "My wife tells me I am a worrier." Maybe that was true. If I could see Sarah face to face on Thursday and have her tell me that she was feeling better, it would relieve my concern.

Later, just before nightfall, I saw three horsemen in the distance coming in the direction of our house. Malcolm and I sat on the front veranda each evening to escape the heat inside the house, but it was the first time I had seen riders come up this late. When they reached the front yard, I could see that they were wearing Confederate uniforms, and all three were officers. Beyond them in the distance, ten or twelve other soldiers were on horses and had stopped at the entrance of our driveway, grouped just off of the main road. I stepped down from where I was sitting and greeted the three officers.

"Good evening, gentlemen."

An officer who was apparently in charge answered.

"Good evening. Are you Alexander Fairfield?"

"Yes."

"Sir, you are commanded to gather your possessions and come with me at this time."

What a shocking request! He had spoken with determination and in a commanding way.

"For what purpose?"

"You are being moved to perform your duties in another location."

"By whose authority?"

"The President of the Confederate States of America."

"When you say another location, what do you mean?"

"To another city."

"I don't understand. Where is John Dabney?"

"John Dabney is not involved. The order has come directly from Richmond."

"No, I cannot possibly leave on this kind of short notice."

"Mister Fairfield, you have made a commitment to our government. I request once again, sir, that you come with me. You are to be in one of the cars pulled by the early morning northbound locomotive without failure."

"Be in a rail car? No, absolutely not. I will give no consideration whatsoever to your request."

He turned and spoke quietly to one of the other officers. That officer then reined his horse about and rode back toward the men who were waiting near the main road. The officer who had been speaking to me looked back in my direction.

"You will either come with us peacefully, or you will be taken by force. My orders are to have you in that car, and that is precisely what I intend to do."

I was stunned, and I was speechless. I thought about trying to get to my Colt revolver inside the house. I glanced at Malcolm and made a very slight movement with my eyes, motioning toward the inside. He knew my intention, and he slowly moved his head back and forth, from side to side. I turned back to the Confederate officer.

"Sir, please understand my current circumstances. I am working with John Dabney and his agent in Marietta on the investigation of a suspicious man from New York. I cannot leave the assignment, it is too important."

"None of that is my concern, sir. My orders have come directly from the War Department in Richmond."

The other men had come up from the street, and it appeared that they formed a squad of cavalry soldiers. It was beginning to look like I would be quickly overwhelmed if I resisted. All the while thoughts of Sarah were coming into my mind, and I kept thinking, "how can I possibly leave her?" Once again I spoke to the officer.

"Sir, at the very least, I ask you to delay this matter for one day."

His attitude did not change.

"I cannot disobey my orders. That will not be possible."

I remained silent and so did he. None of the men talked, and the stillness of the early night was interrupted only by slight movements of some of the horses. It was a very distressing turn of events. To find Sarah after many frustrating months only to be pulled away from her created a feeling of great anxiety, and I could think of no recourse or alternative action that could be taken. Finally the Confederate officer spoke.

"You can bring the darkie with you."

"I need time. I have other considerations to make."

"No sir, there is no allowance for time in the order."

"Can you provide me with any additional information?"

"You are to report to a Mister Marvin Cargill in Richmond, Virginia. Three of my soldiers will escort you on the trip. You must know, Mister Fairfield, that this is a difficult time for all of us, and we must carry out our duties without hesitation or reluctance."

Malcolm stood and looked at me. I could see in his eyes that he was resigned to accepting the orders that had been given by the Confederate officer. I made one final request.

"I must be given enough time to write a letter and drop it off at the courier depot."

The officer thought about it momentarily before answering.

"You can write your letter and leave it with me. From here we will go to a location where you will be housed for the night. You must move quickly. The northbound locomotive will leave early in the morning."

It seemed there was nothing more I could do except go as he was requesting. I stood and told him that we would comply with his orders. He and the other two officers dismounted and followed Malcolm and me to the inside where we began collecting our belongings. In about half-an-hour, we were ready to leave and walked to the outside. Our horse had been hitched to our buggy so that we only had to load our carpetbags and we were set to move out. The three officers rode in front with the twelve soldiers behind us, and we were soon traveling south on the main road leading to Atlanta.

Early the next morning, Malcolm and I were in a rail car accompanied by three Confederate soldiers. I had written a letter to Sarah, explaining everything, and had given it to the Confederate officer. It was sealed in an envelope with her name and address printed on the outside. The officer assured me that it would be taken to the courier depot for delivery to her.

# X.

We began what turned out to be a long and tiring trip. Malcolm was allowed to ride in the same car with me because of the need for security, at least that was my assumption. We most likely appeared to be prisoners to others in the car because of the constant close scrutiny of our escorts. In a conversation with one of the three, after becoming somewhat friendly with the man, he stated that I was needed for a high priority job in a location that was unknown to him. He explained that this was the reason for the urgency used by the officer in his manner of removing me from the house in Atlanta.

After two full days and nights, we arrived in Richmond. At the railroad station, our three escorts were met by two other soldiers and an exchange took place. Malcolm and I were then in a "gentleman's custody" of the new men. We were taken to a building not too far from the station. It appeared to be an abandoned mercantile shop where three men, dressed in civilian clothing, were awaiting our arrival. One of the three men came forward as we entered, and spoke.

"Mister Fairfield, I am Marvin Cargill." We shook hands and he continued. "Please walk with me to the far end of the room. Leave the darkie here."

After we were standing alone, he began talking.

"We have an urgent need for an operative in Washington. We have looked at your file, and you fit our needs perfectly. We believe one of our operatives, a woman, may have become a double agent. It has to be verified quickly, and when it is confirmed she must be removed."

"Is Ed Jenkins involved?"

"Ed is dead. That is the reason for the urgency."

He was ready to continue talking and didn't give me time to think about the sorrowful news regarding the loss of a long time friend.

"I have considered the facts in your file, and I know about your personal circumstances. I regret that it was necessary to bring you back from Georgia, however, our need in Washington is great. It had to be done. I hope you will accept that and give us your full cooperation."

I agreed because there seemed to be no other choice. I asked if I would be allowed to return to Atlanta following the assignment and he responded by saying "possibly," but that he could not address that issue at present. Then he gave me details on how I was to proceed. Malcolm and I were to return to my farm and continue to live there as we had in the past. He identified the woman who was suspected of being the double agent, and gave me details of a plan to be used in my contacts with her. We talked for about twenty minutes after which he asked if I had questions.

"Only one. You have covered everything else thoroughly. My question concerns Ed Jenkins. What happened to him?"

"We believe the woman might have identified him to a Northern agent. Ed was shot by an unknown person." This news jolted me but I remained silent.

He said that Malcolm and I would continue on to Washington immediately. He stated that there were three or four 'openings' in the Union Army picket lines surrounding the city that could be used and we should be able to reach my home within twenty-four hours.

His estimate was right. We traveled during the daylight hours by horses, the ferry, and then again by horseback far into the night. Just after the sun came into view the following morning, we were poised to cross the Navy Yard Bridge and enter the city of Washington. We still had our proper identification papers, and I anticipated the Union Army sentinels would have no problem allowing a "horse buyer" and his manservant to pass.

When Mary Kate saw us, she yelled with joy, and hugged each of us. After a brief conversation I told her we were extremely tired, then Malcolm and I headed in separate directions to get some much needed rest.

Mary Kate came up to awaken me at five in the afternoon. She knew that I had eaten very little during the past three or four days, and she said that she had prepared a good meal for me. She had baked a chicken, and with it she served rice and green beans. As always, her food was delicious. She told me she had taken a very large serving out to Malcolm. She seemed to be holding back a question as she sat nearby and watched me. Finally it popped out.

"What can you tell me about Sarah?"

I told her everything. She listened with great interest as I detailed the whole story, including a limited version of why I had to leave Atlanta and return to Washington. At that point she asked if I could finish the work I had to do in Washington, whatever it might be, and return to Atlanta by the time Sarah's baby was due to be born?

"I hope so. The assignment here is complex, and I can't judge how long it will take."

"When will you begin working on it?"

"Tomorrow."

"Oh, well, it must be important if you are going to start on a Sunday."

"Yes, it is important, and I want to finish it as soon as I can."

The next day, in the early afternoon, I rode my stallion into the city. I went past the Capitol Building and on beyond for another six blocks to the National Hotel. The hotel was on Pennsylvania Avenue, an active area that had gaslights at night. It was known to be a gathering place for Southerners in the past, including some of the elected politicians from the South in the years preceding the war. Even during the present time, although obviously kept secret, connections were being made there among Southern sympathizers.

It was there that I was told to try to make contact with the woman named Laura, the suspected double agent. She sometimes had a room there. She was thirty-five, had coloring of a medium brunette, and was said to be pretty. She had come to Washington with a vengeance after her husband, a Confederate officer, had been killed in one of the early battles of the war. It was easy for her to find the right people, and she was soon an agent for the South.

In the lobby of the hotel, a young man was behind the registration counter. I had thought about the approach I would use before going inside. I had decided that she would most likely be there and have a room because she would be anticipating a contact.

She would know that Ed would be replaced, and she would want to make herself easily found. I walked to the counter and spoke to the young man with confidence.

"I am here to see Laura. Please send someone to her room and notify her."

He used a fake expression to respond. I had seen it a thousand times in poker games.

"Laura?"

"Yes, Laura. You can tell her that A F is calling."

He fumbled with some papers in front of him. While he was stalling I pulled out a ten dollar bill and placed it on the counter. He saw it and smiled.

"Sir, why don't you have a seat? I will send Tim up to let her know."

I sat down and waited. In about fifteen minutes a woman walked in from the area of the lobby that led to the rooms of the hotel. I stood, and she smiled at me, immediately moving in my direction. I recognized her easily from the description I had been given. She was still smiling as she stopped near me, and spoke in a pleasant manner.

"Would you like to go for a walk?"

"That would be nice. Quite a few other people are out for a stroll today."

We walked outside to "the avenue" as it was commonly called, and when we were away from others she asked a question.

"Did you know Ed?"

"I did, in fact he was an old friend."

"Oh? How did you happen to know him?"

"He was from the city where I lived as a boy."

"Poor fellow. It seems the damn Yankees are trying to kill all of us."

"How do you manage to stay out of danger?"

"I don't. This town is full of dangerous people, and..."

She stopped and turned to look at me.

"People are so different when there is a war. Many men have already been killed, and those who are still alive know that it could happen to them soon. They could be here today, gone tomorrow.

The future is uncertain for them. There is no next year to think about. It is all today and now, and nothing else matters. Everything must be done today."

"You are quite a philosopher."

"Not really, just practical. Look around, and you can see it in faces. You can see it in the way people have changed. Can they plan something for a child or a home or much of anything beyond a day or a week? No. We have all been affected."

She was puzzling and obviously a deeply thoughtful person. I needed much more time and information to be able to form an opinion of her.

"Your name is Laura, is that correct?"

"Yes."

"And I understand that your husband was killed about two years ago. I will guess that you have no children."

"You guessed right."

"How long were you married?"

"Ten years. We couldn't have children."

"I have been told that you came to Washington looking for revenge for your husband's death. Do you feel satisfied now that you are doing something to help the South?"

"Maybe, but they took away my husband, and I will always hate them."

"They're not all bad. I had a very good friend here who was a Major in the Union Army. He was one of the best men I ever knew. So, I have come to believe that they have some good and some bad, as do we."

She remained silent. We continued to walk in the direction of the Capitol Building. It was pleasant outside, and not hot. Laura was wearing a dress that did not have a full and large hoop, and she was probably more comfortable than she would have been otherwise. She was, as I had been told, pretty. She had deep blue eyes that were rounded perfectly. I could see that she might easily gain the attention of men who would give her favors. She ended the silence.

"None of us know what will happen. Think of poor Ed and how he came to an end so quickly. I am sorry, and I will miss him."

She was a mystery. Was she lying? My gift of being able to judge people had left me, and my instincts were faltering.

"Do you know the details of how he was killed?"

"I don't believe anyone can be sure about that. I only know that he was shot at a time and place where very few people would have known how to find him. That is the way it was reported by one of the other operatives."

"Do you know all of the other operatives?"

"No, that would be impossible. Many people who are providing information are talking to both sides. Money makes them talk. This city has become a gathering place for lots of disgruntled people, some of whom are deserters from the armies, spies, crooks, and every other type. And now, I am beginning to realize that I, too, probably came here with the wrong thoughts in mind. Maybe it is time for me to give it up and go home."

"Will they let you do that?"

"I don't know. I haven't mentioned it. What do you think?"

"I think you are too involved to leave. You know too much."

"Maybe so. I was hoping the war would be over soon, but now that Lee has been turned back and Grant has taken Vicksburg, I believe it will go on for a long time."

"I agree. Speaking of Lee, are you able to get information about Yankee strategy that is helpful to our people?"

"I have been told that I am doing a good job."

"Where do you live? I am sure that the hotel is not your normal place of residence."

"You're right, it's not. I have a room in a boarding house."

I felt like I might be off to a good start with her. It was helpful because I was scheduled to meet a courier on Tuesday in Surrattsville, across the river in Maryland, to send a message to Richmond with an opinion about her. And that meant, of course, that I would have to move fast. I decided to take a risk and use a bold approach.

"Laura, I need to ask you a few things about Ed Jenkins. Are you willing to answer my questions?"

"Why, yes, that would be no problem."

"Good. Did you -"

She interrupted.

"They suspect me, don't they?"

I didn't answer. I saw a bench a few feet ahead, and I asked if she would like to sit there for a while. She said "yes," and we stopped. After we were seated I looked her in the eyes.

"When did you last see Ed?"

"The day before he was shot."

"And he told you his plans, where he would be the next day?"

"Yes. I had some information for him, and he said he would include it along with the other things he would take to the courier the following night."

"Did you see anyone after that and mention Ed's plans?"

She hesitated. After a long pause she turned toward me.

"That night I was with a Union officer. We drank wine. It seems that he did ask more questions than most men. I honestly cannot be sure whether I said something or not. He did mention that he was acquainted with Ed. It's possible that I could have talked some about Ed. I had quite a bit of wine."

"What is the name of the Union officer?"

"Rigsby. Colonel Albert Rigsby."

The name had a faint sort of significance to me. I tried to recall who he was or how I might have known him in the past, but I could not remember. While thinking about it, I had looked beyond Laura and saw two men standing in front of the hotel who were glancing at us occasionally. The same two men had been in the lobby while I waited for Laura. They obviously had an interest in her or possibly both of us.

I told Laura and asked that she take a good look at them when she could do it without drawing their attention. Also, giving further consideration to the reason I was there, and still being uncertain about her, I had an idea that might help me make a decision.

"How would you like to take a day off and spend the night at my farm?"

She was surprised.

"How do you mean that?"

"It would just be a chance to get acquainted, nothing else."

She immediately had a pleasant expression.

"I would enjoy it very much."

"Very good! I'll walk with you back to the hotel and then I will rent a rig and return shortly. Don't forget to look at the two men in front of the hotel."

One hour later we were riding in a buggy on the road that led to my farm. She told me that she had looked at the two men in front of the hotel and that she did not recognize them. Otherwise, we talked about common things in general terms. I knew that I would have an opportunity later, in a more pleasant environment, to question her about Ed Jenkins.

When we reached my farm and turned into the well-maintained driveway, Laura was pleasantly surprised.

"Oh, how beautiful! Can we stop for a moment?"

"Absolutely."

I reined in the horse. Laura seemed astounded with the view. It reminded me of the first time I had seen the house and grounds when I had been looking for a farm to buy. The long driveway, on flat land leading up to the house, was lined with medium-sized maple trees, spaced twenty-five feet apart on each side. Just beyond the trees, and forming a border along the way, was the white wooden fence that surrounded a green pasture where the horses had grazed in previous times.

And the house, too, was eye catching. Large, with white wooden sideboards covering the two story front, it was typical of the columned plantation-style homes, sitting with pristine beauty behind a circular drive that reached across the width of the house.

As we sat I thought of Sarah, and the number of times in the past when I had entered the drive and imagined that she would be waiting inside the house for me. Laura brought me back to reality.

"Okay, you can go now. How did you manage to get such a beautiful place?"

"Good luck, I suppose."

"Oh, that's right. I don't know much about you except that someone said that you are known as the best gambler in town. Is that how you did it?"

"Yes. That's what I intended by saying good luck got the place for me."

When we stopped in front of the house, I helped Laura down from the buggy, picked up her carpetbag, and led the way through the door. I took her on a tour of the first floor after which we went upstairs where I showed her to the guest suite. I told her I would leave her there to relax for a while, and when she felt refreshed she could join me downstairs. She smiled in appreciation.

"Thank you, Alexander. I will see you shortly."

I returned downstairs. Mary Kate did not come on Sundays, so she would not be there. Malcolm, who still preferred to be in his room in the barn, would come in later for food. I had explained to Laura that she would meet both during her visit, believing that she should know about them in advance, especially Malcolm. And I was glad that Malcolm would have an opportunity to meet Laura. I was convinced that his instincts were exceptional, and his perception of people was very reliable.

Late in the evening, around ten o'clock, Laura and I were sitting on the back veranda. It was comfortable there, and we were both relaxed. Malcolm had come and gone. He had stayed about two hours with us. Laura did not seem to have any concern about being in the presence of a black man. In fact, she seemed to enjoy him, mainly because of his humor which made her laugh quite often.

After Malcolm had left, we had talked about the war for a while. Both of us believed that the South would eventually lose. Then, saying that she was tired of thinking about the fighting, Laura changed the subject back to Malcolm.

"He is an amazing man. I would never dream that a black person could be so intelligent."

"I know. He amazes everyone. But Laura, lets talk a little more about Ed Jenkins. This Colonel Rigsby that you mentioned, his name is familiar to me but I can't place him. Can you tell me all that you know about him?"

"He says he goes back and forth from Washington to the headquarters of the Army of the Potomac. I have known him for only a short while and have spent no more than three evenings with him. I really don't know that much about him."

"I want you to think carefully and try to remember how his conversations originated when you were talking about military matters. Did he bring it up first, or did you?"

She did think carefully. She was silent for what seemed like a full minute before answering.

"He did. I hadn't thought about it much before, but I remember that he liked to talk about some of his experiences with high ranking officers, like he was very proud of it."

"Okay, think carefully again. Did he ever give you information that you did not already have about the Union Army?"

"Little things, maybe, but nothing significant."

"What did you tell him about yourself and why you were there?"

"I told him that my husband was killed and that I was lonely."

"Did he believe you?"

"I doubt it. There may be hundreds of women in Washington telling the same story for the same reason, and I think he knew that."

We talked until eleven, and then we said goodnight. I left a note for Mary Kate on the kitchen table explaining that Laura was an acquaintance helping with a project, and that she was in the house for that reason only. I was beginning to have a rather firm conviction about Laura. However, before passing final judgment, I wanted to consult with Malcolm.

I was awakened in the middle of the night by a startling dream. I sat upright in bed. In the dream, a man had walked up to me and said, "I am Colonel Rigsby." Then I remembered. Ed Jenkins had mentioned his name in one of our conversations. Rigsby was a double agent.

Early the next morning, as was her usual practice, Mary Kate started rattling pans on the stove to let me know that it was time for breakfast. When I got down to the kitchen I was surprised to see that Laura was already there. She appeared to be having a nice conversation with Mary Kate. I sheepishly grinned at both as I spoke.

"I didn't sleep too well – sorry to be a little late."

They both smiled. After breakfast Laura told me that she had to be back in the city by noon to keep an appointment. First, she said, she wanted to take a stroll outside to enjoy as much of the beautiful surroundings on the farm as possible. I told her it would be my pleasure to show her around. Later, as we walked, I mentioned Rigsby.

"Do you think he might be working for both sides?"

"I think he is capable of it, he is that sort of man. He would go in either direction depending on which would benefit him more."

"And he would know that he could only straddle the fence for a short while because one side or the other would get wise to him."

"Exactly."

"Let's imagine that he has been a double agent. We know that he knew Ed Jenkins, and that Ed was sending important information south. With the war taking a quick turn in favor of the North in the last two weeks, do you believe Rigsby might have decided it was time for him to choose one side?"

"It certainly seems like a good possibility."

"Do you believe he is actually a Colonel in the Union Army, or just posing as one?"

"It could be either way. He is cautious in what he allows me to know about him."

"Okay, one last thing. Is he the kind of man who would kill Ed or have it done?"

She thought about it for a moment before responding.

"I can't be sure. I will say this. If he is a double agent, and if he is now making a move to the Northern side, he would probably do whatever was necessary to protect himself. And if that meant disposing of Ed, yes, I think he could do it."

I asked her for a description of Rigsby and where he could be found. She described him very well, and she told me that he could be found in one of several hotels.

Later in the morning we rode in the buggy back to the National Hotel. When we stopped at the entrance, I helped her down, and she looked at me in a pleasant way.

"Thank you for a very nice visit. I assume we will meet again in the near future. You can find me at the address of the boarding house that I gave you."

"I enjoyed the visit, too. See you soon."

She went into the hotel. I walked to my left and went to the corner where there was a telegraph office in the same building. Inside I wrote a message to John Dabney in Atlanta, and because it might be censored, I used vague terms. He would be aware of what I was doing, and he would be able to understand the message. I simply wrote: I am concerned about Mister and Missis D, can you please advise the status of both?

After I returned to the farm, I went to the barn to find Malcolm. When he saw me he smiled and spoke immediately because he knew why I was there.

"I don't think she is guilty. She might have had too much wine and said too much, but it was not intentional. She didn't plan anything to get Ed Jenkins killed."

"I'm glad to hear you say that because I had decided the same thing. Now I can pass the information on to the courier tomorrow, and we will wait for a response from Richmond."

Malcolm was with me the next day when I struck out for Surrattsville to meet the courier. I felt better having him along. My instincts were beginning to tell me that I was involved in a dangerous game, and it was good to have his support. I had confided in him about everything, both my personal life and the work I was doing for the Confederacy.

He understood me perfectly, and he knew that what I was doing was not the result of a desire to see black people held in bondage. It was, instead, my way of passing through a maze of fear, anger, and hatred among others around me. Deciding who was right and who was wrong was no longer an option that would be a pathway into the future. I had made my decision, and I would have to live with it.

As we approached the Navy Yard Bridge on our horses, Malcolm spoke.

"Did you write something to give to the courier?"

"Not yet. I will do it when we get there."

"You can get us both killed, you know."

"How can two fast riders who are tough as nails get killed?"

He grinned.

"How did I ever get mixed up with you?"

I grinned back.

"Just lucky I guess."

We rode on in silence for a while. Intermingled with my thoughts were flashes of Sarah. I missed her and needed her comforting nearness. I was still concerned, remembering that she had not felt good the last day I had visited her home. I wanted to bring an end to my assignment in Washington, go back to Georgia and hold her in my arms again.

There was a small tavern in Surrattsville and it had been designated as the place where I was to meet the courier. The password to be used in making connections was "Black Mountain." The two words could be used separately or in a sentence. It was the code for the week now in progress, then it would change.

When we arrived at the tavern, I went in alone, and Malcolm stayed with the horses. Only three men, plus the proprietor, were there. I ordered whiskey, and it was served. All three of the other customers seemed to be traveling separately. I didn't make a move, staying put and sipping the whiskey slowly, waiting to see which of the three might approach me.

Two of the men resumed what had apparently been a conversation before I had come in. The third man, a rough looking individual, stayed to himself. After a few minutes I found that he was occasionally glancing at me, and finally, he seemed to nod slightly. I acknowledged his signal with a slight movement of my head, and shortly thereafter he walked over near me and spoke so that the others could hear.

"Don't I know you?"

"Maybe. I've been this way before."

"Yeah, I thought so." And he turned so that he was facing away from the others and spoke more quietly. "You got something for me?"

I spoke quietly, too.

"I don't know, it depends on what you are looking for."

"What do you mean by that?"

I looked into his eyes and tried to decide about him. He was large and roughly dressed, and his manner of staring directly back into my face gave me an understanding about him. He was no stranger to a dangerous situation. I acknowledged his question.

"It's simple. I can let you know with two words. Red apple."

"You got that right, mister, red apple. Now, do you want to walk outside and hand me something?"

"Yes. Let's go around to the side, or the back, where we can have privacy."

He smiled and put his glass on the counter. Then, each of us walked toward the door.

Outside, Malcolm was back some distance with the horses, and he watched as I walked to the side of the building with the man from the inside. When we were out of view from the front, I turned toward him.

"Tell me how I am to know you? What does red apple mean?"

"Hell, ain't that the code? You said it yourself. Just give me some documents or papers, and I'll be on my way."

"Tell me the name of the person who sent you."

"That ain't no concern of yours. If you don't give me them papers, we are about to have some big trouble."

His attitude had changed quickly. He was making some body movements that appeared to be aggressive. It was time to put my cards on the table. I quickly pushed my coat back and withdrew the Colt revolver, pointing it in his direction.

"Who are you?"

He backed away, but not too surprisingly, he remained calm.

"Mister, if you was to fire that pistol, some Union cavalry would come down on you like a dog on a rabbit. They's a bunch of them across the road."

"Who sent you here?"

"Can't tell you that. All I will say is that I was sent here to intercept some Rebel plunder."

"Where is the man who was supposed to be here?"

"How in hell would I know that?"

I considered what little information he was willing to give me. He was saying, in effect, that the real courier had been caught, or stopped. He might be bluffing about the Union cavalry, or maybe not. I couldn't be sure. I would attempt to get one other answer, and then I would leave him.

"The man who sent you, was he staying in one of the hotels, Brown's, Herndon House, or the Willard?"

I could sense that he was uncertain about me and what I might do. The Colt revolver, almost sixteen inches long with a heavy appearance, would have an ominous look to anyone facing it. He seemed ready to give way a little.

"I met him at the square."

"Lafayette Square?"

"Yes."

"Was he a military man, an officer in the Union Army?"

"Mister, I ain't going to tell you nothing else. You ain't going to shoot me anyway."

He was right. I had no intention of shooting him. It was time to terminate the conversation.

"All right, we are finished. You can leave now."

He didn't speak again. He walked to his horse, tied to a wooden bar in front of the tavern, and rode off in the direction of Washington. Malcolm could sense a problem as he handed me the reins to my horse.

"Who was he?"

"He wanted me to think he was the courier so he could get papers from me. Somebody hired him to come and pick them up. I don't think he is involved in any other way. He is harmless."

Malcolm was silent. I could sense what he was going to say. His troubled background always moved into his thoughts at such times and prodded him. Three or four minutes later, as we rode back toward Washington, the words came out.

"How much longer are we going to be mixed up in this?"

"Not long. I'm ready right now to go back to Georgia. And this time I'm only going to stay long enough to pick up Sarah and her baby and leave there."

He used his artificial chuckle before speaking.

"Oh? What about DeAngelo?"

"To hell with him."

This time I heard a natural chuckle.

"So, let's see now. You will have both the Rebels and the Union after you, as well as DeAngelo. Did I leave out anybody?"

I grinned at him.

"You getting worried?"

He smiled back.

"Did I say that?"

We stopped in town so that I could see Phillip. He was busy, so I didn't keep him away from his other clients too long. I asked him if he could prepare several legal documents for me.

"Absolutely. Come back in on Saturday, and I will have them ready for you. And plan to spend some time with me. We haven't had a good chance to catch up on things."

It was five-thirty when Malcolm and I got home. Mary Kate had prepared food for us, and we sat in the kitchen together while eating. I thought of what Malcolm had talked about earlier, and I wanted to express some thoughts to him about the future.

"After the war is over, it will be the beginning of hard times in the South. And there will be trouble between the blacks and whites for years to come. Neither will have anything, and they will be fighting each other to get what little can be had. It won't be a good place to be."

"Does that mean you don't plan to be there?"

"No, I didn't mean it like that. I was born there, and it is still my home. I guess I was thinking more about others and the turmoil they will be facing. For a while I think the black people will have more trouble than they had as slaves."

"Maybe, but at least they will be free."

"Yes, and that is the way it should be. But think about it. If you were free, and you had no mule, no land, no money or anything else, where would you turn?"

"I think I would go back to Marse and ask him if he needed a good plow hand."

"And that might work. It all depends on how well Marse himself is doing."

I went into town each day. My first stop was always the same place, the telegraph office on the corner in the same building that was part of the National Hotel. There was no response from

Dabney in Georgia. Every time I asked if there was a message, I did so with a little more anxiety, and the lack of news about Sarah was very frustrating. I sent another message to Dabney on Friday asking about her.

Late Saturday morning I went to Phillip's office, and from there we went together to Mary Carroll's Teahouse. After we were seated, Phillip looked across the table and grinned at me.

"You know you are kind of hard to keep up with these days."

"Yes, I know. And if I don't hear something soon about Sarah, I'm leaving here again."

"Alex, if you're not careful you are going to get your ass shot off."

"Hopefully not. What's your new prediction about the war?"

"My prediction hasn't changed. Look at the facts. How can the South match the men and resources of the North? They can't. The only chance they had has been eliminated."

"What chance are you talking about?"

"Jackson. Without him Lee can't win."

"Do you actually believe that one man could make that much difference?"

"Yes. If Jackson had been with Lee, Gettysburg would have turned out differently. He was a military genius, and Lee knew it. If Jackson had been there on the third day of the battle it would not have ended in failure."

"How do you know these things?"

"I talk to people from both sides, people who are in a position to know what they are talking about."

"How long will the war last?"

"Nobody can predict that accurately. The South won't go down easily. The people who are running things have too much at stake. They will continue to tell their soldiers that the Yankees want to come and take their land and homes. I am guessing that it will last another year, maybe two."

"What will happen in the South when it is over?"

"Fortunately for the South we've got a President who is not only a good man, he is also kind and forgiving. He will help the South recover, but even with his help it will take a long time."

Later, after we had parted, I inquired again at four different hotels, asking if a Colonel Rigsby was a guest. There was no Colonel Rigsby to be found. Did it mean that he had given Laura a false name? I didn't go to the boarding house address of Laura, even though I wanted to talk to her again. I felt it might be a mistake to be seen at her home. And so, I was beginning to realize that I would have to go in a new direction with everything.

When I got home, Malcolm told me that some Union cavalrymen had been there. An officer and four enlisted men.

"They were looking for you," he said.

"What did they want?"

"Didn't say much, just asked if you were here. They asked me if I lived in the house, and I told them no, I live in the barn. I think it was the right answer."

"Yes, it was. What did the officer look like?"

"Dark hair, dark eyes, slender face, medium size. Forty years old. He didn't get down off of his horse."

"How about his rank? Or did any of the men address him by name or rank?"

"No. When they spoke I couldn't hear what was said."

"Do you think they were trying to be secretive?"

"Yes. When they left they didn't go back toward town. They went in the opposite direction."

"Then they might still be out here somewhere."

"Could be. If they come back you better not pull out that big revolver."

"Why not? They will be on my property."

He shook his head from side to side, turned and walked toward the barn. He spoke once again.

"I'll see you tomorrow." He stopped and looked back, "I'll say a special prayer for you tonight."

He looked at me long enough to see my smile, which he returned, and then he continued on his way.

I watched him as he walked toward the barn. He had become as loyal as anyone had ever been in my life. And it would be long lasting. Helping him in the most desperate moment of his life had given me a place in his heart that would always be there. His great physical strength was equaled by his resolve for fairness among men, regardless of color. The feelings he must have had at one time, believing that all white men were his enemies, would have been softened.

The Union cavalrymen did return. It was at dusk. I was sitting on the front portico when I saw them turn off the main road into my driveway. As they rode toward me, I could see that it was an officer with four enlisted men following closely behind him. They appeared to be armed in a manner according to their rank. I stepped down into the yard to meet them. The officer pulled up on his horse when he was near me and spoke.

"Mister Fairfield?"

"Yes."

"I have come to notify you of a new law just signed by the President. All men must report for duty with the Union Army."

"All men?"

"What is your age, Mister Fairfield?"

"Thirty-one."

"Yes, all men thirty-one must report for duty."

I could see his rank by looking at the insignia on his uniform.

"Colonel, I have been commissioned by the Federal Army to procure horses for the Union. The commission is documented and states that I am to be exempt from military duty in order to provide other needed services."

"Who signed the document?"

"Major Dale."

"Major Dale is dead. Your document is void."

"I beg your pardon, Colonel. A record of my commission is in the office of the War Department. The document states that the order is to be executed until revoked by that office."

He was immediately perturbed and embarrassed in front of his men. He spoke again, impetuously, as if he wanted to strike back at me.

"What were you doing across the river in Surrattsville a few days ago?"

His question surprised me. I did not expect him to boldly reveal his knowledge that I had been there.

My answer was already in place because of previous statements. "Looking for horses."

He paused, and realized he had made a mistake. It gave me the opportunity to think about who he might be. I decided to risk a question and use a name.

"Colonel Rigsby, how is it, sir, that you are aware of my whereabouts recently? I did not see you the day I was across the river."

I could see in his facial expression that he knew he had spoken too quickly without giving it enough thought. I anticipated that he would avoid answering and try to cover up his error.

"How I gain my knowledge is none of your concern. I will check into the validity of what you have stated about your commission. If you have lied, you will be placed under arrest."

"Fine."

He jerked the reins of his horse, used his spurs, and headed back in the direction of the main road at a gallop. He obviously was upset and angry.

Early the next morning I rode into town. I went directly to the address of the boarding house where Laura was staying. At the door a heavy-set woman, possibly fifty years old, had a friendly greeting for me.

"Good morning, sir. Are you looking for quarters?"

"And a good morning to you, madam. No, I am not looking for living quarters. I have come to see Laura McKinnon. Is she in?"

"No, sir. And she won't be anymore, she has moved out."

"When?"

"Yesterday."

"Do you know where she was going?"

"No. The only thing I can tell you is that she seemed to be in tight with a Union army officer. He came yesterday morning, riding in a fine buggy, and helped load her belongings, and they rode off."

I had to think quickly to give her a reason for further questions.

"I am sorry I missed her. I have some important news for her. Can you suggest anything that might help me find her?"

"Well, let's see. The only thing I can think of right now is that she seemed to be settled about the officer coming to get her, like he might be going to take care of her or something along that line."

"Can you describe the officer?"

"He was sort of dark, his eyes and hair, and he was medium size. About forty years old I would say."

The description fit my visitor from the previous night, Rigsby. And I believed it to be him because he had not rebuked me when I used that name.

"And so she left no forwarding address?"

"None whatsoever. From what little I know about her, I believe she had moved around some before she got here."

"Thank you. I will be on my way now. Have a pleasant day."

"And you do the same, sir."

Shortly thereafter, as I rode along The Avenue, I tried to reason out everything. The woman at the boarding house had made a puzzling statement about Laura. It seemed that she had a "settled" feeling as the officer had taken her away. If Rigsby had come for her, how could she have a settled feeling? Did Malcolm and I both misjudge Laura? If she was cunning enough to fool us, what was her motive?

I stopped at the telegraph office, and it was the same. No message from Georgia. At that point I made a decision. If by the end of the week there was no message, I would head south.

Over the following two days, there was no new contact from Cargill in Richmond. Apparently the courier who was to meet me in Surrattsville had been intercepted, and he most likely was dead. With no means of communication with Cargill, I would be completely inept. My duty to the Confederate States would be at a standstill.

Friday, about mid-morning, I walked out to the barn to find Malcolm. He was involved with a minor project, and after a greeting I asked him to come with me for a walk. He looked puzzled as he followed me out toward the back pasture. I turned in his direction.

"I thought we might have a talk. It's a nice day, and it might be a good time to walk back toward the briar patch where you took shelter when you first came."

"Yes, we can do that, but I believe you've got a serious look on your face, Marse."

I smiled.

"It's serious, but I am sure you can handle it."

Malcolm's keen sense of perception had gone to work. I could see he didn't want to wait all day to find out what was going on.

"Whatever it is, why don't you just go ahead and let it out?"

We passed through the gate and walked onto the green grass of the pasture, and I began telling him about my plans.

"I'm going back to the south. The way things have turned out here, I'm not accomplishing anything. If I can go through Richmond, I will try to find Cargill and let him know. But my intent is to go to Roswell, Georgia and get Sarah. From there, I don't know where I will go. It will depend on what Sarah wants." I paused to look at him. "Do you have any questions so far?"

"No, but I know you haven't told me the whole story, so just keep on talking."

"Okay. Here is where you come in. You can stay here and be safe. I have already made arrangements with Phillip. You are protected, and you will be provided for permanently. Or, you can go with me, and I know I don't have to tell you that the picture would be different in that case."

He chuckled.

"You brought me back here in the middle of the pasture to tell me that? And ask me that kind of question?"

I stopped and looked into his eyes. I knew what his answer would be, but I wanted to be sure that he understood everything.

"Yes. And you need to give it some thought before you decide. The south, for a black man in the future, is going to be pure hell. What would you do if somebody got to me and you were left on your own?"

"I would get out of there. I've already done it once when I left McCleskey's place."

"So you have. I had forgotten that temporarily. And you feel you could make your way back to Washington successfully?"

"Certainly I could. And you could too. We would both make it back to Washington."

"And you are saying that you want to go with me?"

"Yes."

"Somehow, that does not surprise me." I smiled at him as I continued, "All right, some time in the next day or so I will explain everything to Mary Kate and Bradford. They can take care of things here like the last time. Then we will set a date to leave."

"What about the Rebs, the people you have been working with? Won't they be a little upset?"

"Maybe. But they have left me stranded. I don't even have the new code word. It would be hopeless to try to continue without any connections or guidance. There are hundreds of spies in Washington, and they probably won't even miss me. In addition, the spies are working back and forth making it impossible to trust anybody."

We turned and went back through the pasture toward the house. When we got to the gate, Malcolm headed back to the barn, and I walked on alone. My thoughts turned once again to Sarah. All other things seemed minor compared to the problem of getting her away from DeAngelo. Phillip had drawn up a document that was certified that stated that she had been abducted from her home by DeAngelo causing her to be absent with great distress and held against her wishes. If I should be stopped and questioned after leaving Roswell with her, it would give me some ammunition in warding off others who might interfere with us. Nonetheless, I knew that high risks were involved.

Would documents drawn up in the North be good in the South? Would she be able to travel with a baby? How much of a problem would DeAngelo be? He would use the fact that she had married him as an advantage. But, it actually didn't matter. I had reached the point that I wouldn't let anything stop me from taking her away from him, regardless of what I had to do.

## XI

It was a Tuesday afternoon when Bradford hitched a horse to the big rig we had in the barn and pulled it up to the front of the house. It was an old fashioned six-seater and had been sitting idle for several years. Bradford had wiped away the dust, and I climbed aboard in the front seat. Malcolm sat in the seat behind us. We were going to the station where we would board a late afternoon rail car for Baltimore. There were three rail trips daily from Washington to Baltimore. I had picked the one that would leave around six, assuming it would be a less conspicuous time for us to travel. I knew the town to be full of devious people, and we could no longer consider that we would be safe under any conditions. In a sense, I felt no regret in vacating Washington for a while; my beautiful home and farm notwithstanding.

In the rail car, Malcolm was allowed to sit beside me. It was, I believed, for two reasons. Some people assumed him to be a manservant. Secondly, and more likely, the attitude of the people was changing. Following the success that was achieved by the Army of the Potomac at Gettysburg, there was more confidence, and more open support for Mister Lincoln. Consequently, the President's call for the blacks to be treated with more consideration was beginning to be accepted by many of the people. Others, however, were moving steadily in the opposite direction. Still in evidence was the disgruntled attitude of many Southern sympathizers who made up a slight majority of residents in the Washington and Southern Maryland area.

The car we were in gradually became filled with people. Military men and civilians were present. Some ladies were traveling alone, something that would not have been seen in ordinary times.

Eventually all seats were taken. A moment or so later, two additional people came in, a man in a Union Army uniform accompanied by a woman. He was on crutches and the lower part of his left leg was missing. Most people were watching as the two made their way slowly along the aisle toward the middle of the car where we were sitting. When they realized that no seats were left, they stopped. Malcolm, who was sitting in a seat on the aisle, immediately got up and offered the soldier his seat. The man stared momentarily with an obvious contempt and hobbled on toward the rear of the car. The woman who was with him looked squarely into Malcolm's face and spoke in a spiteful tone.

"It's all your fault, you, and all of the others like you."

Malcolm sat down next to me, and I spoke quietly.

"Don't worry about it. They are bitter right now."

"I know."

Less than two hours later we arrived in Baltimore. There were no other incidents along the way. Two soldiers in the rear of the car had given up their seats to the crippled man and the woman who was with him. It had been, however, an omen of things to come. The black man was going to be mistreated no matter where he turned.

On our previous visit to Baltimore, I had seen a sign in the front yard of a big house that read, "Rooms For Travelers." In small print below was an added notation: "accommodations for servants." It was near the rail station so we stopped there. Inside, I made arrangements for both of us, a room for me within the large residence and a room for Malcolm in a building in the rear.

The next morning I sat next to a young man while having breakfast. We were at a table where the food was served family style. We introduced ourselves. He told me his name was Charlie Daws. He was youthful, possibly twenty-five, and I could not decide where he was from based on his accent or lack of accent. He was well-experienced in meeting and talking to others, and he was quite knowledgeable about current events.

I had the feeling that he knew many things that other people might not know, and might never learn from him. He did not solicit any information from me. I mentioned casually that I was planning a trip southward during the day. He glanced about, and then, speaking softly, he asked his first question.

"Are you by chance going beyond the State of Maryland?"

I nodded. Again, speaking quietly, he responded.

"If you have finished your meal why don't you walk with me to the outside? I might have information that would be of interest to you."

Shortly thereafter we were standing alone on the portico, and he seemed more comfortable and spoke with a little more ease.

"Are you planning to leave this morning?"

"Yes. I have a black man traveling with me."

"That's fine. I know about him. I have a coach, and I am looking for passengers. I am going to Richmond, and if you are interested you can travel with me."

"How did you know about the black man?"

"I saw you yesterday when you got off the rail car from Washington."

"When are you leaving?"

"As soon as possible. I just need to have passengers in my coach to get through the countryside. The Yankees have tightened up, and it's much harder to get past them now. If I have passengers it works out better."

I realized then that he was either a courier, or he was moving something that had to be concealed as he went through the areas where conflicts between the North and South might occur. This was neither surprising nor disturbing. The country had been turned upside down by the war, and many people who were operating within the Washington, Baltimore, Richmond triangle were suspect. They were not to be trusted until a reasonable assessment of them could be made. In that regard, I had one or two more questions for Charlie Daws.

"I don't care about your reasons for going to Richmond, but if we are stopped and searched, will we be able to pass?"

"They will find nothing about me or my coach to delay me. How about you?"

"No, we have nothing. I have a revolver, but I have papers that allow me to possess it."

"Very good. Why don't you find your darkie and get your bags? I'll bring the coach around, and we will be off."

During the day it became obvious that Charlie Daws was well known along the route toward the Potomac. Even some of the men of the Union cavalry units on patrol in the area laughed with him and greeted him as "Wild Charlie." We had no trouble on the road, and the day of traveling was completed when we arrived very late at the Star Hotel in Bowling Green, Virginia. It was where Charlie said we would spend the night. The hotel, a two story building with a portico that completely circled the structure, was picturesque with large white columns holding up the overhanging roof, making it appear similar to some of the large homes on southern plantations. I was given a room on the second floor.

Malcolm was taken in and given a room in the lower level, an area of rooms below the main lobby of the hotel just above ground level. About thirty minutes after I had placed my bag in my room, I walked down to the lower level to be sure that Malcolm was safely in place. He greeted me at the door and obviously had something to tell me.

"Did you know that this hotel is a main gathering place for Rebel agents?"

"How do you know?"

"I talked to a man who works here, a black man. He told me it is a stopping off location and a meeting point for most of the operatives going to and from Washington."

"I'm not surprised. What else did he tell you?"

"Our driver, Mister Daws, takes information directly to the office of Jefferson Davis."

"How does the man know that?"

"He talks to the daughter of the owner of the hotel, a young girl about sixteen who is trying to be the sweetheart of Daws. Daws tells her what he does, and later after he is gone and she wants to talk to somebody about Daws, she corners the man who talked to me and confides in him."

"That doesn't surprise me too much about Daws."

"One other thing. She thinks Daws is finished now and will go back to Canada. He has found out that Yankee agents in Washington are on to him."

I stopped talking, momentarily gazing beyond Malcolm to the back of his room as I considered what he had just said. He noticed.

"What's going on, Marse? You've got that look in your eyes again."

"Canada. That's what's going on. We will take Sarah to Canada." He grinned.

"Okay. I hear it's cold up there but maybe we can get some 'long draws.' Yes, I can think of no reason we cannot do that."

"I'm going to ride on the outside of the coach next to Daws for a while in the morning." I smiled at him. "I think we might have to buy some 'long draws' when we get to Richmond and maybe he can tell me how to find them."

We were on the road again the next morning at daybreak. The proprietor of the hotel, knowing the tendencies of his guests, began serving breakfast at four-thirty in the morning. By daylight the rooms in the hotel would be emptied out. It was a time when men were faced with circumstances of danger, and it demanded the full use of each day by all.

The early morning air of the Virginia countryside was fresh and had a clean smell. Vegetables and fruit trees were nearing full term and the scent given off was exhilarating. When I had suggested to Charlie Daws that I would like to sit next to him on the driver's seat, he had seemed to be pleased. We had left the Star Hotel at five-thirty, and Charlie was pushing the horses rather hard, alternating between a gallop and a slower pace when there was an incline in the road. He was using four horses to pull the coach, and I commented on it.

"How much time do you gain by using the two additional horses?"

"I can cut one-third off of the time it would take with only two horses. I can make the trip between Baltimore and Richmond faster than anybody."

"I can believe that. How long have you been at it?"

"Six months. It's coming to an end though. Things have changed, and I am getting out of it."

"Are you going to be a soldier?"

"No, I'm not a native of this country, Mister Fairfield, and I will leave it to the others to do the fighting. I am going home to Canada."

"Canada? What part of Canada?"

"Montreal. It is not my home, but many of the people here who have become my friends are going there."

"Is it easy to go there? I mean by that, would it be a problem for someone like me to travel through the northern states and pass over the border to Canada?"

He turned and looked at me. In his glance I could recognize that he was aware of my circumstances and that my question was based on an impending need.

"It would be easy, and you would have no problem."

I thought it would be best to throw a cloud over my tracks.

"I have given it some consideration because my profession has become limited in this country due to the war. In the past I have bought and sold fine horses, thoroughbreds. However there is no longer a need for such animals, at least not in the way they were sought out in the past."

"I understand." I hadn't fooled him. I could see it in his eyes. Then he confirmed it.

"Maybe you are like me, Mister Fairfield, and consider it to be a safer place these days."

"That could be." My instincts were telling me that he knew more than he had indicated previously. "I think we might be in the same boat."

He didn't answer immediately, and he seemed to be weighing what he should say. He continued to look at the road ahead. After half a minute he turned toward me.

"I know about you, Mister Fairfield."

"How much?"

"Just about everything, I believe. I know you got out of Washington just in time."

That got my attention in a hurry.

"How do you mean that?"

"Rigsby was assigned to get you."

"He was not a double agent?"

"No, he only pretended to be. Cargill found out about him after Ed Jenkins was killed. The Yankees found out about nearly all of the southern operatives so Cargill had to shut down contacts with everybody. He will have to reorganize everything."

"That's very surprising. What else can you tell me?"

"They are going to take your farm. Confiscate it and move some of the rabble off of the back grounds of the White House to your location. There are squatters from the back door of the White House to the river. Mr. Lincoln has not been willing to have them removed, but Mister Lamon wants them out of there. I heard that somebody thought your farm would be a good place."

"I'm not surprised. I've been thinking they might take my property if they caught me."

"Do you have other assets, like money in the bank?"

"Before leaving I made arrangements for my money to be protected. I will operate with gold certificates that are non-negotiable by others. But tell me, how did you get so much information?"

"I worked in Washington for a while and made some friends who were in sympathy with the South. About six months ago, I met Cargill, and he asked me to start driving the coach between Baltimore and Richmond. But things have changed, and it is getting much more dangerous, so I have decided to give it up and go home."

"Do you know a woman named Laura McKinnon?"

"Yes. I met her some time ago at a social event."

"What happened to her?"

"She was given a release from performing further duties and sent home."

"I guess being a nice looking woman must have helped her."

"Exactly. I think Rigsby helped her, and she probably paid him off well."

I thought about what he had told me and nothing was too surprising. I had expected most of the things to happen. I would miss the beautiful farm, but without Sarah there to share it with me, I was not greatly disappointed. I continued talking to Daws.

"It seems like you and I have been caught in the same whirlwind."

"You're right. I guess the good thing is that we are a jump ahead of some of the others."

"Where will you go from here?"

"Deeper into the South. I have some personal business to take care of there."

"Do you mind if I ask about your darkie?"

"No."

"It doesn't seem like you are a master with a slave. You are more like friends."

"And that is the way it is."

"Well, I must say, that is amazing. How did that come about in this day and time?"

"We both come from rough backgrounds. I helped him when he needed it, and he has never forgotten it. Since that time he has helped me."

"He sure seems to be bright for a black man."

"He is. Actually he had the benefit of special training for many years. He is dependable and a man I would trust under any conditions."

"Well, I hope things work out well for you. Going south with a black man nowadays could be trouble."

"I know. In fact, you don't even have to go south. But, we will only be in this part of the country for a short while and then we will move on."

Although I considered that we might go to Canada, I realized that it would be best not to leave that thought in the mind of Daws.

When we arrived in Richmond, I asked Daws to take us to the rail station, which he did. Also, I asked him to tell Cargill that I would be continuing on to the south, and based on what Cargill was undertaking in reorganizing his operatives in Washington, I felt that he would have no immediate concerns about me. Consequently, I changed my previous plans to try to find him. There would be no need.

When Charlie delivered us to the station, he did not stop directly in front. He pulled down a ways and brought the coach to a halt so that Malcolm and I could get out with our belongings. He then stepped down from the driver's seat. He stood facing us as he prepared to bid farewell.

"Let me give you some advice. I have brought people here before, and I have picked up travelers who have just come off of the trains. First of all, you have to be master and slave at all times. Don't forget it. Malcolm has to carry both bags and he always walks behind you," and he looked directly at me, "the time will never come when he is beside you or talking and laughing with you. The only thing Malcolm ever says is 'yas-suh' or 'naw-suh', and the rest of the time he stays quiet. And you bend over backwards to be polite not only to the ladies but to the men as well. And Malcolm stays about ten feet away from all of the white ladies. If somebody calls him a nigger he says "yas-suh". When you go up to the counter to pay for your passage you state that you are traveling with your manservant. And if it gets complicated, you can say that you are on official business for the Confederate States. Do you still have those papers you told me about?"

"Yes."

"Good. That will probably get the tickets you will need. Malcolm will ride in the baggage car. But depending, of course, on how many wounded soldiers will be trying to get on the railcars to go home, you may have to wait a day or so to even get the tickets. Take the food you brought with you, and stretch it as far as you can. You won't get anything along the way. You might be able to get water, but that will be all. Always give up your seat to the ladies and wounded soldiers. And last, curse Lincoln and Grant in a loud voice every chance you get. Any questions?"

He had covered things pretty well. Malcolm and I glanced at each other and back to Daws, after which I commented.

"No, I think you have told us all we need to know. Thank you, and good luck to you."

"And to you as well."

He climbed up to the driver's seat of the coach, tapped the horses with the long leather reins, and moved away. And if the information I had received about him at the Star Hotel was correct, he would be on his way to the office of Jefferson Davis. Malcolm and I stood momentarily facing each other. Charlie Daws was a colorful individual, and I wanted to make a few comments about him.

"You know the thing he said that surprised me the most?"

"No, what?"

"Laura McKinnon. She fooled us both."

"She might not have fooled us. She could have just been trying to save her hide. I think she was ready to give it up, and Rigsby gave her that opportunity. I don't know if she lied to us."

"Maybe not. It doesn't matter now anyway."

We turned toward the depot. Quite a few people were moving in and out of the building. I suspected that it would be crowded inside, and I felt it might be a problem to even get a place on a south bound rail car. I decided to have in hand the papers that would identify me as an official servant of the Confederate government. I believed it to be our best opportunity to get a ticket. We walked in the direction of the entrance. There was nothing about us, a gentleman and his manservant, that would attract attention. I prepared mentally to deal with the problem of getting tickets because it seemed likely that there would be a large number of others who would be there for the same purpose.

The inside of the station was, indeed, crowded. The first glance around answered the foremost question in my mind. There were other blacks in the very large waiting room. Most of them seemed to be at work helping people with their bags and possessions. Black nannies were there, attending the white ladies who were with men. In a few cases, they were traveling with other women. In any event, Malcolm would not stand out as the only black man.

Babies were crying, people were moving about and speaking loudly, and in general, it was a scene of chaos. A long line had formed that was leading up to a counter, and it obviously was the place to go to secure tickets. I walked to the end of the line with Malcolm following closely behind me and stood next to the last man. He turned, and I questioned him.

"Is this the line to buy a ticket?"

He smiled.

"This is the line where you try to buy a ticket."

"So, it's hard to get a ticket?"

"Yes, sir. If you see the man walk away from the counter, you know he has sold out all seats for the next two days."

"When does he return?"

"In the morning."

I started thinking about what the alternatives might be. I first thought of horse drawn carriages and whether any would be going south. And even if there should be, would it be just as difficult to obtain a seat? While considering these questions I realized that I was getting a look at the new conditions in the South. Things had changed in just the past few weeks. It was, of course, due to the battle at Gettysburg. Large numbers of people had been affected and many thousands of lives had been disrupted. I turned and talked quietly to Malcolm.

"Did you hear what he said?"

"Yes. What can we do?"

"The only thing I can think of at this moment is a freight car. Maybe we could climb on one of those, catch it on the run."

"I think they have soldiers on those cars. We would be shot before we could get within a hundred feet of one of them."

"Yes, you are probably right. I guess that just leaves horses. We might have to ride horses. Do you think we could make it like that?"

"We can make it, but you will need more than one horse if you ride hard."

"We could pace ourselves. Some of the locomotives only make ten-miles-an-hour. We can do that on a horse without pushing them faster than a trot."

"Whatever you say, Marse."

"Okay, let's stay here in the station for twenty-four hours. If we don't get on a rail car, I will buy two horses."

As usual, my thoughts turned to Sarah. There was a pressing urgency in the back of my mind about her. She would have come to full term with her baby. The nagging comment of Doctor Stiles, expressing a concern about her, persisted in creating an on-going anxiety for me. It made one thing certain about the future. I would never allow her to be separated from me again.

Gazing about the great room, I saw a panorama of change. Men who were farmers were now soldiers, and some were already missing arms or legs. Women who had been wives were now widows, or caretakers of crippled men. People of dark skin were tentatively seeking hope, uncertain about how and when it would come. All were cast together, and all were a part of the greatest tragedy of our nation. It was the time of a low tide in America, and a deepening despair would evolve before a healing could begin.

Thirty minutes after I had become a part of the ticket line, the man behind the counter vacated his position. It meant he was through for the day. None of the people in the line moved, and it told me that they would hold on to their positions until the man returned in the morning.

I thought about the people who were caught in the drama in the room and others like them scattered throughout the South. Regardless of how they felt about having slaves, they were becoming hardened and more determined, and they were willing to accept great sufferings and hardships in support of the cause. The majority had been considerate and kind to the slaves. Some of the blacks even became like family members, but the great tragedy had occurred when they had mistakenly believed that holding another human being in bondage was acceptable.

After all, as they had assumed, slavery had been in existence for thousands of years going back to biblical times, so what could be wrong with it? It did not originate in the South. Now, people from the outside, people who would force them to makes changes and destroy their homes and farms were engendering fear and hatred in the people of the South.

This would cause the people to become more unified and more determined that it would not happen. Even so, freedom of the slaves would happen. And the end result would be just. Not the death nor the suffering, but no man should be held as a slave. Mister Lincoln was right. It was only the painful process of accomplishing a very difficult task that would divide the people and cause a great misery that would undoubtedly be in existence for many generations.

I had to decide whether I would stay put in the line until morning. To leave would set me back at least a day, possibly two, in getting up to the counter. I whispered quietly to Malcolm.

"I'm not sure what I should do. If I leave this line, we will be here much longer, and we might be stuck here in Richmond for three or four days. What do you think?"

"I think you are right. What about the document you have, would it help you?"

"If I could get to the right person. But showing it to the man at the counter might just create a problem, he might call in somebody who would want to investigate us. After thinking about it, I'm not sure it is a good thing to do."

"Yes, I agree. Why don't you stay in line and let me talk to some of the other blacks who are working here? Maybe I can learn something that will help us."

"A good idea. But be careful, and be sure you stay where I can see you at all times."

"Okay, I will. And will you promise me one thing?"

"What?"

"Don't pull out that big revolver." And a wide grin spread across his face.

He walked away. I did as the others in the line and sat down on our bags. I needed all of the patience I could muster. Waiting with uncertainty was very frustrating. The man ahead of me, who was also sitting, turned and began a conversation.

"Well, looks like we will be here for a while."

"Yes, so it does. Are you traveling alone?"

"Yes. I'm returning to Alabama."

"Have you been visiting relatives?"

He looked down, and I realized that I had asked him the wrong question. I was about to change to something else when he answered.

"You might say that. I came to say goodbye to my son. He was killed at Gettysburg."

"Oh, I'm very sorry, sir. I should not have asked you the question."

"It's all right. In a way I want to talk about him. He was a fine boy. Just eighteen."

"That's too bad. Were you able to find out what you wanted to know?"

"Yes. I talked to a soldier who was with him. He said that my son was most likely buried near the battlefield. I would like to tell you about him if you would like to hear."

"Yes, sir, I surely would like to hear."

"He was in the unit that charged Little Round Top on the second day. They made several charges up a steep hill and were thrown back each time. They had marched hard to get there and were not as well rested as they might have been normally, but they pushed on up that rocky ground anyway, trying to reach the Yankees who were holding on to the top of the hill. Their commanding officer told them that the hill was very important. They needed it to control artillery fire over the fields below where the main battle was shaping up for the next day. So our Alabama boys kept it up, kept going back again and again. But those Yankees were just as stubborn, and they were on the top and didn't have to put as much effort into climbing up for the fight, and they were able to hold on. Finally our boys just played out, and it was all over."

"I'm very sorry, sir."

"Yes, so am I. He was a good boy. I am proud of him, and what he tried to do. We have no slaves, and I don't pretend to know if slavery is right or wrong."

And he looked me straight in the eyes. "I can only be certain of one thing. I will always know that my son had the courage to give his life for his country."

He had become slightly emotional, and I didn't speak. He clearly represented the unyielding resolve that had become a part of every Southern heart. They would not give in or surrender, and the North would have to shed a great deal of blood to subdue them. Whether they were right or wrong, they were setting an example of valor unlike anything that was known about wars from previous ages. History might record them as people who fought for the wrong cause, but in no sense would any person in the future be able to question the great courage of the people of the South.

About an hour later, I saw Malcolm coming in my direction and his expression told me he had good news. I stood to make it easier for him to speak to me in a way that would not be conspicuous. His voice reflected an eagerness as he spoke.

"There is a military shipment leaving for Petersburg in about two hours. I think there is a good chance we can get on one of the rail cars."

"Where is it?"

"Out in the back. There are some officers there. I believe your papers will work with them."

"Okay, let's go."

Malcolm told me which direction to take, and we walked out of the depot. We crossed several tracks and approached some rail cars where there was considerable activity. I could see soldiers and many blacks who seemed to be loading boxes into the freight cars. When we were within about one hundred feet of them, a corporal in a Confederate uniform stepped in front of us and gave a command.

"Halt!"

We stopped, and he spoke again.

"Who are you, mister? You are in a restricted area."

"I am Alexander Fairfield. I am working for the Confederate States of America."

"Stand where you are, and I will send for an officer."

We did as we were told, and a second soldier moved away immediately. Within five minutes he returned with not only a major, but also two captains. The major spoke.

"Your name is Fairfield?"

"Yes."

"You are in a highly restricted area, Mister Fairfield. I hope you can give a good explanation for being here."

"I can. Will you allow me, sir, to withdraw my papers?"

"Yes, of course."

I reached into the pocket of my coat and brought out the document that had originated in the office of President Jefferson Davis, and handed it to the major. He looked at it carefully, turned and took several steps away. The other two officers followed, and all three considered the information on the document. Then they had a quiet discussion that lasted about five minutes. At that time they turned and walked back to face me. The major spoke.

"Why is the black man with you?"

"To create an image. I will be traveling, and later working, as a gentleman with a manservant."

"What is your destination?"

"Atlanta."

"These cars are not going to Atlanta. From Petersburg we will go to Chattanooga, and from there we will continue on to the west."

"Would we be able to go as far as Chattanooga?"

He thought about it and conferred quietly once again with the other two officers. Finally they were in agreement, and he turned to me.

"Sir, your papers seem to be in order. You can travel with us. We are moving supplies to Corinth, Mississippi, and you will be able to go as far as Chattanooga. You will have to find a place in one of the cars where there is room. There will be two armed soldiers in each car, and you will take orders from them. At Chattanooga you will leave the car and be on your own. You will be provided with rations during the trip. Do you understand and agree to these instructions?"

"Yes. And I appreciate your assistance, major."

"Very good. I will write out authorization for you to be in a car with your black man. Now, I suggest you go and try to find an available space."

We did as he said. The soldiers who were near the cars where we were standing with the major had seen us talking to him, and they were courteous and helpful. We were told to go to a specific car, and found there was room for us there. We climbed aboard and were all set for the trip. There was hay on the floor where there were open spaces, and I felt it was left there by previous riders. I jokingly made a quiet remark to Malcolm.

"Looks like we are going on an old-fashioned hay ride."

"What's an old-fashioned hay ride?"

"Oh, it was something we did when we were young. We would hitch up a wagon and fill the back with hay, and then we would take the girls for a ride."

"I bet that was some ride. What did Mama say when you got back home?"

"Not too much. She had the same kind of ride when she was young."

I tried to calculate in my mind how long the trip to Chattanooga would take. I didn't know how many rail miles we would be going, but if what I had been told was true, that some locomotives only averaged ten-miles-an-hour, we were most likely in for a ride of some thirty-five or forty hours.

After we were under way, I estimated that our locomotive was moving faster than the speed I had projected. The supplies in the cars were probably urgently needed in Mississippi. I noticed that when we passed the sidings used by oncoming locomotives, we were always allowed to pass and never had to wait.

The only stops we made were for new supplies of wood needed for the steam engine. Otherwise we moved along well, many times exceeding the ten mile per hour speed. There were no unusual incidents, and the two young soldiers in the car with us were cooperative. I had the feeling that they had been instructed beforehand by one of the officers to treat us with respect.

We arrived in Chattanooga at ten on a Sunday morning. We departed the car, thanked the two soldiers, and walked into the depot. It was almost empty, and was quite a contrast to the scene in the station in Richmond. I immediately felt good, believing that we would be able to get on a southbound car easily.

My assumption was correct, and when the attendant returned to his window at one o'clock, he told me that seats were available for passengers going to Atlanta. He said it was a night time trip for a locomotive pulling eight cars, leaving Chattanooga at eight in the evening and arriving in Atlanta at ten the next morning. He said it would be permissible for Malcolm to remain in the waiting room of the depot unless a large number of men and women should come in. In that case he would have to move into the baggage room next door. And he was very adamant in his instructions: Malcolm was to take leave of the room at the sight of the first lady. It was not an entirely new attitude although it was expressed a little more forcefully.

Oddly enough, the station remained empty through the early afternoon hours. I believed it to be for two reasons. People preferred not to travel on Sundays. Also, the worst part of the war was not yet nearby, it was in the north, far enough removed to not cause an uprooting of the people.

Late in the afternoon, a man came in who was being assisted by two other men. All three were wearing Confederate army uniforms. The man being assisted looked gaunt, and was barely able to walk, even with the two other men assisting him on each side. He was helped to a seat and then one of the two men walked over to the ticket counter. I could hear part of his conversation with the attendant, enough to learn that the frail looking man who was being assisted had some sort of travel permit that would allow him to have a seat on a rail car. The man behind the counter suddenly raised his hand and pointed to me, and then to Malcolm. Following that the Confederate soldier came in my direction, and when he was near he spoke.

"Sir, we need your help. The man we brought in wants to travel south on the same cars you are planning to be on. He was wounded at Gettysburg and is going home to Marietta, Georgia. He arrived here on a car three days ago, too weak to go on, and he had to be brought to our encampment. He believes he can travel now but will need some assistance. Will you be kind enough to help him?"

"Yes, I will help him."

"Very good. I know he will appreciate that, sir. Can you come with me now and take over with him?"

"Yes."

I got up and walked with the soldier to the seat where the man was resting. His name was Ed. At close range I could see that he was in a bad condition. I wondered if he could actually travel and asked him about it.

"Sir, are you sure you can travel?"

"Yes . . . I believe I can make it. If I have trouble I will get off of the car at one of the stops. The people have been good to help me along the way."

"I am going to Atlanta, and I can help you get to Marietta. If you have no objection, my darkie will help also."

"Oh, no, I have no objection. I never had a problem with a darkie in the first place."

"Will someone be there to meet you?"

"Yes, my wife. She has been advised that I am on the way home. She will come to the station when I get there."

I turned to the two soldiers and told them that I would be able to take over. I wanted to know more about Ed before they left, and I questioned the Confederate soldier who had spoken to me earlier.

"Was he wounded in a battle?"

"Yes, sir. Gettysburg. He was hit in two places, but I think the blast of a cannon did the most damage."

"Did he describe it to you?"

"Yes, sir. He said on the third day, when the big charge took place, he made it to within twenty yards of the Yankee lines, and then a cannon was fired directly into his line of men. Two pieces of the canister shot hit him causing flesh wounds. But it was the concussion of the cannon that put him down. He said he was unconscious for a while, and when he woke up everything was over. His friends were either on the ground or gone. The ones still alive were most likely herded off as prisoners. He said three Yankees came up and stood over him, and he asked them for water. They gave him some water and then one of them said, 'Why don't you go on back, old timer?' He said the three of them helped him up and turned him back toward the field he had just come across and let him go."

"That's amazing. I guess there must be some good Yankees after all."

"Yes, sir. Well, he's fifty-one years old, and they could see that he wouldn't give them any more trouble. And I think they already had all of the prisoners they wanted anyway."

"Okay, Corporal, we will take over now. Thank you for helping him. I think he deserved it."

"Yes, sir, I agree." Then, he and the other soldier walked away.

The station master came by and visited with us. He said that his wife was sending some food over and it would be there at five-thirty. He was gracious in his remarks, and said it would be fine for Malcolm to remain in the waiting room.

At seven-thirty, a man who worked in the station came in and announced that boarding of the cars could begin. Ed had been asleep for about an hour, and I gently aroused him to let him know it was time to leave. A few other people had arrived, and they all stood back and watched as Malcolm and I lifted Ed by holding his upper arms on each side and walked with him in the direction of the rail cars on the outside.

Two young men picked up our bags, and they came along behind us. The people stood quietly as we passed among them, paying their respect to Ed. He had come home, and he was among his own. He was being honored as their hero, a man they looked upon with pride, a soldier who had served his country well.

After the locomotive was on its way, Ed seemed to liven up. He realized, of course, that he was on the last leg of his journey. He appeared to be anxious to talk, and I listened as he told me about his family and other things connected to his background. Eventually he got around to discussing the war.

"I was at Chancellorsville in General Jackson's army. We could hardly believe it when we heard he was down. He was truly one of the best, and it was said that he was responsible for contributing to many of the decisions that were made by General Lee. He had an amazing way about him; it was almost like he knew ahead of time what was going to happen."

"Yes, sir, I have heard the same thing from others. But, if I may ask, do you mind talking about Gettysburg and what happened there?"

"No, I don't mind. We had been fighting for two days. On the third of July, which was also the third day of the battle, we knew it was going to be settled. It was hot that day, and we stayed back in the woods for most of the morning. Our boys were ready and anxious to go. The Yankees knew we were forming up and that we would be coming soon. Early in the afternoon, Colonel Alexander opened up with his artillery. You never heard such a roar, and it lasted about an hour. By then there was a line of our men for as far as you could see. The boys were whooping and hollering, and raring to go. I was in a unit on the far right, and the officers said that we would oblique to the left as we approached the Yankee line. It would put a large number of our men at the weakest place in the Yankee position."

He paused, seemingly to reflect on what he had described. I didn't know if he wanted to continue because he was coming to the most difficult part of the battle, so I remained silent. Finally, he spoke. "It was their artillery. We didn't expect it. Almost from the time we reached the first rise, they poured heavy fire on us. Even so, our line never broke, and we had to cover about a mile to get to them. Only a few made it, and as I walked back I saw thousands of our boys dead or dying. I made it back to the woods and collapsed. When I woke, quite a while had passed."

I didn't comment and waited to see if he wanted to continue, finally he did.

"You know, Mister Fairfield, I almost died. Canister shot hit me in the arm and leg, but thankfully the injuries were not bad. I realized I couldn't catch up with 'Uncle Bobby' and what was left of his army, and I didn't try. I knew he had to get them away from there, back across a river somewhere before the Yankees decided to come after him. I walked as best I could back the way we had come, and even though my wounds were no longer bleeding, I couldn't go very far, so I just decided to lay down on the side of the road. I was so weak and tired that I just didn't care."

"What happened?"

"A farm couple, Pennsylvania people, took me in and helped me. They saved my life. I had lost a lot of blood, and the wounds were still bleeding at times."

"Sounds like you just happened to be at the right place at the right time."

"Yes. You are right. They gave me nourishment and treated my wounds. I stayed with them for about eight or ten days. I had a lot of time to think while I was there. And I had some good talks with the people who were helping me. One day the missis asked me why I was fighting for slavery, and I told her that I was not fighting for slavery. I had no slaves, and she said, 'Well, God has spared you for a reason and you must lay down your arms and go home and try to do good things for others for as long as you live,' and that is what I intend to do, Mister Fairfield."

Thirty miles south of Chattanooga the locomotive stopped the cars for a short while for the "convenience of the passengers." Ed was asleep. I asked Malcolm to accompany me to the outside of the car to talk. I had a thought that I wanted to discuss.

"I think we should leave the rail car at Marietta. It will be just about as easy to get to Roswell from there as it would be from Atlanta. What do you think?"

"It makes sense. Have you thought about what you are going to do, how you will handle things with DeAngelo?"

"I am going there to get Sarah. I don't know how or when because I don't know what has happened about her baby. I know she wants to leave him, and I am going there to take her."

"She is still his wife."

"I have a document drawn up by Phillip that makes her marriage to him null and void."

"Is it good here in the State of Georgia?"

"As far as I am concerned, it is good anywhere."

"Where will you take her? Were you serious about Canada?"

"If she wants to go there, yes, we can go to Canada."

# XII.

We arrived in Marietta the next morning on schedule. It was eight o'clock. There was to be a one hour stopover that was needed to replenish the supply of wood for the steam engine of the locomotive. It made no difference to us, of course, because we had decided that we were at our final destination. I was tired, as was Malcolm. Ed was the only one who had slept, and he was able to do so only because he was so exhausted when he got on the rail car in Chattanooga.

We helped Ed get out and into the depot. Malcolm went back into the rail car and brought out our possessions. Ed spoke to Malcolm and me.

"Thank you. It would have taken much longer if you had not helped me." Then he surprised me. He reached out to Malcolm first to shake hands. It was, I believe, symbolic of his changed feelings and his plans for the future. Malcolm realized what was taking place and a happy look came over his face. In a pleased manner of speaking, he addressed the man who was still wearing a Confederate uniform.

"Good luck to you, Mister Ed."

"And good luck to you, Malcolm. I am very grateful for your help." Then he turned to me. "And, my thanks to you as well, Mister Fairfield. I don't know what your mission might be, but I hope you are successful."

By then other people had come up and gathered around Ed. They knew who he was, what he had done, and where he had been, and remarks of praise were beginning to flow freely. I motioned to Malcolm, and we moved away. We had delivered Ed back to his people and it was time to take care of our own affairs. But, we needed rest before heading for Roswell. I told Malcolm.

"I think we need some sleep before we do anything else. I will see if I can find a place where we can rest."

He was agreeable. There was a hotel adjacent to the depot, and we walked to the entrance. Remembering where we were once again, I asked Malcolm to wait outside. At the desk on the inside was an older man, possibly in his sixties, and my instincts told me that he was most likely the owner. He did not set forth an engaging manner as he spoke.

"What can I do for you?"

"I am looking for a room for one night. Also, I need accommodations for my manservant."

"I can provide you a room and bed."

"How about the black man who is with me?"

"He will have to stay in a different location. I can place him in the care of a negro man who is my employee."

It seemed to be all right, and it was settled. The man behind the counter told me to come back in an hour. He would have arrangements completed for both Malcolm and me. In response to my question, he told me that a livery stable was close by, and I felt we could make good use of the time we were to wait by going there and renting horses for the ride to Roswell the next day.

I found a friendly man at the stable who told me as we talked that he owned another stable in Alpharetta, a small community several miles north of Roswell. He said I could return the horses there if I should so desire. He also told me there were three hotels in Alpharetta. My plans to reach the home of Sarah were finally becoming a reality.

Early Tuesday morning Malcolm returned to the hotel from the home where he had spent the night, and we were ready for the ride to Roswell. At the livery stable the horses were saddled and ready, and by nine o'clock we were mounted and on our way. I had been thinking about Sarah, and there was one aspect of her situation that I was not sure about. I mentioned it to Malcolm.

"When we get there… there is one thing that concerns me."

"You concerned? Why, Marse, I didn't know you ever got concerned." He grinned.

"Well, now you know." I smiled back at him. "It involves the legal rights of a married woman."

"What about her legal rights?"

"She doesn't have any. Everything is in the hands of her husband."

"How do you know that?"

"By talking to Phillip. After she was taken last fall her father came to Washington, and we went to see Phillip and he warned us about every conceivable thing that could go wrong. So we told him to go ahead and prepare documents to protect her assets, which was done. Sarah's father and Phillip are the guardians of her trusts. Of course, we didn't know at the time that she would end up being married. Even though her assets are still protected, it seems that women have very few rights in a court, in fact, a woman normally does not even become involved in legal matters."

"So what are you concerned about?"

"When Sarah married DeAngelo, she gave up just about all of her rights to him. He knows that, and he will try to use it. Fortunately, the trusts in Washington are still protected, so he can't touch her assets there. But everything else, including her marriage, will be decided by Georgia laws."

"You've got the papers stating that she was taken against her will."

"And I think that would have worked if she hadn't married him."

"Why did she do that, marry the man?"

"She said she was desperate. She was going to have a baby, and she was in a hopeless situation. Being alone and having so many needs that she could not possibly handle was just too much. She said she finally gave up and reluctantly decided that she had no other choice and agreed to marry him. She thought it was something that could be dissolved later."

"And she had all this trouble even though the baby was not her idea?"

"Yes. Women are more easily affected by things like that. She told me that she didn't know if she would ever be able to get away from DeAngelo anyway."

"So now you feel like he might have an advantage with the local authorities?"

"He might. It depends on how a local solicitor would consider it. But, based on what Phillip told me, I'm not sure she would even have a chance to tell her story in front of a judge, or whoever might make a decision. I first thought that I would just take her and run. Now, I have decided that would not be best. Getting her on a rail car, or traveling with her by any means would be very difficult, and I doubt that I would be able to get away with her."

"Yes, I think you are right. Is there any way you can bluff him?"

"I've thought about that, and so far I haven't been able to come up with anything. He has been thinking, too, you know, and he probably has made some plans of his own."

"How about money, can you give him money?"

"No. I offered him money in Washington for other reasons, and he had no interest. I think he already has plenty of money."

It was a hot day, so we didn't push the horses. My thoughts were concentrated on Sarah, and with nearly every turn in the road my anxiety seemed to build. I had received no response from Dabney after sending four telegrams. Was he reluctant to give me bad news? And, foremost in my mind were the comments of Doctor Stiles and his concern about the condition of Sarah. I was at a point that I almost dreaded what to expect when the time would come for me to walk up to the door of her home. Malcolm noticed.

"Are you worried, Alexander?"

"Yes, I am. Knowing she was ill the last time we were there and not having any further news since then makes it hard to deal with."

"I know. I've been watching you for a long time now, and I know you pretty well. I know what she means to you."

"I can give up a farm. I can give up money. Those things are like being in a poker game. But the only thing I cannot give up is Sarah. Nothing could ever replace her."

"You won't have to give her up. We can handle it."

I looked around at him and smiled.

"I am glad you are with me, Malcolm."

"It's good for me, too. I was lucky you were standing on that portico the day the bounty hunters were after me."

"So am I. We've both been down some dangerous roads. Maybe we can make it again."

"We will." He spoke in a confident way, not in a manner that was artificial.

At one o'clock we had reached the bottom of a long hill in the road ahead. We stopped under the shade of some trees next to the road to give the horses a rest. Malcolm spoke.

"When we get to the top of that hill and make a right turn, we will be about three minutes from her house. She's going to be there and everything will be fine. I know it is going to happen."

"I hope you are right. When we get there, let's ride to the back of the house and wait under the trees for a few minutes. Maybe Lula will see us and come out."

Malcolm's keen sense of perception was at work as he responded.

"I think you are dreading the very first few words you are going to hear. I can understand that. Okay, let's do it your way and see if somebody comes out."

And very shortly thereafter we did exactly as I had suggested. We dismounted under the trees and tied the reins of our horses to a post. Then, we stood watching the back door of the house.

Within two minutes, Lula came out with a broad smile on her face.

"Law have mercy! Mista Alex! I sho' am glad to see you!"

I moved forward to meet her and spoke at the same time.

"Is she all right?"

"She's fine, Mista Alex, just fine. But she sho' does need somebody like you."

"She had the baby?"

Her expression changed some as she spoke.

"Yes sir, she had the baby. But it aint here." And she paused as if she might not know how to continue.

"What do you mean, Lula?"

"It was stillborn, sir, and she had to give it up."

I was shocked and it took me a moment to respond.

"Oh, I'm sorry to hear that. But is she all right?"

"She is all right except in her mind. She cried all day after the baby came, and since then she don't want to eat nothing, or come out of her room. But she sho' is going to be happy to see you. I think that was what was wrong with her. She just didn't know if you would ever be back."

"Thank God she is all right. I can't begin to tell you how I have worried. Did she get my letter?"

"No sir, she ain't got no letter from you. She didn't know what happened to you."

"That's terrible. I had explained everything to her in the letter. When did the baby come?"

"About seven or eight days ago. It was a little early."

"Where is she now?"

"Upstairs in her room. She takes a nap about this time every day."

"Where is the . . . Mister DeAngelo?"

"He gone. Been gone for two days. He don't tell her nothing 'bout where he is going but I have done found out. He gone to Savannah."

"How do you know?"

"Uncle Shad. He drove the master in a buggy to the railroad station in Atlanta and put his traveling bags on the car that was going to Savannah. I told Miss Sarah and she say she is not surprised."

I wondered why he would leave Sarah, knowing that she might try to get away. I asked Lula.

"Oh, he ain't worried about that, he knows she can't go no place right now. She can't travel, Mista Alex. Doctor Stiles say she has to rest in bed."

"Yes, that explains it. Well, I'm very anxious to see her. But I know she needs rest, so Malcolm and I will ride on up the road a ways and make arrangements for a place to stay, and then we will come back. It should be about two hours from now."

"That will be fine, Mista Alex, and she sho is gon' be happy. I can't wait to tell her."

"Thank you, Lula. I know you mean a lot to her."

"She's my baby, Mista Alex."

Malcolm and I grinned at each other and prepared to leave. After we were mounted I could tell that he was eager to say something, and I looked at him in a quizzical way.

"What?"

"Didn't I tell you?"

"Yes, you did. And you want to know something?"

"Yes, tell me something."

"I believed you."

We pushed our horses some as we rode north to Alpharetta. We found a hotel and the situation was similar to what we had found in Marietta. I was given a room in the hotel, and Malcolm was told how to find a black family who would put him up as a roomer. In my room I bathed and put on a clean shirt and trousers. At three I went down to meet Malcolm, and he was there, at the prearranged time, on the outside with our horses. I was excited and in high spirits, and Malcolm noticed.

"You look like a new man, Marse, and I don't just mean your clothes."

"I feel like a new man, Malcolm. It's like a new life has just started for me."

He grinned. We mounted up and headed south toward Roswell. Twenty-five minutes later we were tying our horses to the hitching post in the rear of Sarah's house. I was turned in a direction away from the house when I heard a familiar voice.

"Alex!"

I knew it was Sarah, and I turned quickly. She had seen us from the inside of the house and had come out the back door. She came down the steps, moving carefully, and I walked forward hurriedly to meet her. She was beaming, and I was smiling too. We met in the middle of the back yard, and each of us eagerly reached for the other. She put her arms around my neck, and I reached around her upper body and we held on tightly. We were both too emotional to make a sound, and it seemed to be the most wonderful moment I could imagine. To have her again, to hold her, and to know that she was safe were all of the things I had so desperately been hoping for. Even though I had just learned about the tragic loss of her baby, the joy of holding her was foremost in my mind for the moment.

I pulled her close, rubbing my face against hers, and I could not turn loose. It was the same for her, I could feel it in the way she was holding on and pressing against me. And then we were kissing. Neither of us could hold back as we continued to pour our hearts into the touching of our lips and bodies. Our love was overflowing, and it was the fulfillment of dreams that were long awaited. Finally we pulled apart, and I looked at her. She was even more beautiful than I had imagined. She was smiling, and she was finally able to speak.

"Alex, I can't begin to tell you how wonderful it is to see you."

"And it is the same for me, Sarah, it seems I have been longing for this moment forever."

She reached down and took my hand and guided us toward the house. Then she remembered something and turned back.

"Oh, Malcolm, please come with us. And please forgive me, I forgot to greet you."

He smiled.

"Don't worry about it, Miss Sarah, I think you might have been thinking about some other things."

She laughed.

"Yes, I was. But please come inside where you will be more comfortable. Lula can fix some tea or lemonade for you."

She turned again to look at me, smiling in a way that described her happiness. I held her arm as we climbed the five steps up to the back veranda. Lula was waiting there, grinning, and spoke to Sarah.

"Now you take Mista Alex right on in to the parlor, and I will bring in some lemonade. You gon' have to sit and rest yoself. You don't need to get wore out."

Sarah was still smiling broadly.

"Okay, but I don't think I will get to be worn out on this day."

In the parlor Sarah guided us to a long couch that had a velvet-like surface. We were still holding hands, and even as we sat down she didn't take her hand away. It was as if she was afraid that I would suddenly be gone again. After we were settled she looked into my eyes.

"Alex, we have so much to talk about."

"Do you want to talk about the baby?"

I couldn't judge her reaction too well as she answered.

"Yes, I think so. Now that you are here it makes everything different. When it was born and Doctor Stiles told me it was stillborn, I cried in a way that was almost hysterical. I couldn't stop. I had nothing to hold on to, or anyone to give me the comfort

I needed. Since that time, it has been a real problem for me. You could not have come at a better time."

"I'm glad. Maybe the worst is over. I wrote you a letter but Lula said that you didn't get it."

"No, I didn't get it. I was heartsick when you didn't come back. I knew something had happened to you and that just made it worse."

"I was commanded by Confederate troops to return to Washington. They refused to let me come and tell you. I left the letter with the commanding officer, but I suppose he never mailed it."

"Either that or it was intercepted."

I had not considered that and had somehow overlooked it. I thought of DeAngelo.

"Where is Michael?"

"Savannah. Lula found out from Uncle Shad that he drove Michael to the rail station in Atlanta and put his bags in a car that was bound for Savannah. I think he is trying to buy passage on a ship."

"Do you know where he plans to go?"

"No. He doesn't tell me anything. Lula finds out things about him . . .he has been careless a few times . . .and I believe he intends to take me out of the country."

"We will stop that. Don't worry about it, I'm not leaving here again without you."

She reached over and kissed me, and I was able to hold her briefly once again before she leaned back and spoke.

"Alex, there is something I want you to know. I wanted to tell you before when you were here but we had such a short time together I never did have the chance." She paused as if to gather her thoughts, and continued. "First of all, let me explain about the marriage. When I realized that I was going to have a baby, I knew that I needed to be settled somewhere and be under the care of a doctor. By then I was convinced that Michael was determined to keep me with him. He brought me here, and it was like I was halfway around the world from Washington. After that first week in Baltimore . . . when he forced me . . . when the baby was conceived, he became a different man. Even though I hated him, I will have to admit that he was as kind and considerate as any man could be to a woman. It didn't mean that my feelings changed about him, it just meant that he was no longer a beast. Do you want to ask me anything so far?"

"No. And Sarah, please understand that you don't have to tell me this story."

"I want to tell you, it's important to me."

"Okay, tell me as much as you want me to know."

"I told him I was going to have his baby, and he actually seemed happy. He said he would like to marry me, and I think he thought the baby would convince me that it was the best thing for me to do. He was right. I thought that it would be wrong to bring a baby into the world without a father or a proper name, and so I agreed. At the time I believed that I could somehow become separated later, or get a divorce. That was the main reason I made the decision to marry him." She paused to let me respond, which I did.

"When you told me about it, and after I had time to think about it, I was certain that you did it for the reasons you have told me, and it was so frustrating, not being here during that time to help you."

"When I decided to go through with a marriage, I had reached a point where I believed that you would never be able to find me because he plans so well. Like having me write you the letter and having it mailed from Canada."

"It did fool me. I made plans to go there to look for you. But, as always, people make mistakes, and I found out it was a ploy."

"Let me finish, Alex, because there is one thing I want you to know. In Baltimore, after the first week he kept me there, he changed, becoming much more considerate, and actually, an entirely different kind of man. He has not been in bed with me since then. He said it would only happen in the future, with my permission."

She stared into my eyes with a sweet expression. I could tell that she felt a great sense of relief and that a long lasting burden had just been lifted.

"Thank you for telling me. I know this is very important to you, letting me know. I appreciate it very much."

"You're right, it does mean a lot to me. And you made it easy for me to tell you." Staring into my eyes with a sweet expression, she continued. "You do know that my love for you has never changed, don't you?"

"Yes, I do know, but it's nice to hear it again."

Lula came in and brought lemonade and cookies. She sat down on the edge of a chair and looked at Sarah as she spoke.

"My, my, I don't believe I have seen such a happy face in a long time."

We both laughed. I thought it might be a good time to tease Lula.

"Now Lula, I better warn you again about Malcolm. He's a dangerous man around women."

She laughed hard as she stood to leave.

"Aw, Mista Alex, you just carrying on. He ain't no dangerous man."

After she left the room, I turned to a more serious subject.

"How long will Michael be gone?"

"I'm not sure. I know he must be in Savannah to try to work something out for a sea voyage, but it will be difficult because of the blockade of the ports. He might have to go on to Charleston. In either case, it won't be easy, and it will take him a while."

"And when he has everything worked out, he will come back for you?"

"Yes, I am sure that is what he is planning."

"Well, that will never happen. But it does mean that I have to go to work in a hurry. I will contact a lawyer in Marietta tomorrow. We will need some sort of order to prevent him from taking you out of the country."

"Why Marietta?"

"Because it is the central office for this district, which includes Roswell."

"What can you say, or do?"

"I'm not sure. You mentioned a divorce and maybe that is a possibility, although it could be risky."

"Why?"

"According to Phillip, a woman is rarely seen or heard in a courtroom, and Michael would be in control of things. He might be able to stop it."

"But I know there are divorces. I heard about several in Washington."

"Yes, that's right. I will just have to get more details and be guided by a lawyer." I looked around at her. "But let's don't worry about it today."

She agreed, and began telling me other things, details of her life during the time she had been with DeAngelo. Finally she mentioned the baby.

"At first I was completely mortified. I thought that I could never face my family and friends again, even though it was not done with my consent. But then I realized that I was only thinking about myself, and that was wrong. God had created what was to be a human being, and he had chosen me to bring it into the world. It changed me. I can't say that I was ever thrilled about it, but I did think of it differently, and I accepted it."

"Do you know what happened, why it was stillborn?"

"No. Doctor Stiles said afterwards that in the last trimester the baby seemed to be less active, and possibly the heartbeat was not quite as distinct. He said that he could not determine a reason, and that he felt that we did nothing wrong. He says that stillborn babies are a mystery to doctors in nearly all cases."

I thought about DeAngelo and what we had discovered, the packets of a granular substance that he had been receiving in Marietta that had a chocolate smell. I also thought about what we had been told by Lula, that he would sometimes take hot chocolate up to Sarah on certain days. Did it mean that he had given her something that was wrong for the baby? We would never know, there would be no way to prove it. I decided that I would not tell Sarah; it would accomplish nothing and might upset her. There had been a pause in our discussion, and she suddenly turned toward me with a rather excited expression.

"You know where I would like to go?"

"Where?"

"South Carolina. Back home. I might like to stay there. How would you like to live in South Carolina?"

"I would like to be anywhere with you."

She really seemed to mean it.

"You could have a horse farm. And Malcolm and Lula could go with us."

I smiled at her.

"How long will it take you to pack your things?"

She laughed.

"I can be ready in about thirty minutes."

# XIII.

In the late afternoon, Lula came in and told us she had a meal prepared, and we should go directly to the dining room. She said that her food was the favorite of the people who lived in Roswell and that it would give us "Yankees" from Washington a taste of real Southern delights. And it was good. She had baked chicken with seasoned rice, field peas, potatoes, and corn. She was a marvelous cook, and everything was delicious. Sarah and I both ate heartily, and Lula could not have been more pleased.

After we had finished the meal, Sarah and I walked through the house to the outside. The heat had subsided, and we decided to take a stroll through the back grounds. Sarah was not wearing one of the large hoop dresses and consequently was not burdened by the extra weight that was a part of that type of dress. I commented on it.

"I'm glad to see that you don't have on one of those heavy hoop dresses. I've heard that they add about ten pounds when you wear them."

"You're right. I don't know how they ever got started. I just want to be comfortable. I don't care about being stylish, at least when I am at home."

"When we get to South Carolina you can wear anything you want to, and it will be fine with me."

"Do you really think it can happen, Alex? Even when I am free from Michael, we will still have the war to worry about."

"Yes, and I'm afraid the war is not going to turn out well for the South. We've probably got some troubling times ahead of us."

"What will happen to the people if we lose?"

"I guess nobody knows at this point. In addition to the whites who will have problems, there are over three million slaves scattered through the land. They will be free, but they will have no place to go. Washington is covered up with them now, and it is only a drop in the bucket."

"Will Malcolm stay with you?"

"Yes. He is a good and loyal friend. I will always take care of him."

"Maybe that will happen to others. Many people love their darkies, and I don't believe they will turn them out."

"Neither do I. The problem for both blacks and whites is that neither will have anything. Maybe the government will help. I have heard that President Lincoln does not hold a grudge, and most people feel that he will offer some kind of help."

"Do you think there is any chance at all that the South can win?"

"Oh, there is possibly a chance. But think about it. The Yankees are now in control of the Mississippi River, and they have closed off the ports with blockades. More importantly, they have the men and resources that the South does not have. The only thing left in the South is spirit and determination, and I don't know how far they can go with that."

"It is so sad. Just think of how things were two or three years ago. Will we ever see those days again?"

"Oh . . . maybe." I didn't want her to become too discouraged. "At least we can be together and that is the most important thing."

She turned and looked at me and smiled sweetly.

"Alex, can you stay here in the house with me tonight? We have plenty of room."

"I would love to stay, Sarah, but I would be concerned about how it would look."

"Nobody will know. Lula is the only other person who is here. She can prepare a place for Malcolm on the back veranda, it is nice there at night. It just scares me to death to think that you might leave like you did before and not come back."

I thought about it and wanted to stay. But I wanted to be sure that it would not cause a problem.

"Sarah, you know how much I would like to stay, my only reluctance is whether there is any possible way that Michael could find out about it."

"He won't. You can put your horses in our barn. There are no other homes close enough to give anyone an opportunity to see anything. Michael does not talk to the people who live nearby, anyway."

"Okay, we will stay. And I am really glad we will have more time together."

"Me, too!"

She was glowing with happiness. And it was understandable. It was the end of a very stressful and discouraging nine months for her. We sat in the wooden chairs under the great oak tree and continued our discussion. I asked a little more about Michael and the things that had happened just after he had taken her. I wanted to have as much information as possible before talking to a lawyer.

"When Michael brought you from Baltimore who did he have along to help him?"

"Two men. I don't know their names. He avoided using their names in my presence. I can describe them if that will help."

"Yes, it will help."

"One was young, maybe in his early twenties. The other one was older, probably mid-fifties. The young man was large, heavy through his upper body. He had dark eyes and hair, even a dark beard. He apparently left the rail car at a place called Big Shanty. The older man stayed with us until we arrived in Marietta. Both of the men seemed to be familiar with the area. Michael goes to Marietta often, and I think the older man might still be there."

"So you believe that Michael might still be in touch with the men?"

"He might be. Michael has plenty of money, and he has never told me how he got it. The two men who were with us as we traveled seem like the type to do things that might not be right. If Michael is involved in some sort of illegal business he would want to have them helping him. But I am only guessing, Alex, and I don't know anything about what Michael is doing. I just know what he did to me, and I think he would be capable of doing just about anything."

I didn't tell her what I knew about DeAngelo. I didn't want to scare her. Finally, I asked a question to confirm what she had already said.

"Are you sure you want to go ahead and file your petition for a divorce?"

"Yes! Absolutely! As soon as possible. Now that you are here to help me, I want to get it done."

"All right, I will talk to a lawyer about your intent and your request. As soon as papers can be drawn up, I believe a lawyer will have to come here for your signature. We have to be careful and be sure that the information you provide will be irrefutable. What will you state as the reason for wanting the divorce?"

"The whole thing. He forced me to go with him against my will; he forced me against my wishes to be with child. He is keeping me here in Georgia against my will."

"All of those things are true, but remember, he will be in the court and you most likely will not. He will deny all of those things."

"How can he do that and get away with it?"

"Because he is a man and the court recognizes him as the head of the household, and as such, he is given the authority to speak for you. What we need is something that will play on the sympathy of the judge, something he cannot dismiss."

"I don't know what it would be if I cannot be there."

"If we could somehow convince the court that he is trying to remove you from your home here in the South, it would have a big effect. He is from New York, and when that is pointed out, right now it could work against him. How can we do that?"

"We could say that he went to Savannah to book passage on a ship."

"He would deny it. He is so cunning he would most likely say that he was trying to buy supplies from the blockade runners for our boys fighting in Virginia. We will have to have tangible evidence. Where does he keep his papers?"

"I have no way of knowing anything about his papers or his personal affairs. Maybe he has a place in Marietta, and possibly he goes there for that reason."

She seemed to be getting tired, and I felt it was time to conclude our discussion about Michael.

"Don't worry about it, I'll take care of everything. Let's talk about our farm in South Carolina."

She smiled.

"Yes, we can start planning now. How many acres of land do you need for your horses?"

"About three hundred. I want plenty of pasture land."

We talked until ten o'clock, and then I suggested that she should go to bed. Lula had been out once, and Sarah had asked her to get the guest room ready for me and to prepare a place for Malcolm. I helped Sarah up from the chair, and we locked arms as we walked into the house. The guest room was downstairs, and Sarah walked with me into the room to be sure that everything was in order. Then I went with her to the bottom of the stairs where we stopped, and I held her again and kissed her softly on the lips. And then, as we were ready to part, she gazed contentedly into my eyes and spoke.

"This has been one of the happiest days of my life. Thank you for being here. Goodnight and sweet dreams."

"Good night. And Sarah, I love you."

She smiled and turned to go up the stairway.

Early the next morning, Malcolm and I were saddled up shortly after dawn and were under way to Marietta. Lula had left each of us a large piece of cornbread in the cupboard, and we ate it as we slow-walked our horses away from the house. In making general observations from the driveway, I decided that Sarah was right, it would be difficult for others in the surrounding houses to see us. After finishing the cornbread, we pushed the horses some, using the early morning coolness to cover as much distance as possible while the animals were fresh. By most accounts it was a four-hour ride from Roswell to Marietta, however, we hoped to make it in three.

We didn't miss our targeted time by very much, arriving on the outskirts of the city at ten o'clock. I had seen the courthouse when we had been there previously, and I knew where to go. Inside the building I began questioning the people who were working there, inquiring about whom they would recommend as a lawyer. After speaking to four different people, each of whom gave me four or five names, I found that one name was repeated in all discussions - James L. Burke. I was told that his office was only a few doors away. It took us only five minutes to walk there.

I went in alone and Malcolm stayed with the horses. At first glance in the office I almost decided to leave. Everything was in complete disorder. Books, files, papers, cardboard boxes, and various odds and ends were scattered all over the room. A man of about sixty was there, and was walking across the room holding a hand full of papers up not too far out in front of his face. He was talking quietly to himself, apparently reading from the papers.

He was slightly overweight. This was made more prominent as he was wearing an open vest. He was getting bald, and as was often done by men in such circumstances, the hair on the sides of his head had been left long to flow downward over his ears. His clothes matched his office, and I would guess that his attire had been gathered up and put together in a last minute rush with no effort to establish a fine look.

I stopped just inside the room and remained quiet, watching as he paced from one end of the room to the other. Finally, without looking up from the papers, he spoke.

"Yes?"

"Mister Burke?"

"Yes." He did not look up. He continued to walk and talk to himself.

"Sir, if you are busy I can come back later."

"No! No! State your business. That's the trouble, most people don't have the nerve to get something done."

"Mister Burke, I need help, and I am wondering if you might have the nerve to get something done for me?"

He stopped and looked at me, and then he smiled.

"Yes sir, I might. Why don't you sit down and tell me about your problem?"

I did. For twenty-five minutes I talked to him, leaving out nothing. I had decided to do that, hold nothing back, and trust that I could pick the right man. He listened patiently, and my instincts told me that he was indexing every detail into his mind. I began to realize that my critical assessment of him earlier was done in error; his appearance had nothing to do with his ability. When I finally paused he was thoughtful before speaking.

"You have a difficult case, Mister Fairfield. We need something that you have not yet been able to give me. Do you understand?"

"I believe so. We don't have enough hard evidence to win."

"Well, I wouldn't state it just that way. What I will say is that the odds are not in our favor."

"Are you willing to try?"

"Oh yes, yes, sir. But I want you to try to learn more about this man, DeAngelo. We have a couple of things in our favor. We've got a man from New York who is disrupting the life of a fine Southern lady. If we can just find a way to convey that to a judge, it will certainly go a long ways. The big problem, of course, is what your lawyer friend in Washington told you: she is not going to be able to come into the courtroom to counter what he says. It's just the way the law works, the husband is always in control."

"What is the next step?"

"I will have the petition prepared and let her sign it. I believe, and this I am not sure of, that we will then go before a judge and present the case. The judge will make a decision based on what he hears. A lot of short cuts are now being taken, Mister Fairfield, due to the war, and cases are decided quickly to get them out of the way."

"And she will not be allowed to come into the courtroom to make statements?"

"It is highly unlikely. I don't believe I have ever seen it in this kind of case. If it was a criminal case it would be different."

"When should I come back for the papers?"

"Ah, let's see, I have a young man who is very good with a pen. If I can start him today, he will be finished by tomorrow. Come back in two days."

"I'll be here. I can pay your fee whenever you wish to receive it. A draft will be drawn on a bank in St. Louis."

"Don't worry about the fee right now. Just get something for me on this man from New York."

Outside, Malcolm had walked across the street with the horses to a park where there were trees, and I went there. Water troughs were spaced about the park, and it offered the opportunity for the horses to become refreshed. When I was near to Malcolm, he spoke.

"How did it go?"

"All right. I think he is a good lawyer, and he will take the case. He wants to have more information about DeAngelo. It seems to be the key to our success. I will have to go to work on it immediately."

"How about Dabney? He had started an investigation of DeAngelo before we got shipped off to Washington. He might have something by now."

"That is a good possibility. I will send Dabney a telegram from the depot while we are here, and maybe he will respond this time."

We rode the short distance around the park to the depot. Inside, I sent a short message to John Dabney: "Critical that you investigate Michael DeAngelo who is now in Savannah attempting to arrange passage on a ship that will take him out of the country. Please acknowledge this message." Under my signature I put the name of the hotel in Alpharetta.

We found a mercantile store, and I bought crackers and some fresh, locally grown peaches. Then we headed back to Roswell. We walked the horses most of the way back and didn't arrive at Sarah's house until five-thirty.

After hitching our horses in the back, we were greeted by Sarah and Lula, and we all gathered on the back veranda for a few minutes of relaxation. Lula brought tea for us and, about fifteen minutes later, Sarah and I went into the parlor. I started at the beginning and described every detail of the events that had taken place during the day. I tried to make it sound encouraging to her, and it seemed to work.

"I think you are off to a good start, Alex. Don't you think so?"

"Yes, I believe so. And now, Sarah, there is something you have to consider. As soon as Michael returns he will be given a copy of your petition for a divorce. How do you think he will react?"

"Oh, he will be extremely upset and angry. I have been thinking about it, and I believe I should go ahead and move out of the house."

"So do I. Do you feel well enough to move?"

"Yes, I can move. I want to move, I hate this house."

"Good. We will get you out very soon."

We talked about various places she could go, considering locations that we felt would be safe and comfortable for her. I asked if Lula could go with her.

"No, unfortunately she cannot. She is still an owned slave. She is working here because her owner contracted with Michael for her services."

"If you want her to go with you, I will pay for her freedom. I will pay the owner, and the lawyer in Marietta can draw up the rest of the papers that are needed."

"Oh, that would be wonderful, Alex! I love her. She has been so good to me, and it would be easy for her to come because she has no family."

"Okay, I'll take care of it. Does it matter to you which city you are in while we are still here? I think you should get away from Roswell. How do you feel about living in Marietta until the divorce is settled?"

"Fine. I just want to be where you will be."

"And that is what I want. I will go back to Marietta in a day or so and start looking around at houses. In the meantime, I want you to be careful. If Michael should surprise us and come back early, let me know as quickly as possible."

"Yes . . . I will do that."

I could sense that I had most likely created some anxiety for her, so I wanted to reassure her.

"You won't have to worry about anything, Sarah, I will be close by at all times."

"I know you will, and it is certainly a good feeling."

Malcolm and I returned to Alpharetta later in the evening. I was very surprised to learn that a telegram had come from John Dabney. It was brief: "Received your message today and will comply with your request. Have excellent agent in location mentioned by you. I am investigating matter in another city but hope to return soon." It was good news.

On Friday I tracked down the man who owned slave rights to Lula, and I found him to be a reasonable person. And my good luck prevailed once again. There was a paragraph in the agreement he had with DeAngelo that gave the option to DeAngelo to buy

Lula for fifteen-hundred dollars. I paid him the money, leaving ownership in the name of DeAngelo. It allowed me to avoid becoming a slaveholder, and I was greatly relieved. I would take the document, which outlined the details of the sale, to James L. Burke in Marietta and leave the rest to him. Lula would soon be a free woman.

I made sure to stop by as often as possible to see Sarah. I not only wanted to be with her, I wanted to be sure that she was safe. Malcolm and I were continuing to have conversations occasionally in which we would try to anticipate what plans DeAngelo might have made. I recognized him to be a sly and resourceful adversary. I knew he was a very dangerous man.

Saturday morning I went back to the office of James L. Burke. He greeted me in a friendly way, and we exchanged brief comments of a general nature. He had cleared out a space in his office where two chairs were positioned next to a small table. We sat in the chairs and he got down to business immediately.

"After giving careful thought to everything you told me about Missis DeAngelo, I decided that there is only one strong argument I can make in her behalf. So, the petition for divorce will be based solely upon the intent of her husband to remove her from her home here in the South. Due to the war, and the bitter feelings that exist among the people here at present, I believe I can persuade the court that her loyalty to her homeland must prevail and that this man who is from New York, a state that is among the forces fighting against the Confederate States of America, must not be allowed to take her from her homeland."

"That sounds good, Mister Burke, but I am wondering if he will not deny that to be true?"

"Yes, of course he will deny it. And that will give cause for the judge to make a decision about who to believe. But think about it. She is asking for nothing. No money. No property, nothing. She is only asking that she be allowed to remain in her beloved homeland, and the logic of the petition is strongly in her favor."

"What if he says that she has no proof that he plans to move her?"

"That will be one of the most tedious parts of the case. I will use all of the information you have given me, and although it is circumstantial, perhaps it will carry some weight."

"What about me? We know he will say that she wants a divorce because of me."

"That will be his strongest argument, and we will have to stretch things a little. We will counter by saying that you were acquainted with her in Washington because of your horses. She had considered buying one of your fine horses, and it was simply coincidental that you called on her in Roswell. You were there looking for land for a horse farm, and you happened to learn that she was a resident there. I will secure a written statement from Doctor Stiles that will confirm it, and the doctor will be considered a credible person."

"Will you use the information I gave you concerning the fact that DeAngelo forced her out of her home in Washington and brought her here?"

He looked at me and smiled.

"Yes, I will use it, but not in a way they will suspect. I will turn it around and use it against them."

"How can you do that, sir?"

"I will paint a picture of her as the perfect wife. She had the baby of her husband, and she provided him with a happy home. It was only when he renounced the Southland and told her that he would take her away that she made the heart-breaking decision to petition for divorce. And Mister Fairfield, if we happen to be in the courtroom of Judge McMillan, which I understand that we will be, I can assure you that Mister DeAngelo will be in some hot water. You see, the son of Judge McMillan, Captain Edward McMillan, served in Jackson's army and was killed by a Yankee sniper at Chancellorsville."

Even though he had disclosed the sad news of a death, I was feeling encouraged about our outlook.

"Mister Burke, I am very happy that I found you, sir."

"Thank you, but we must not become over-confident. The other side will be making plans just as we are."

"Have you decided about me? Will I be allowed to be in the courtroom?"

"Yes, I will need you there to council with as we go along. It was a difficult decision because it gives them something to use against us. I am quite sure that DeAngelo is going to say that his wife wants a divorce in order to become united with you, so it is a risk. However, your advice during the arguments will be valuable to me, and we will counter what he says by stating that you are simply a friend in her time of need."

"When will the court be able to schedule the case?"

"As soon as possible. Of course we have to wait for Mister DeAngelo to be given a copy of the documents and to have time to prepare for the appearance in court."

"Missis DeAngelo has expressed a fear of him, so I have suggested that she should move out of the house. Do you feel that there could be a problem with that?"

"Ah... no, I don't believe so. I can think of nothing wrong with it."

"Do you by chance know of a house that is available for rent here in Marietta?"

"Yes! I do know about a house! A favorite client who is a large cotton planter told me just yesterday that he and his wife will return to their farm for three months during the harvesting season. He was concerned about leaving their home here unattended during that time, and he asked me to keep an ear open for a good renter. I am sure that he will be most happy to accommodate Missis DeAngelo. He said that the house will be available as soon as he can find a suitable renter, so it will solve his problem and hers."

"Very good. If you will give me his name and address, I will go to see him as soon as I leave your office."

When I saw the house I was very pleased. It was located on the road leading north, only a short distance away from the center of the city, and the mercantile stores and other shops could be easily reached. There were nice homes nearby, and it was most likely considered the best residential area of the city. About two hundred feet behind the house in a wooded place, there was a one-room structure that appeared to be quarters for a servant. On beyond, there was a small stable. Everything seemed to be working out well for us, and it reminded me of some of the times in years gone by when I had been gambling consistently, and the cards had been "running good" for me.

Sarah was elated when I described everything to her. She was eager to move, and we decided to set a time of ten on Monday morning to leave for Marietta. It would give me time to rent a carriage in Alpharetta and pick her up in Roswell. Sarah, along with Lula, could ride inside the carriage unseen, and I would plan to be the driver. In that way, no one else would know about her or her destination. Malcolm would follow one hour later in a rig with the personal possessions of Sarah and Lula. Neither the carriage nor the rig would attract the attention of casual observers, or others, who might otherwise notice that the two were connected, or bound for the same destination. Sarah had accumulated very little that she cared enough about to take, and it would make a move much easier to carry out. The planter and his wife had preferred to rent the house furnished and that, too, would be a big advantage for Sarah.

The move on Monday was accomplished without a serious problem. The time we were on the road was longer than I had anticipated, and we did not arrive at the new location until late. I was not experienced in driving a carriage and we were slowed some because of that, however, we had no mishaps and reached our destination in Marietta around five-thirty in the afternoon. Sarah was exhausted, and Lula insisted that she immediately go to bed for a while.

I waited for Malcolm to come in the rig, and we unloaded the cargo. We then returned the carriage and rig to a stable in Marietta where I had previously met the owner. He had told me previously that we could turn in the carriage and rig in Marietta instead of taking them back to his stable in Alpharetta. I rented horses for Malcolm and me, and we returned to the house where we had taken Sarah and Lula. Malcolm was planning to occupy the one room structure in the rear of the main house, and I would plan to rent a room in the hotel next to the depot. It was the end of a tiring but productive day.

The next few days were happy and pleasant. It was almost like DeAngelo was already out of our lives. I felt good about having Malcolm on the premises of the house where Sarah was located; he would provide some security that otherwise would not have been there. And he enjoyed it. The little one-room structure provided him privacy and a relaxing place to be. One day when he was with me he commented, "Marse, you think this place might be for sale?"

Sarah and I were together most of the time. She was regaining her strength at a fast pace, and she appeared to be just about back to normal. She was exceptionally happy, and her moods were such that she enjoyed teasing me in some manner each day. The estate was large enough so that we were able to take a stroll through the wooded area of the back when it was cool late each afternoon. It was a time when I felt that we both were as happy as we had ever been, and to finally have her all to myself was the link in my life that had been missing. It was what I had been seeking almost from the first moment I had met her.

We sat in the wooden chairs in the backyard in the early evenings. At times we were content not to talk and just listened to the sounds coming from around us, the music of the night creatures, some singing their songs with an unequaled beauty. The katydids were bidding for attention by calling out enthusiastically with their shrill chimes, and off in the distance near a pond, frogs were booming their speeches as if in competition with each other, trying to be heard in the most distant and faraway places.

One evening, as we were sitting together, I wanted to let Sarah know again how much she meant to me. I hesitated because I had already told her in many ways, and I did not want to overdo it, or let it become like a nuisance. Just then, she happened to turn in my direction, grinning.

"What are you thinking about? You've been quiet for the last five minutes."

I smiled back at her.

"You. I've been thinking about you, trying to decide whether I should tell you again about the way I feel. Are you tired of hearing it?"

"Oh, Alex, a woman never gets tired of that."

"The first time I ever saw you, the night at church when I backed into you and turned around to see who it was, I couldn't believe it. I had seen other attractive women over the years but nobody like you. You were the woman I had always imagined that I would find, and to suddenly bump into you seemed amazing. And then, as we talked, I realized that you had an inner beauty also. I had never experienced anything quite like it. Later, when someone said that you were a misses, I was really disappointed. But in the end, of course, I learned that you were a widow and that I would have the opportunity to get to know you. I think I must have realized that first night how much I would someday care for you, and as it later turned out, I was right. And now, all I can say is that I will never let you go."

"Thank you, Alex, that means so much to me. And you don't have to worry, you won't ever have to let me go."

Saturday evening when I returned to the hotel, the young man at the counter advised that there was a letter for me. He handed me an envelope and I took it along as I walked up to my room. I turned up the lamp so that it would give off adequate light, and read the enclosed message. It was brief. "Mister Fairfield, please plan to be in my office Monday morning. James L. Burke." I was reasonably certain that it could mean only one thing. DeAngelo had returned.

Sarah and I went to church on Sunday. We questioned whether to go and be seen together. In the end, we decided that since I would be seen in the courtroom sitting beside her lawyer, it wouldn't make any difference. We spent the rest of the day together. During the day I didn't mention the note from Burke or what I suspected was about to happen, and she had another happy day. She seemed to be more carefree each time I saw her.

Early on Monday I walked into the office of James L. Burke. He smiled as he greeted me and asked that I be seated. Never one to play around with words, he immediately got to the point.

"DeAngelo has returned. He undoubtedly found the note by Missis DeAngelo advising that she wants a divorce. He came to the courthouse Friday and requested a copy of the petition, and as I understand it, he has hired a lawyer."

"Who is the lawyer?"

"Tom Wade."

"What do you know about him?"

"He has won some criminal cases. He will take any kind of case, and he is, how can I put this… 'unscrupulous' might be a good word."

"So he would do anything to win a case?"

"I believe you could say that."

"How do you feel about going up against him in the courtroom?"

"Oh, I've been up against nearly every type in my thirty-eight years of practice, Mister Fairfield. He might be a little more dangerous than some; otherwise he is just another opposing council. His presence doesn't disappoint me as much as what I have heard about the judge who will hear the petition. It will not be George McMillan, it is going to be Judge Blalock."

"Why does that concern you?"

"Judge Blalock doesn't really concern me. He is a very fair judge. It is only the loss of a man, Judge McMillan, who I know has a resentment for folks from the North right now. You know, because of what I told you about his son being killed by a Yankee sniper. But no need to worry, we will move ahead as planned and do our best. And by the way, we are to be in the courtroom at ten on Thursday to begin the procedure."

When I left Burke's office, I decided that it was time to explain everything to Sarah. The petition for divorce would soon be heard and settled, and she would need to know the details beforehand. Based on everything Burke had said, I felt that we had no better than a fifty-percent chance of winning. Then, my thoughts turned toward a picture of myself standing in the courtroom and hearing the judge order that Sarah was to return to Roswell and resume her life as the wife of DeAngelo. This brought about a quick mental reaction. I would not allow it under any circumstances. No matter what had to be done, I would be sure that she would never return to live in the same house with him again.

We needed to make some alternate plans just in case things went wrong. I considered whether Sarah should leave at once to go to South Carolina to the home of her parents. She could travel by rail. I had seen a diagram in the depot showing rail lines in operation in the South. It appeared that by going to Savannah and on to Charleston she could make a connection there to a rail line that would take her in the direction of the middle of the state. She could take Lula, who could ride along as her nanny, and Malcolm could go with them and ride in a car in the back. After going as far as possible by rail, she would be within about thirty miles of her parent's home, and she could send word to her father who would come and get her.

Mister Burke had stated that he would ride out Tuesday morning to meet Sarah and have a discussion with her. He wanted to make a first-hand assessment of his client, and this was understandable. I knew that he would be favorably impressed, and I was happy to know that he planned to interview her.

When I returned to the house and saw Sarah, she knew at a glance that I had some new information, and she asked about it.

"What is it? I know you have something to tell me."

"Michael came back last week, and he knows about your petition for a divorce. He has hired a lawyer."

"Fine. I will be happy to get it over with and be rid of him."

"Sarah, we need to talk some. And by the way, Mister Burke will ride out in the morning for a visit with you. Let's go out to the back veranda and sit in the swing and I will tell you about my discussions with him."

She looked puzzled.

"What is it? Has something happened that I don't know about?"

"No, it's not that." We walked out and sat next to each other. "Mister Burke has pointed out some things to me that take place in court, and I wanted to let you know."

"Okay."

"He says that the lawyer for Michael will deny everything. The lawyer will say that you came with Michael because it was your desire."

"That is absolutely ridiculous. You know that is not true."

"Of course I know. And Mister Burke believes it is not true as well. The problem is nobody will be in the courtroom to verify the truth; we have no witnesses."

"Everybody in Washington knew what happened."

"You are right, but because of the war most of the communications with Washington have been closed off, and we will have no statements from anyone there to support you."

"Oh good heavens, that's absurd. How could they possibly call it fair if they do not know the whole story?"

"I know - Believe me - I know. The problem is when a woman marries a man, she gives away nearly all of her rights. Her husband takes charge of everything, and he is in control. Right or wrong, that is the way it works."

"This can't happen, Alex, we have to do something."

"I agree. Mister Burke knows it is not right, and he has a plan he thinks will work. But we have to face the fact that it is possible that we might lose. And that brings me to my question. Would you want to consider leaving and going to the home of your parents in South Carolina before the case is settled?"

"No! Absolutely not! I am not going to run away. And I can tell you with complete certainty that I will never go back into that house with Michael. I don't care what the court rules."

"And you won't have to do that. I will keep it from happening no matter what I have to do, so don't worry about it."

James L. Burke arrived the next morning at nine forty-five. He was riding a horse and was accompanied by the young man he had referred to as being "good with a pen." I had come out to Sarah's earlier in order to be on hand when he arrived. I introduced Mister Burke to Sarah who greeted him warmly, and then each of the others was made known to each other. Sarah invited everyone to go into the parlor. Mister Burke began the conversation after we were settled.

"Well, it is nice to be here again. I have visited here on several occasions with the owner and his wife. He owns a large cotton farm in middle Georgia, although he and his wife spend most of the year here to be near their daughter and her family." Then he turned toward Sarah. "But I know that you would like to discuss the petition you have filed, so we can move on to that if you wish."

Sarah responded.

"Yes, of course, Mister Burke, that will be fine."

He then talked at length about the petition and his strategy to offset what he felt would be encountered from the lawyer representing DeAngelo. He assured Sarah that he had no doubts whatsoever about her description of what had happened, and I could see that it made her feel better. Finally she asked about whether she could win, and what he thought might be our weakest part of the case.

"The fact that you married him. And Sarah, if I may respectfully address you by your first name, I can assure you that I understand completely how that came about. Mister Fairfield has done an excellent job of describing it to me, and I truly believe that if you could appear in the courtroom and describe the events that took place, the judge would be able to make a decision in your favor immediately. Unfortunately, that cannot happen. And of course Mister Wade, the opposing lawyer, is aware of that, and he will contrive a story to counter yours, so I have decided to take a risk. I am going to state that you married him of your own free will."

"Oh, Mister Burke, you cannot do that!"

"Well, my dear, it is actually what happened. All of us here know why you did it, but trying to convince Judge Blalock that you were forced into the marriage, I am sure, would be a mistake. Also, I am hoping that we will be able to take them by surprise. Wade will undoubtedly be preparing to defend DeAngelo against charges that you were forced to go with him and that you were later forced to marry him. I am going to try to convince the judge just the opposite – that you have been a good wife and your reason now for asking for the divorce has to do with his desire to take you away from your home here in the South."

Sarah was disappointed, and it showed on her face. She almost seemed near to tears. After a few moments, she looked back into the face of Burke.

"All right. I don't like it, but I am sure that you know best."

"Very good. And Sarah, I will promise you that I will do my very best. Now that I have met you, I can see that you are a very gracious lady, certainly deserving of everything that you are asking."

"Thank you, Mister Burke. I know that you will represent me well."

Burke and the young man left. I asked Sarah if she would like to go for a walk and she said "no." She said that she would just like to relax in the house. I then asked if she would like to be alone. She quickly responded.

"No. I want you to be with me, Alex. You are holding me together right now, and I don't know what I would do without you."

She moved over and sat next to me on the long couch. I put my arm around her shoulders, and she leaned inward so that her upper body was next to mine. It was very comforting to her, and she finally became relaxed.

# XIV.

At fifteen minutes before ten on Thursday morning, Mister Burke and I walked into a room where we were told to go in the courthouse for the divorce proceedings. It was a rather large room with a table centered next to the back wall. To the right was a table with two chairs, and to the left was a similar table and chairs. Mister Burke and I walked to the table on the right and sat down.

Within two or three minutes others arrived, including Michael DeAngelo and a tall, bushy-haired man about thirty-eight or forty years old. They proceeded to the table on the left. After a first glance at DeAngelo as he had entered the room, I did not look at him again. There were two young men who had come in about the same time, and they sat at a long table to the left of the center back table. I assumed both to be court recorders.

Within another three or four minutes, a bailiff came through the rear door and announced that Judge Blalock would enter. We all stood until he was settled in a chair behind the large table in the center of the back wall, and then as he motioned we were all seated. Stacks of papers were on the table in front of him. He glanced over them, seemingly to make sure that all things were in order. Then he raised his head and spoke.

"Good morning, gentlemen."

We all responded. I tried to analyze Judge Blalock. He appeared to be about sixty-five. His facial expression and demeanor conveyed years of experience in a courtroom, and I had the feeling that he would be thorough. He seemed to be the type who would not render a decision without due consideration of all facts. There were no others in the courtroom as the judge spoke.

"Gentlemen, I am Judge William R. Blalock. This procedure, conducted in the District of Cobb County within my jurisdiction, will be ruled upon by me at the end of all arguments. My decision will be final. We will move along quickly, with some measures of protocol being removed to save time. However, I emphasize to you that the law will be strictly adhered to, and a fair procedure will take place. In order that we can come to a conclusion expediently, I will allow a controlled cross-conversation between opposing parties, and I in turn will participate. In other words, gentlemen, we will be less formal than might otherwise be expected, and both sides will be given the opportunity to express any and all pertinent facts. My intent is to allow you to bring before the court any issue that relates to the important decision that is to be made. All right, Mister Burke, you are bringing the petition to the court, so you may begin by making your opening statement."

"Thank you, your honor." Burke pushed his chair back and stood in place. "Today, I bring to this room the petition of a heartbroken southern lady. She has been a good homemaker, and an obedient wife. She has borne the child of her husband, a baby which unfortunately was stillborn, and only now at this time is she recovering from that tragic event. And it is now, just at this most grievous time, that her husband, Michael DeAngelo, a native of the State of New York, has announced to her that she will be taken from her beloved home here in the Confederate States of America.

"He has not told her where they will go, only to some distant place: possibly even back to New York from where he has come. Therefore he has attempted to force her to discard her love of the Southland, ignore her loyalty to the men who wear the Confederate grey, and choose between remaining his wife or a loyal lady of the South. She has chosen to remain here, your honor, and by doing so her only option is to petition the court to allow her to become divorced. We pray that the court will grant her request and allow her to remain."

He paused briefly and continued. "And now I would like to ask if we will, under the terms that you outlined earlier, sir, be allowed to make cross-related statements as we move along with the procedure?"

"By all means, Mister Burke. It is my intent that the right decision will be made, and we will use whatever methods that are necessary to achieve that goal."

"Very well, sir. In that case my opening remarks are concluded."

The judge turned in the direction of Wade.

"What say you, Mister Wade, in response to these remarks?"

Wade, who obviously had been surprised by the statements of Burke, replied.

"May I have just one moment with my client, your honor?"

"Yes, but I suggest that you make it very brief."

Five minutes passed as Wade and DeAngelo whispered back and forth. Finally, the judge spoke.

"All right, Mister Wade, that will do. Let us now have your response."

Wade stood. He was rather tall, and his appearance, as well as his deep voice, would be intimidating to some. He walked around the table where he had been sitting and stopped midway between the judge and our table. He looked first at me and back to the judge.

"May I ask, your honor, why the man sitting next to Mister Burke is here in the courtroom?"

The judge answered impatiently.

"He is here because he is authorized to be here. You have the papers that Mister Burke filed. Have you read your papers? And by the way, he is to be addressed by his name, which is Mister Fairfield."

"Yes, sir, your honor. The papers state Mister Fairfield to be an advisor to Mister Burke. Can we know a little about him, his background? Is he here to give legal advice?"

"His background is outlined in the papers, Mister Wade. He has been approved by the court. Now, either make a challenge concerning Mister Fairfield, or proceed with your response to Mister Burke."

"Yes, sir, your honor, we will move on. The remarks made by Mister Burke relating to Mister DeAngelo almost constitute slander. Let us consider each point individually. First, he stated that Mister DeAngelo is from New York, inferring that a resentment should somehow be related to that. The fact is that Mister DeAngelo remained in New York at great risk only to be able to provide the manpower needed by Southern planters and manufacturing concerns. He was a broker there of laborers, sending large numbers of workers to the South in order that men in the South would be available to leave their farms and shops to wear the Confederate uniform. He is a dedicated and loyal Southern sympathizer, and he has been for a number of years. When he realized that the North would shut down his brokerage firm in New York and prevent him from further supplying manpower to the South, he decided to move to the South and continue his support of the Confederacy here.

"Secondly, for Mister Burke to state that Mister DeAngelo has advised his wife that he will move her away from the South to some distant place is absolutely false. Why would Mister DeAngelo voluntarily move to the South and then suddenly state that he was planning to move again? Why not just go ahead and move to some distant place directly from New York? I can tell you why: because of his patriotic effort to continue to supply manpower to the South and his support of the Confederate cause."

He paused, seemingly to try to determine the effect of his remarks on the judge. Burke used the opportunity to stand up and ask the judge a question.

"Your honor, have we reached a point that we may begin the cross-conversations?"

"Yes. You may proceed, Mister Burke."

Burke turned to Wade.

"It has come to our attention that Mister DeAngelo recently traveled to Savannah for the purpose of attempting to arrange passage for himself and his wife for a voyage on a sea-going vessel. This, of course, bears out our contention that he planned to take her to some distant place."

Wade answered promptly.

"What proof do you offer, Mister Burke?

"The man who drove Mister DeAngelo to the depot in Atlanta when he was leaving for Savannah provided us with the information. He stated that Mister DeAngelo instructed him to be on standby in the future. He was to make himself available on short notice to drive Mister and Missis DeAngelo to the depot when called upon."

"And who might this man be?"

"A man who is known by the name of Uncle Shad."

"Uncle Shad? Uncle Shad indeed. And would Uncle Shad by chance be a black man?"

"Yes, he is a black man, a reliable black man."

Wade turned toward the judge.

"Your honor, please. Mister Burke knows that hearsay cannot be accepted in this room."

The judge spoke.

"I agree, Mister Wade. Mister Burke, I am going to ignore your last statements."

Wade spoke again.

"With your permission, your honor, I would like to advise the court regarding a recent trip to Savannah by Mister DeAngelo."

"All right, go ahead."

"Once again, disregarding his own safety, Mister DeAngelo did travel to Savannah. It was for the purpose of finding a blockade runner who would be willing to continue to bring in manpower, blacks who could replace men who left their work to go into the Confederate Army. Mister DeAngelo knows that the need for men in the Confederate ranks is becoming more critical each day, and he was willing to risk his life to provide help."

Burke was silent, and it appeared that he could not think of an adequate response. After a few moments the judge spoke.

"What say you, Mister Burke?"

"Your honor, I have spoken with Missis DeAngelo at length, and she is a very gracious and truthful lady. I feel there is something amiss here."

The judge responded.

"And what might that be, Mister Burke? Tell us because we cannot make decisions on guesses and hunches."

Burke was silent again. Wade used the opportunity to speak.

"Your honor, if I may proceed, I would like to question Mister Fairfield."

"Well . . . Mister Fairfield does not come here as a witness, so I will permit it on a very limited basis if it is pertinent."

Wade took a step in my direction, stopped, and spoke in a loud voice.

"Mister Fairfield, how long have you been acquainted with Missis DeAngelo?"

I thought for a moment before answering.

"About two or three years."

"Oh, so you must know her very well. I believe you lived in Washington at the same time she did, is that right?"

"That is correct."

"Did you visit in her home there?"

"Yes. We were members of the same church and –"

Wade interrupted.

"No need to go into that, Mister Fairfield. How would you describe your friendship with her? Friendly? Very friendly? How?"

"We were casual friends."

"How did it come about, may I ask, that you came to Roswell, Georgia, where she was living? Is it quite likely that you came specifically because she was here?"

"I went to Roswell to consider buying land for a horse farm. While there, I called on Doctor Stiles and learned in that way that Missis DeAngelo was living there in the town, and I thought it would be nice to visit an old friend."

"By the way, Mister Fairfield, are you married?"

"No."

"So you were looking for a horse farm? From my understanding, it seems that Tennessee or North Carolina might offer better pastureland for horses. Can you tell me, sir, once again, how you happened to pick Roswell, Georgia to look for a horse farm? Was it because of Missis DeAngelo, did you go there because of her?"

Burke stood immediately and spoke.

"Your honor! I object to these questions and insinuations. Mister Wade is certainly deviating from the prepared outlines of the petition. And I feel it is quite out of order to question an individual about visiting an old acquaintance in any event."

The judge did not respond immediately, and it seemed as if he would allow Wade to continue. It gave Wade an opportunity to quickly speak again.

"Your honor, if I may offer an explanation, we are moving into what is considered by my client as the most critical issue involved. I hesitate, sir, to make allegations without first establishing reasonable cause. Therefore, I request your permission to continue questioning Mister Fairfield with that in mind."

Blalock did not speak. He obviously was giving serious consideration to the request by Wade. We had lost ground, and we were about to lose more. I touched Burke and motioned for him to lean down near my face, which he did as I spoke.

"Ask for a recess. We need to stop Wade."

Burke rose up and spoke.

"Your honor, it seems that Mister Wade intends to embark on covering some new ground, something that is far removed from the outline, and guidelines of the petition filed. Mister Fairfield did not come into this courtroom prepared to be questioned as a witness; he came only as an advisor. Now, to suddenly be called upon to become a participant in the proceedings without having previous notification would deny him his lawful rights. Therefore, we respectfully request a recess until tomorrow."

Blalock responded immediately.

"You are right, Mister Burke, and your request is granted. We will recess until ten in the morning. But I will allow a continuation of the questioning of Mister Fairfield at that time. Good day, gentlemen. The court is no longer in session."

Burke and I walked out together, and when we were alone, he spoke.

"I have to admit, Alexander, it doesn't look good."

"I know. If the petition is denied, what will take place?"

"Judge Blalock will most likely order the bailiffs to make arrangements to have Sarah escorted back to Roswell immediately."

We parted. I knew that Sarah would be eagerly waiting to see me and hear the details of how the court session had progressed. I didn't know what to tell her. I didn't want to lie, but I didn't want to tell her the truth.

When I reached her home and saw her, Sarah greeted me with a big smile.

"How did it go?"

"Okay. It was a short session. I think the judge just wanted to get everyone oriented."

"Did you see Michael?"

"Yes."

"Did you talk to him?"

"No. I was never that close to him."

"Could you see him well enough to know how he feels?"

"Not really. I only saw him come in, and when it was over Mister Burke and I left immediately. I think I know how he feels anyway."

"Does Mister Burke still feel confident?"

"Oh, I believe so, although it's too early to be sure about anything."

Her perception was too good for me to fool her.

"Alex, tell me the truth. Is there a problem?"

I stared back into her tender and innocent expression and decided to answer as best I could without deceiving her.

"Well, as we have said from the beginning, there is the possibility of a problem. But, Sarah, I promise you faithfully that you will not go back to that house with Michael."

She seemed to be relieved, and we changed to other subjects. Later, I walked back and found Malcolm in his quarters. He put down the book he was reading and smiled when he saw me.

"Well, look here. You finally decided to come around and see me."

"Yes. Thought I had better check up on you and make sure you are staying straight. How is everything going?"

"Okay. I might need some new reading material soon."

"Maybe not. We might have to leave here. Quick."

"It didn't go well today?"

"No. And it could get worse tomorrow."

"What do you have in mind?"

"South Carolina. The four of us might have to move out in a hurry.

"How?"

"I don't know. Be thinking about it."

"How much time do we have?"

"It might happen tomorrow. But don't mention it yet. I don't want to worry her."

"Okay. Oh, there is something I intended to tell you. You know the man you talked to in Washington, the one called Heavy that you met behind the saloon?"

"Yes, I remember him. I believe he lives in Big Shanty."

"I think he rode by here today. I was cleaning off the front steps and saw him. He didn't stop, in fact, he didn't even look at the house, but I am sure it was him. It was like he was checking to see how much of a ride he would have to get here from wherever he would come from."

"So, he is still working for DeAngelo. He would probably come to get her when the court session is settled. At least he thinks he will do that."

He smiled.

"Don't worry, Marse, he won't leave here with her no matter when he comes."

I smiled back.

"I know. With you back here, I'm not worried."

When I returned to the large house, Sarah and I sat in the chairs in the back yard after the heat had subsided. She had always been able to read me like a book, and when she looked at me with the telltale expression, I knew what was coming.

"Alex, tell me what you will do."

"What do you mean?"

"You know exactly what I mean. You never were able to fool me, and you're not fooling me now. I know there could be a problem."

"Well, we talked about South Carolina; what do you think about that?"

"It would be fine. But how would we do it?"

"I don't know yet. We can't travel by rail; they would stop us. And a horse-driven coach would be too slow. I think we will just have to hide close by and wait for a while."

"There will be four of us, right?"

"Yes. Malcolm and Lula will be with us."

She seemed to feel better. Just having an answer, having it settled helped and she did not appear to be anxious. At nine I told her I would leave and go back to the hotel. After a long embrace, and just before leaving, I wanted to reassure her again.

"Malcolm will be here. I told him to stay alert, and he will."

"I'm not worried. I have never been worried when I know you are nearby."

"Goodnight, Sarah."

"Goodnight. And Alex, I do love you."

When I returned to the hotel I was told that I had a telegram in the office next door at the depot. It was from John Dabney, and I was immediately encouraged. It read: "Will arrive Marietta eight AM by rail Friday. Meet me at depot. Very important."

I knew that Dabney had a particular disliking for DeAngelo. Also, I knew he had set a personal goal for himself to find a means of determining the real story behind the man from New York and bring out the absolute truth about his activities. Nothing would please him more than finding good reason to take DeAngelo into custody. Dabney knew about the petition for divorce filed by Sarah. He had been advised by his agent in Marietta, and he knew it was urgent for him to become involved while the court procedure was still in progress. All of these considerations gave me cause to believe that John Dabney was bringing help.

I could hardly sleep during the night. Once I got out of bed and tried to read. Finally, at about two-thirty, I drifted off to sleep for several hours. At ten minutes past eight the next morning, I was standing on the platform on the outside of the depot when the locomotive arrived from Atlanta.

John Dabney stepped down from a rail car almost before it stopped, and seemed as eager to see me as I was to see him. He was accompanied by a man who appeared to be about forty and had a rough countenance, one that might have been the result of many days that were spent in weather that would drive most people inside. He reminded me of the few men I had seen from the West, men who had lived hard and showed it. He was, nonetheless, friendly with a quick smile and an easy-going manner. He spoke with an Irish accent.

We walked from the depot to the hotel where I had made arrangements for a meal. During our breakfast, John gave me the details of what he had, and his companion withdrew a document to support what John was saying. It was sensational, and I could hardly contain myself. As soon as we finished the meal, we walked in the direction of the office of James L. Burke.

He was in his office and after introductions, Dabney and the man with him, who was called Harry, presented their information to Burke. He was very elated, and for the first time since I had known him I saw a real smile come over his face.

At ten o'clock all were present in the courtroom of Judge Blalock, with the exception of Dabney and Harry who were waiting in the hallway just outside. Judge Blalock stood and began speaking.

"All right, gentlemen, we are ready to proceed. Are there any statements or requests by either party before we begin?"

Burke stood at once.

"Your honor, I have a request if you please. The core of our petition is based on the intent of Mister DeAngelo to remove his wife, against her wishes, to a far and distant place. Although this intent has been denied by his attorney, Mister Wade, we have not heard directly from Mister DeAngelo. Therefore, I request permission, for the record, to speak directly to Mister DeAngelo."

Judge Blalock knew that the legal protocol would support the request, and he readily agreed.

"Proceed, Mister Burke."

Burke turned and looked into the face of DeAngelo.

"Mister DeAngelo, have you at any time contacted the Captain, or Master, of a sea going vessel inquiring about passage for you and your wife for a voyage to a foreign country?"

DeAngelo answered quickly.

"No sir, I have not."

"Mister DeAngelo, have you signed a document, and have you made payment in advance, for passage on a sea-going vessel for you and your wife that is bound for a port in a foreign country?"

"No, sir, I have not."

Burke turned to the judge.

"And now, sir, if you will give me just a little more time, I will complete what I have started here."

Blalock seemed to be getting interested. He replied immediately.

"Why yes, Mister Burke, I feel you must have good cause to make this request. Proceed."

"Thank you, sir. Next, if you will permit the bailiff to bring in the two men who are waiting in the hallway, I will introduce them to the court. The reason for their presence will be self-explanatory."

The judge nodded to the bailiff who in turn walked out of the room into the hallway. He was back immediately, and was followed by John Dabney and the man called Harry. Burke took a few steps in their direction and escorted them down to the front where chairs were located. After they were seated, Burke turned back toward Judge Blalock as he spoke.

"And now, sir, I will introduce these two men to the court. First, we have Mister John Dabney," and he motioned for John to stand, "who is a highly respected servant of the Confederate States of America. John, if you will, please, hand a copy of your credentials to Judge Blalock in order that your status can be verified."

John withdrew a document from his pocket and walked a few steps to the table where Blalock was sitting and handed him the paper. Blalock looked at it carefully, and when his eyes reached the bottom of the page he spoke quietly, saying, "Oh, I see that this document has been signed by the Honorable Alexander Stephens. Very good. Mister Burke, your witness is accepted by the court and his testimony and evidence will be considered admissible."

Dabney retrieved his document and returned to his seat. Next, Burke introduced the second man.

"Your honor, sitting next to Mister Dabney is Mister Harry Donovan. He is a native of Sligo, Ireland, but in recent years he has served as Master and Captain of the sea-going vessel named Victoria. He has successfully by-passed the Yankee blockade of our ports on a regular basis bringing much needed supplies to the Confederate States of America. His ship at the present time is docked in Savannah undergoing maintenance and minor repairs."

Burke motioned, and Harry stood. Then Burke continued.

"Mister Donovan if you will be kind enough to hand me your commission as Captain of the ship Victoria, I will pass it along for observation by Judge Blalock."

It was done. The judge looked quickly upon the document and commented.

"Everything seems in order. Proceed, Mister Burke."

"Yes sir." He turned toward Dabney.

"Mister Dabney will you tell us why you are here today?"

"I am here to conclude a case that I have been working on for a lengthy period. We received a report several months ago about a man who was involved in slave trading in the past who recently turned to receiving goods from overseas which he stored in warehouses in Savannah. The items involved are non-existent here in the South and consequently were being sold at unbelievably high prices, resulting in wartime profiteering.

"My orders were to stop it as quickly as possible, and I went to Savannah immediately to investigate. Not long after arriving there I learned the name of the man I was seeking. I also learned that he had become aware that he had been discovered and had made plans to leave the country with his wife. It was then that I contacted Mister Donovan who confirmed that the man had made arrangements for passage for himself and his wife on the return voyage of the Victoria to England."

He paused and looked at Burke, who spoke.

"Mister Dabney, will you give us the name of the man you have described?"

"Michael DeAngelo."

Wade was on his feet immediately, and his deep voice resounded strongly throughout the room.

"Your honor! I most strenuously object to this make-believe act. It is hearsay and obviously an attempt by Mister Burke to discredit an honorable gentleman."

The judge remained calm as he spoke.

"Sit down, Mister Wade. I want to hear the end of this story. You may continue, Mister Burke."

Wade sat down and Burke continued.

"Thank you, Mister Dabney. And now, I would like to ask Mister Donovan a question. Would you tell us, sir, if you sometimes take passengers along on the return trips to England?"

"Yes, sir, we do."

"I assume you have limited space, your ship being primarily a freight-carrying vessel, and I am wondering if you therefore might have made arrangements with passengers in advance?"

"We did that, sir."

"How did you go about it? How could you be sure the passengers would show up?"

"We required their payment in advance, sir."

"Did you recently make such an arrangement with Michael DeAngelo?"

"I did."

"What evidence do you have to show us that such an arrangement was made?"

"I have the contract that was signed by Mister DeAngelo, showing payment received for a stateroom to be used by him and his missis on our return voyage to England."

"Will you be kind enough to show the document to Judge Blalock?"

"Yes sir, that I will do."

He stood, withdrew a document from his pocket and walked to the table where Blalock was seated. The judge eagerly reached out to receive it. I glanced at DeAngelo. He was nervously moving about in his chair. Judge Blalock finished reading the document and returned it to Donovan, who had remained standing nearby. Donovan returned to his seat, and Burke spoke.

"Your honor, that concludes the matters that gave me cause to request the time that you have extended. Thank you, sir."

Burke sat down, and Blalock looked at Wade.

"Mister Wade, do you wish to offer a response?"

"Sir, will you allow me a moment to have a discussion with my client?"

"Yes."

Whispering began immediately between Wade and DeAngelo. It lasted only briefly, and Wade stood up facing the judge.

"Your honor, we respectfully ask for a recess to further consider the ridiculous allegations that have just been made."

The judge spoke firmly.

"Your request is denied. Please be seated. And now, gentlemen, I will announce my decision regarding the case we have considered. The petition of Missis DeAngelo contains two requests. She asks that her marriage to Michael DeAngelo be dissolved and a divorce be granted. Secondly, she asks that her previous name, Sullivan, be restored. In both matters I rule in the affirmative. The petition is granted. This concludes this court procedure. All are free to leave except Mister DeAngelo. Bailiff, please come forward and stand beside Mister DeAngelo and await further instructions. Good day, gentlemen."

Burke and I stood and shook hands. I then walked to where John Dabney and Donovan were standing, and we also shook hands. There were smiles among all of us, and we each excitedly poured out our happy thoughts. Actually, however, I couldn't wait to leave. I wanted to get to Sarah and give her the good news. Shortly thereafter, I was able to explain to the others and made my way toward the door. I did not look at DeAngelo again, and I felt as I left that I had probably seen him for the last time.

When Sarah saw me, she immediately broke into a huge smile, and for a moment I thought she might take a great forward leap into my arms. She spoke, very excitedly.

"Oh, Alex! We won! I can see it in your face!"

"Yes! Yes, Missis Sullivan, we won!"

We reached for each other and embraced, holding on for a long time. Then we backed away, and I could see small teardrops in the corners of her eyes. Nonetheless, she was still able to speak enthusiastically.

"Alex, I am so proud of you. What on earth would I have done without you?"

"Oh, maybe you could have just settled for Jennings."

She smiled and reached out to give me a slight push with her hand. She was bubbling as she spoke again.

"This is wonderful news. Let's go tell Lula and Malcolm."

We did. And they too expressed their pleasure and happiness. Sarah and I were together for the rest of the day. After the evening meal, as usual, we went out to sit in the chairs in the back. When a pause occurred in our conversation, I turned toward her, and she immediately moved her face around to look at me. I smiled at her.

"And now, Missis Sullivan, I have a question for you."

As always, she knew exactly what was coming.

"All right, Mister Fairfield, I will answer your question."

"Will you do me the honor of becoming my bride? Will you marry me?"

"Yes! I will marry you! And not only will I marry you, I will love you every day for the rest of my life."